A BED ON BRICKS

& other stories

A BED ON BRICKS

& other
stories

M.A.Kelly

modjaji books

Published in 2022 by Modjaji Books
www.modjajibooks.co.za

Cover photograph by Janine Lessing
Cover artwork by Monique Cleghorn
Book design and layout by Andy Thesen

ISBN: 978-1-928433-42-2

Contents

For Sibylla and Conrad

Mother's Milk

Through the dusty second-floor window of the head of department's office, Margo idly observed the throngs of students noisily leaving the Faculty of Social Science's scattered buildings for the day, heading out into the sunlight that was still blindingly brilliant in the late afternoon. Groups of threes and fours stuck to covered walkways where they could, intently consulting their phones and conversing with each other simultaneously. All Margo could make out from above were the shaved heads, the weaves and braids, the few natural styles and the many baseball caps.

The Head of Sociology was still talking, as he had been doing for a considerable time now without interruption, about how she might have to alter some of her expectations and commit to doing more fieldwork than she had originally intended on her arrival at his institution. He had a low, monotonous voice and was keen on repetition. This – along with the background hum of the ancient air-conditioning unit, her persistent sinus infection, and the insistent circling of a fat, noisy fly – was beginning to make Margo feel drowsy. She just wanted this pointless meeting over with, *please Lord*.

Now, by the slight change in his tone, she sensed that maybe Dr Phampa was winding up at long last and so she snapped her attention back to him in bright encouragement.

But he wasn't done quite yet.

"Just because you are African-American, you must not make the mistake of thinking you have anything in particular in common with us, Miss Michaels, so I am trying really to give you the benefit of my experience, do you follow me? One way or another, you are going to have to go out into the communities and explain your work in order to get the kind of results that will contribute to sound-enough research."

She bristled inwardly, both at the reference to her race and the "Miss", which she assumed was being used specifically to rile her. She was not used to feeling so stealthily outmanoeuvred, especially by someone she considered her intellectual inferior, despite the letters after his name on the door. Dr Phampa's way of speaking was at all times so slow and deliberate it seemed as if he had once been asked to deliver a keynote address and had subsequently forgotten how to shift his register back to something less formal. Indeed, Margo had found herself unconsciously adapting her own words to mirror his over-articulation during the course of their many conversations to date, face-to-face interactions necessary because Dr Phampa had never learned to accommodate the convenience of email in his dealings with his colleagues.

"It's not primarily rural and disadvantaged sectors of the community that I wish to engage, Dr Phampa. I want to interview a broad cross-section for my research, including urban populations, which are usually side-lined in this type of work. I thought we had decided long ago that my proposal had made that clear."

Margo's toes in her espadrilles were curling with frustration and with the effort of employing cheerful uptalk to try to move their conversation towards an acceptable, amiable conclusion. She didn't understand why they were going around and around repeating the same arguments and counterarguments to no good purpose. It wasn't just Phampa – she had found herself having the exact same circular discussions with a number of other colleagues here, as well as with the people running the guesthouse. It was never sufficient to say something once when a repetition or two could be effected.

Cutting to the chase, she had swiftly detected, was considered both rude and an unserious way to go about business.

"A case in point, Miss Michaels. You state there, I believe, that you wish to include the stories of middle-class people, but this does not mean that they will necessarily want to tell them to you, do you see, just because you are the same colour as them. We Batswana are a reticent people generally. Town and country alike. You will find that we don't open up to strangers as easily as you seem to suppose we shall. We don't have that, what can we call it, that confessional impulse that you Americans all share."

Margo resisted the temptation to remind Dr Phampa, yet again, that she was originally from Trinidad and simply smiled in the face of his dogged rejection of her research methodology. It was a continuation of the resistance he had been articulating with truculent stubbornness from the first day she had set foot on his campus. In no apparent hurry to wind up this interview, it appeared as if Dr Phampa wanted her to go back to the beginning *yet again* and explain the work she wished to do for the *umpteenth* time, as if in doing so the patent futility of her proposal would eventually be revealed to her.

"I know that you did read the short introductory text I have prepared as a preliminary to my interviews? Where I set out how I feel it's important to facilitate the people of Botswana in uncovering the value of preserving and sharing their patrimony? I am sure educated people will appreciate the importance of this work, keeping the stories of their ancestors alive and accessible to future generations?"

All Margo's research up to that point had been conducted within American urban communities. So, the last thing she wanted to do was to have to rent a foreign (and no doubt ancient) car – the workings of which would be incomprehensible to her when it inevitably broke down – and drive on the unlit, dangerous backwoods tracks of this vast country. Then be forced to ingratiate herself in remote villages where creature comforts would be thin on the ground and she might have to depend upon the hospitality of strangers. She had been in the country less than a fortnight, and already her skin was sloughing off, leaving behind an unattractive mosaic of scaly dryness almost as soon as she had finished moisturising each morning. She couldn't imagine making like Jane Goodall, or whoever, and doing fieldwork in some hinterland where cleansers and tampons would be difficult to source. She simply wasn't *that* kind of academic.

Worse than that, she had already been told that she would have to take a translator along if she ventured outside the city, and the thought of spending days on the road in prolonged, enforced proximity with a Motswana who wanted to know her life history, her income, and her household and domestic arrangements, was deeply unappealing. Contrary to Dr Phampa's belief, not all Americans were sharers, and she was keen to avoid having to prove this to someone and be thought of as rude or arrogant.

Margo had been warned by one of her elderly colleagues back home that apparently any African one became even slightly friendly with would decide that their unannounced arrival at your home would be welcomed at some point in the future, or that you would be prepared to sponsor their studies or assist with visa applications, and so on. And although she found it hard to credit, she had also been advised that overseas sociology researchers who did not avail themselves of locals to help them navigate the complexities of unfamiliar territory risked basing their entire theses on sets of partially fictitious data. Not that the local Africans were serial fabulists, *naturally*, it was just that they had a collective tendency to tell you what they believed you wanted to hear. Subsequently, a great deal of information innocently phrased to please and ease social relations would then undergo a further, fatal transmutation as you struggled to collate evidence of dubious veracity.

Neither of these bits of anthropological wisdom came to her first hand – it was simply that people she was acquainted with knew someone else it had happened to in the past. She was torn between following her own advice of always taking seriously the views of colleagues more knowledgeable than she was, or of dismissing these frankly rather racist generalisations as bits of unsupportable, arcane academic folklore.

❧

Lebogang sighed. How many scholars from abroad had come to his university over the years with patronising offers to share their overvalued expertise? With the objectives of enhancing capacitation, creating linkages, mapping intersecting identities, interrogating new paradigms, and all the other wilfully esoteric abstruseness in which they traded. As if his young faculty wasn't already delivering valuable, rigorous and innovative work of its own. (Although, alas, recently he had noted with distaste the tendency of certain students, who clearly relied too much on the internet for their research, to start parroting these useless phrasings as well. He had only the other day discovered some particularly egregious examples in a gifted girl's work and during a brief tutorial he had therefore impressed upon her that he had neither the time nor the resources to go through her essay and interrogate the interstices between pretentiousness and plagiarism. She would have to rework the entire thing.)

Here was yet another one of these disdainful liberal westerners, descending on his world as if from on high for a term or two. Somehow though this woman was worse because she was black and so had, he assumed, come to get in touch with her tribal roots and use her purported common ancestry as an additional mother lode of cultural capital. Let her find out for herself that cultured Batswana who wouldn't know an ethnic artefact if you beat them over the head with it were climbing over each other in an effort to distance themselves from the old ways. The last thing they would want to revisit would be the stories some decrepit old village crone told them back in the day, before anyone local had even heard of Black History Month.

Moreover, what was this funny way she had of articulating each sentence as if it were a question directed at a mentally deficient child? Phampa sighed once more.

His PA had left for the day, and Lebogang found he couldn't bring himself to extend the natural courtesy of asking Margo if she would like him to prepare a cup of tea for them both, so he changed the subject instead, hoping this would bring the pointless deliberations to an end so he could go home.

"Are you settled in your accommodation, Miss Michaels? And is there anything more I can do to help you initiate your work?"

"I am, thank you for asking. As regards my work, and to reiterate, my main challenge is going to be meeting with the range of people I need to interview in order to make my research relevant. At this point I think I just need to get out there and make a start?"

Dr Phampa got up without explanation and began consulting a drawer in his filing cabinet. This gave Margo a rich opportunity to appraise, really for the first time, the extraordinary person who was her only real acquaintance in Botswana to date.

A tiny man – his wrists so fragile-looking that she possessed an urge to grip them and see what they looked like against her far more substantial hands – he reminded her of the Kenyan long-distance runners she used to watch on TV as a child, dominating the field at the Olympics as their emaciated-looking bodies drove them on with unstoppable, unbeatable momentum. She had observed already that certain of his well-padded colleagues, male and female, wore rather snug outfits, but Dr Phampa appeared to be on a one-man mission to reverse the trend. Every day he enveloped his slight frame in one of a series of lightly-sheened, boxy double-breasted suits that completely swamped him. She wondered if these were given to him by a much-bigger relative or friend or if, strange though it would seem, he actually bought them or had them tailored this way.

His features, too, seemed ill-fitting – his little conical ears stuck out at right-angles to a tall bald dome of a head, and his eyes were most unfortunate in their protuberance. As if to draw attention away from these, he wore a comically luxuriant moustache. God forgive her, but she was reminded of a self-important gremlin.

Next to the filing cabinet was a wide metal bureau, on top of which stood a large colour photograph in an elaborate, gilded frame that she hadn't registered on her previous visits to his office. The picture showed Dr Phampa in, she guessed, the 1980s, appearing to weigh as little as he did today while wearing an almost identical but even shinier suit that entirely swallowed up his adolescent figure. A slightly wilting carnation decorated his buttonhole, and his hair was sculpted in a splendid, cascading jheri curl. He had his arm draped with obvious pride around the shoulder of a stunning young girl a little taller than him, who was wearing a party dress with padded shoulders and a waterfall hemline, the iridescent fuchsia material trimmed all around with black lace. The girl also had an elaborate up-do and was wearing black lace gloves and a band of black lace looped around her head and tied in a big bow to the side of her centre parting. The couple was standing before an impressionistic backdrop painting of Paris by night, and they seemed to be cringing a little with the self-consciousness of teenagers dressed up as adults but simultaneously fully self-possessed and aglow with promise.

Margo had already discovered that Dr Phampa was a widower with no children. This old photograph was one she assumed had been taken on graduation day (did they have such things three decades ago in Gaborone?) and she could only surmise that of all the snaps that had been taken of him with his lovely wife, this was the one he had decided showed them at their best – their happiest and most hopeful. How long after the portrait was taken had things taken a tragic turn, she mused a little sadly.

"My apologies, Miss Michaels. I can't find a copy of the documentation I am looking for here. Will you excuse me while I try to locate it elsewhere in the building?"

Margo nodded her assent, quickly turning her head so that Dr Phampa wouldn't know that she had been staring at the photograph. Once he had headed off down the long corridor to a far-flung administrative office, she found herself thinking some more about the professional progress of the boy in the giant's suit in the picture to the middle-aged man still wearing the same style of outfit who was slyly sabotaging her work here now.

Before she had left the USA, her parents had organised a cookout to celebrate her departure. As her father had fired up the barbecue in the well-kept yard of their bungalow on the wooded lot outside Galveston, her mother chopped coleslaw and chatted in their little kitchen. Margo recalled something Carla had said as she made the salad with that absentminded care that results from long experience.

"There comes a point in your life when instead of looking forwards into your future, you spend your time and energy looking back into the past."

That Saturday afternoon, Margo had had no reason to think that Carla wasn't talking about herself and her husband. And perhaps dropping an unconscious hint about the dwindling number of years that Margo had left to find herself a decent man and raise a grandchild or two for the couple to spoil and indulge.

Now, a few weeks later, Margo was able to see that the comment applied just as well to the way that she examined the procession of years that constituted her own career. Which photograph would be the one that she could tell people represented the most notable day in her life? Where was her personal highpoint? She was pretty sure it hadn't happened yet – perhaps it was the PhD she was slogging towards now, but maybe it would always be some way off, in the future that was being used up month by month, term by term, paper by paper. Endlessly deferred until the menopause, or the family curse of sudden cancer, or her diminishing powers of reasoning put an end to the ephemeral professional plans that she hadn't really ever formulated but which, she just assumed, were waiting to be fulfilled along the way.

After her relatives and friends had left, and the aluminium foil serving platters had been scraped and piled in the trash, Margo sat with her parents in the TV area of their open-plan home. Justin, her father, had fallen asleep almost immediately in his La-Z-Boy recliner

– Margo was distressed to note that his catering responsibilities that afternoon had completely exhausted him. As she watched him slump into a deep slumber, she understood that perhaps now – or the next time, but sometime soon – would be the last time she ever saw him. He was, no question about it, an old man now.

Carla, on the other hand, had been energised by the company and the sociable buzz, and she suggested that they put on one of Margo's favourite movies and chat awhile before tackling the washing up. They both knew this was actually an excuse to gossip about the afternoon's visitors.

Some way into *Julia*, a young and fiercely lovely Vanessa Redgrave strode across a college quadrant at Oxford. Her pale, ardent eyes ablaze and arms swinging, the confidence of youth rang out from every firm movement of her tall, purposeful body. Julia's friend, Lillian Hellman, was delivering the voiceover and explaining that, at 19, Julia would never be so magnificent again. This was the very pinnacle of her powers and her beauty, when an ardour for learning left no room for vanity or even the consciousness of physical appearance: her "perfect time of life".

It was the expectation of such a moment that had driven Margo on through her academic life. That complete trust in a life's direction, that totality of identity when the mind and the body harmonise their energies and desires to produce the best ever version of one's selfhood.

It was a moment, she suddenly saw now, that she was still waiting for – even as she had been unable to perceive, until just a moment ago, that perhaps her time had almost run out.

As she examined her many interconnected difficulties, which Dr Phampa had been so fastidious in reminding her about today, Margo felt overwhelmed by an incapacitating ennui in the face of all the tasks ahead of her. It had all seemed so simple at the end of last year. A doctoral advisor in Chicago had let her know that the university was keen to have a PhD candidate do some work overseas for a change and that he could hook her up with the necessary people. She was still single, wasn't she, so the logistics wouldn't be too complex?

It was arranged that she would rent a nice room with Wi-Fi in Gaborone from an ex-student of his, and she was assured that a simple announcement on the university radio there a few weeks before her arrival, stating that she was recruiting volunteers for her interviews, would bring crowds of Batswana to her, more than eager to share their stories. "Tales of the Ancients in a Maturing Democracy: Towards a Re-evaluation of the Uses of Myths and Narratives in Botswana" – they had even thrashed out her basic premise together over a bottle of Pinot Noir. It was painful for her to remember now how excited she had been less than five months ago, when she had been firing on all cylinders and had been reinvigorated, intellectually, at the thought of a new environment and new work theme to pursue.

She had waited for news of potential interviewees to begin appearing in her email inbox and, when this didn't happen, put it down to a communications glitch she could fix on her arrival. Instead, a few days before she was due to depart, while she was trying to type up a list of all the things the cat sitter needed to know, she got a less-than-sufficiently-apologetic email from the ex-student cancelling the rental agreement. Apparently, he and his wife were getting a divorce and were going to sell the property. There you go, she had told herself, the problems caused by the constitutional unreliability of Africans that she had been warned about so many times (except in this instance it turned out that Nadezna and Clive were not, in fact, Batswana at all, but white South Africans).

Her contact at the university, Dr Lebogang Phampa, had promptly faxed her the details of the guesthouse where visiting academics would usually stay if the duration of their trip was short and where she could have a room at a reasonable rate until she managed to make other arrangements – which had been helpful of him. He had then sent her a rambling, troubling message on her answering machine outlining the difficulties she was going to have finding enough subjects for her interviews. This was also, she admitted, kind of helpful to know in advance, but nevertheless frustrating and demoralising. She suspected later on that he had taken a slightly malicious glee in dumping all over her plans before she had even arrived in the country.

On the day after she had flown in, when Margo was still poleaxed by fatigue after travelling for more than a day and a half, Phampa had insisted on bringing her along to a second-year lecture. There, he had introduced her as "Miss" and she had made a point of correcting this immediately to "Ms", to his evident displeasure and to no apparent effect. He had then requested that the students ask around their circles of friends and family to see if anyone would be willing to be interviewed by Miss Michaels for her research. A simple matter of meeting at a time and place convenient for them, answering a few background questions to establish context, and then telling her a story (or stories) that had been handed down through their family. They could choose the story, and she would sit and record it and then ask any questions that occurred to her. There might be a further follow-up session if anything else crossed her mind later that maybe needed clarification, but that was basically it. *Why*, she'd asked herself as he took it upon himself to sketch out her plans to the bored-looking class, *did he make it sound as if he couldn't care less if they participated?*

Through this process she had located a grand total of ten volunteers and she needed at least fifty to stand a reasonable chance of accumulating enough viable material. Maybe once she started her work with these few individuals, they would put the word out and more subjects would materialise. If not, Margo was going to have to mobilise her famed resourcefulness and step everything up a gear.

Perhaps she would have to explore the option of reaching out through Facebook or Myspace or something. But for the time being, she simply couldn't imagine finding the reserves of energy necessary to initiate this task, let alone processing the feedback she hoped it would produce. Just being in this godforsaken place had robbed her of any initiative or goodwill. What's more, the guesthouse food she was consuming every day was leaving her dyspeptic and sluggish – carbohydrate-heavy meals that sat uncomfortably in her stomach for far too many hours.

Dr Phampa returned empty-handed – he had been unable to locate whatever it was he had wandered off to find. The way that he didn't re-enter his office but stood instead on the threshold with his hand on the door handle gave her to understand that their meeting was at long last over.

☙

A few days later Margo was summoned to Dr Phampa's office once again. She made a mental note to ask him where he got his few prints and cloth wall hangings before she left Botswana for good – something to embellish her own workplace on her return and hint heavily at her credentials as an academic with experience of working outside of the USA. There would be no harm in a bit of late-in-the-day diplomacy towards her colleague here before she departed, in order to maintain at least a pretence of collegiality between their two institutions. After an offer of tea, Dr Phampa announced that one of his students had given him an idea that would potentially deliver more interview subjects than she could handle. He told her this welcome news with less smugness than she might have anticipated.

"There is a pool of potential interviewees living here that we perhaps haven't considered, Miss Michaels. Uneducated people without access to modern technology perhaps, who won't be able to hear about you through the adverts on social media that you are proposing."

Margo resented his use of the word "advert" but let it slide; by now she strongly suspected that Dr Phampa was a committed technophobe. She leaned towards him slightly over her steaming mug to indicate that she was paying attention.

"A good many students here will have at least one maid and garden boy employed by their family. Perhaps even a driver, too, a few of them. If we offer these people a meal and pay for their transport home, doubtless you will have a queue passing right outside the campus main gate by the end of the week. And they will have come from all around the country originally and will represent a range of ages and tribal backgrounds."

Margo stifled a wince at the use of the word "tribal", though it did cross her mind to raise an objection to "maid and garden boy". However, to do so would only compel her to listen to a lecture from Phampa about how the contrast between her western PC liberal assumptions and the realities on the ground in the developing world was going to cause her unlimited problems unless she could learn to reconcile them, at least for the duration of her visit.

It seemed an unlikely, even unorthodox, answer to her dilemma, but in desperation – and rather against her better judgment – she looked into it further. What she discovered made her re-evaluate her adversarial relationship with her colleague. Were they really struggling with mutual antipathy, or was it all on her side, in fact? It seemed likely that he had, indeed, presented her with a neat solution. It wouldn't cost so very much to set this all up, it seemed: a roll of white bread containing pink, polony-like meat, or a magwinya, plus a soda at the campus café turned out to be ridiculously cheap. Margo told herself that any outlay involved in this process could be offset against the diesel budget she had reluctantly set aside for the fieldwork she was so anxious to avoid, since in effect, and to her great relief, her rural subjects would be coming to her, as opposed to the other way around.

As Dr Phampa had predicted, the response – once she had put out her call for these new interviewees via the students – was overwhelming, and Margo spent the next fortnight going through the details of the volunteers with an enthusiastic and clever first-year assistant, separating the men and women who had responded out into cohorts in order to make sure that – so far as was possible – she interviewed a representative spread of them, young and old, and covered all the minor ethnic groupings, along with the majority Tswana.

☙

Which is how she came to be at a small but funky café in town late on a Thursday afternoon, sitting under an inadequate shade umbrella opposite a middle-aged woman of significant proportions whom she knew from her notes to be Charity Montle of the Kalanga people, aged 55. On the phone the night before, Charity had explained in clear English that she had an interesting story to tell but that she was leaving town the following afternoon to visit her sister's stepdaughter in Zimbabwe, and if Margo wanted to hear this story it would be best to meet in town before Charity caught the bus through. They had greeted each other in the doorway of the café a few minutes after the appointed time and had sat down at a rickety metalwork table in the interior courtyard and completed the necessary introductions. Charity then ordered a plate of fried chicken and chips, a Coke, and a side order of rolls and butter, which Margo quietly asked the waitress to bring as quickly as possible, please.

Charity was dressed with flair in what Margo assumed might be cast-offs from her employer or a friend's employer: a very tight pink T-shirt with a vaguely Hawaiian design picked out in peeling gold that flattened her large breasts against her ribcage; a long, stiff denim skirt that was straining against her impressive thighs; a pair of very old but nevertheless expensive-looking trainers; and a nylon headscarf. Unlike most of the other domestic workers Margo had interviewed already, Charity had a self-possession and evident pride in her appearance that made her, well into middle age, sexy and even glamorous.

They continued the required greetings, at which Margo had already become adept, enquiring after the wellbeing not only of each other, but their families – perfect strangers of course, to both women. Then they talked around various subjects while Charity consumed her greasy-looking, substantial meal with speed.

Margo was slightly surprised to discover that Charity was candid and pleasant company. Although she had had only the most basic education and had always worked as a cleaner and nanny, she was voluble and articulate in English – despite the fact that it was only her third or fourth language – and knowledgeable about national events and even some international news. In fact, Margo doubted that she had enjoyed such a companionable conversation since she had arrived, a full month ago now. She felt herself warming to this woman so quickly that she wondered later if her longing for relaxed social intercourse had made her rush to establish an intimacy with Charity that, under normal circumstances, she would have been more reticent about. Margo desperately wanted to impress on this domestic worker that the rigid economic stratifications of local society did not position her outside of sisterhood or respect, at least so far as the woman from America was concerned. Looking back subsequently on her over-eager, ingratiating efforts to break the ice, Margo found herself shamed slightly with retrospective embarrass-ment at her condescension. But it could not be denied that Charity's wide, humorous face and gappy, easy smile invited confidences.

Then Charity finished the last of her meal and, as she carefully wiped across her forehead and then around her mouth with the small paper serviette provided, Margo cribbed from her preparatory state-ment, explaining the purpose of her work. She replaced words she now recognised as inappropriate – like "heritage" and "patrimony" – with others that she felt Charity would understand without a patronising explanation and tried not to suddenly sound too formal. Then she opened her notebook and asked if she might switch on the tape recorder. Charity sat back in her chair, nodded her compliance, then with good grace shifted her own focus to the purpose of their interview.

She cast a dubious glance at the tape-recorder and then leaning towards it, asked, a little too loudly, "Can I begin now then? I must go across to catch the bus soon."

"Yes, Charity. Please begin my dear. Just tell your story to me as if you were talking to someone you know very well, and I'll only interrupt you if there's something I don't understand. I'll save my questions to the end mostly."

"Ah yes. Well, you know now, I used to live in the village. That village is up past Serowe, far, far from here."

Margo had opened a small map out on the table in front of her now that the plates had been cleared, and before she had a chance to turn the map to face Charity and ask her if she knew how to locate her home, the woman had stuck a plump finger down on it near to a feature called the Makgadikgadi Pan. Margo was glad she hadn't had to drive all that way to interview this subject, even though she already had a suspicion that her story would be pay dirt compared with some of the muddled, evasive and repetitious tales she had heard so far.

"So yes. I was staying there, and my auntie told me this story many times, from when she had been a just a bit older than a teenager. My auntie, her name was Linda, but now she is late. She told me this story on nights when there was no moon, and I was small. She liked to scare me, and I liked to be scared, you see? It was only later, when I was older, and she told the story in a different way, that I realised it had happened to someone she knew. And only much, much later now, when she was then an old lady, that I found out it happened to someone she had loved. This made me confused in my heart then.

"Anyway, let me say that Auntie Linda used to look after the child of her husband's first wife's cousin."

Margo stopped the recorder to ask a question that wouldn't have occurred to her until very recently. "Was this cousin an *actual* cousin or …?"

"Yes, no, they actually were relatives. The first wife's father's brother's second child. Her daughter."

By now Margo had ceased to be amazed at the ability of Batswana interviewees to recall the details of family dynamics going back sometimes many generations before they were even born. She turned the recorder back on as she wrote out a few notes.

"These women – the first wife and the cousin – were also both late in an accident with a train. But before the mother of the child died in the hospital there, this cousin said that she wanted the family of the first wife's husband to raise her baby. Those people had money, and they were good people also. The husband's mother then took the little baby in her house. So it came that when Auntie Linda married the first wife's husband a few years later, she ended up with this other child to mind, and the real name of this child is not known to me, but everyone called her Mamsie. My Auntie Linda was just married then and had a lot of work she had to do to show her new husband that she could be a good wife to him and keep the house so nicely. She already had one son, and another child would be soon on the way so, you know, she did not really have the time to look after this Mamsie when she came to live with them. Just make sure the child was safe in the day, because Mamsie was five and could go about by herself around the village already then."

Charity interrupted herself to order another large Coke, and Margo asked some apposite questions relating to the structure of the household, the complicated family arrangements (which she drew out as a quick family tree in her notebook), and what they did for a living. She also considered venturing some diplomatic enquiries about the advisability, even in gentler times, of letting a tiny child wander around a village in the African countryside by herself but thought better of it. The story was developing a momentum of its own now, and she did not want to present too many obstacles to its flow.

Charity resumed. "I used to live in Kimberley, you know. In South Africa, and also here, it can be that children are not raised by their mothers and fathers. This is not only something that happened since those times when people started getting sick. If my mother has only daughters and her sister has only sons, then maybe some of the children go to the other house and grow up there. This is something people from overseas don't understand, they think it is wrong to send children away to be raised by someone not their real parent. But if the children are raised by people who love them, does this really matter or not matter? In our culture this sometimes is the way. Some people can even ask for a child to come to their house and stay. And that's what happened with my Auntie Linda. When she married her husband and found out that he had a sort of daughter already living with his mother taking care of her, she begged him to bring the child to live with them in the village. All her older brothers only had sons, and she wished so much for a girl child to play with because she was only just stopping being a child herself, even though she already had that one child. Trust me, she loved that Mamsie as if the girl came from out of her own body. She did."

The Coke arrived, and Charity emptied half the glass with a sigh of deep satisfaction, the ice cubes clattering against her pretty teeth. Margo took the opportunity to draw a few arrows onto the notes she was making to indicate where events Charity was relating out of sequence would need to be re-ordered chronologically.

Since it was becoming apparent that Mamsie was the protagonist in this particular story, Margo had another type of question, "So what was this Mamsie like, Charity? What was her character, do you know?"

Charity looked a bit nonplussed at this. Margo had learned by now that the narratives she was collecting tended to be driven by events, by accidents and sudden actions – often supernatural, involuntary or unconscious. An interesting part of her thesis was going to be pointing up the lack of human agency or characterisation in the stories as they were told to her.

"This family, the family of my Auntie Linda's husband, was not poor. They were in the village, but they had things – people today don't know this sometimes, but you can be in the village and not be so poor. Mamsie had toys she brought with her when she came, and Linda got her things too. She could go and play by herself when my auntie worked in the house. Her favourite toy was a baby doll, you see? Linda told me that this Mamsie, from the day that she came, was like a little mother to the other children in the village. This was her character, I suppose then – that she looked after all the children, even older than her – as if she was already so grown up.

"One day she asked Auntie Linda for a baby's bottle. My aunt thought at first that the baby doll had come with a doll's bottle that had got lost, and asked Mamsie this but no, Mamsie still had this one toy bottle but now she wanted a real baby bottle too, like the one Linda was using for her second born. Now Linda had told me that she was worried that Mamsie was so grown up already. It was helpful she looked after the other kids, this is true, but still Mamsie should have a chance to be a child. Now she looked like she wanted to drink milk like the second born, and so Linda got a spare bottle and got her a drink from one of the cows, and Mamsie went off. Lots of children do this, I think. They see a baby, and they want to go back to being like a baby and be getting that attention. My Auntie Linda was so, so busy, you know, that she was pleased to give something new to Mamsie to do, even though she had to give up one of the bottles from the real baby.

"A few days later, Mamsie came there to my aunt and asked for another bottle with milk. Now Linda was angry because she thought that the first bottle would be lost, but Mamsie said she still had that one but wanted the other bottle to play with as well. She had this baby doll, but now that toy bottle, it got broken or lost somehow, so Linda gave her another real bottle of milk to go play with the doll and also have some fresh milk for herself. And every day Mamsie would ask for these things, the two real babies' bottles of milk, and she would go play so nicely by herself for many hours until it was time to start helping making supper.

"One day, my aunt didn't have much work to do for some reason, and the new baby was sleeping, and she felt like she had not been paying so much attention to Mamsie. And anyway, she wanted a break from working in the house. She would go find the child and speak with her or see what games she was playing or some such. She knew where Mamsie went in the bush, along a path that went under a twisted tree, one of the only shade trees there that side. So Linda went along the path so quietly, thinking she would see Mamsie and her games before Mamsie knew she was coming. Oh, oh. I forgot to say that Mamsie was not good with hearing. She had that thing with her ears so she could only hear people if they were close by."

"Mamsie was deaf?"

"Mmmm. Could it be from measles, I think? Then Linda was peering at the child over the top of the long grass, and what she saw made her stop still as if she had died and stayed standing up, like some people do. Mamsie had the baby's bottle of milk she was drinking from. But she was also holding the other bottle up to give the milk to a cobra that was standing up taller than her head under the tree. Linda could not believe what she saw. Ayeee! This she could not believe. She watched and watched, and the child Mamsie gave the milk to the snake as if it was a baby and was talking to it as if it was a baby, stroking the yellow neck and wiping the side of the mouth with the teat of the bottle when some milk fell there. These animals, you know they grow sooo long. So even though the snake was taller than Mamsie, in fact it was not even yet an adult – it was going to grow a lot bigger in time. You know it makes me go cold to just say these things, shuh. The hood of the cobra was down. Do you know what this means?"

Margo had no idea.

"The hood being down means that the snake was happy, he was relaxed. He was not going to bite. Linda was always a strong person. She was sensible, and she grew up on a farm. She loved that child also, though she was not her own. She knew that if she ran out or made a shout, the cobra would just go strike, even before Mamsie heard her. These animals are nervous, you know? Because people, they are always trying to kill them. Even if she just gave Mamsie a surprise by running out then, the sudden movement of the child could make the snake go bite. So Linda went back by the path, and went to her house, and was trying to figure out what she could do, because definitely this was not just a regular snake. It had to be a special one that you couldn't just treat the same as the others that they killed all the time on the farm with pangas.

"When her husband returned to the house from the cattle post soon after, he asked why Auntie Linda was sitting on the stool outside the hut with her hands covering her face and crying. Before she told him the story, she warned him not to go off running through the bush and making such a scene – of course she was worried that the snake would still go bite, though she made sure not to mention the cobra when she first began the story. She just made him promise not to do anything foolish until she had finished all of what she wanted to say about Mamsie.

"But now the husband – Benson was his name – was sure that Auntie Linda was going to confess that she had harmed the child in some way. Otherwise, why could she be crying so much? It can happen that a stepmother can be jealous of a child or be forgetting to look after it or what. So, the husband was now already in a state in his mind, he was not really listening to what Auntie Linda was saying, just thinking to himself that something was very wrong and that he was the man and was going to have to deal with it. You know how husbands do not listen to what the wife is saying sometimes, even if the wife knows more than them.

"So as soon as he heard the word 'cobra' though, he could not help himself. He jumped up and ran off and went to the back of the hut where there was a little store and got his big panga and ran down the path in the bush. My Auntie Linda was running after him, but she had not long had a baby, and could not keep up. When she got to the tree, she could see that Mamsie was not there at all but that her husband was chop chopping at the ground and she looked and there he was cutting at the neck of the cobra.

"And ayeeeee! The snake was wriggling and squirming in such a nasty, nasty way, pushing the dust up in big clouds, its tail was all wrapped around the arm of Benson, but he was standing on the body more towards the head, and the snake could not escape.

"And slowly, slowly the snake stopped with its wriggling, and the tail let go of Benson's arm, and soon it was lying so dead and limp on the ground. But this was a tough and special snake. Benson had not used the panga for a while, and in the rains it got blunt and rusty. So where he had tried to chop the head right off the body of the snake, in two, it was only chopped off under the skin, you see, where the bones were, so that snake still looked whole, with no blood or cuts from the blunt knife. And, and this was the horrible thing now: the head was turned right round, twisted backwards where it was no longer joined to the body underneath the skin, like when you wring the neck of a chicken. This was an ugly, terrible thing to see and proved the snake was under a spell or was a spirit.

"My aunt and her husband were so happy now. They had rescued their Mamsie that they thought of as their daughter from the evil snake. They would go together to find her and tell her not to play babies with the wild animals anymore but to rather stay near the house where Linda could see her, and she could help with her younger brothers.

"They searched and searched. They called her name out as loud as they could, because only then could she hear them. They ran to their neighbours and asked if anyone had seen Mamsie. It was growing darker, and still they had not found her, but Linda was thinking that maybe Mamsie had seen what her father had done to her cobra and was hiding because she was sad or thought he was angry with her. They went together to the most obvious place that Linda could think of – a place beyond the village where Mamsie hid when Linda wanted to beat her for something bad she did.

"In the high banks of the dry riverbed were lots of holes. Some were very tiny and in groups, made by birds that nested in sorts of tunnels in the sand. Some were big and untidy, made by the porcupines looking for things to eat. And a very few were smooth and just as wide as my leg, and these were made by the snakes. Walking up the riverbed they finally saw Mamsie and raised their voices up to praise God. She was resting there with her head up against the sandy bank. They were so relieved and crying, and it was getting dark so quickly, that it was only when they got right up next to her that they saw Mamsie was even sleeping and that her head was part of the way down inside one of these holes made by the snakes.

"Then they started to be too scared. Her father gently reached down to grab on her ankles and pull her out, but when he touched her feet, he already knew Mamsie was not going to wake up when he did this. With the biggest sigh he pulled anyway. And of course, when her head came out of the hole, it was on backwards, just like the head of her cobra baby."

It was clear that Charity had finished her tale. With an unfocused gaze Margo stared, as if hypnotised, into her own empty glass, eyes wide with some unreadable fear of her own.

After some time, she cleared her throat. "That's a true story, Charity?"

She could feel that the fine hairs on her forearms were standing straight up, and she was chilled through, though the sun was still fierce, and the sweat had been dripping down the inside of her shirt a moment ago. Still Margo couldn't turn her eyes back towards the storyteller; they remained fixed on the frosting of condensation on her glass. She was struggling to emerge from the spell that the story had cast. Judging by the long silence between the two of them, she wondered if recounting those horrific events hadn't had the same effect on the narrator as well.

"True that my auntie told me, or true about the snake and Mamsie?"

"Both. I guess."

Charity shrugged with her whole body and drained her glass of the water from the melted ice cubes. Margo thought then that if this maid was having a huge joke at the expense of academe – just for the sake of a meal in a café into which she would never normally have set foot – it was unlikely that she would now burst into laughter and admit as much. On the other hand, if Charity believed this story implicitly, as Margo suspected she did, then no amount of questioning would ever get her to rehearse some objective explanation, supernatural or otherwise, for the death of the little girl. The events – as Charity had matter-of-factly shared them – were as much as Margo would ever know concerning the tragedy of so long ago.

The story was in essence true, she supposed, so far as anything passed down from throat to throat over many years could be said to be completely true. Charity needed it to be true, too, and this was the understanding at the heart of their encounter: *I have given you this gift that you didn't even know would be a gift,* she seemed to be saying by her shrug, *and now it is up to you to use it wisely, and pass it on or not as you see fit. But you cannot betray the faith I have placed in you by treating it as if it is some silly folktale.*

Margo could already see that Charity was gathering herself to leave and catch the late bus to the border. She carefully switched off the tape recorder and started to thank her by extending her hand in what she hoped would be perceived as a sincere, thoughtful gesture. Charity was already standing, and Margo was trapped in a seated position at the table by the proximity of another patron right behind her, so their handshake was very awkward in the end. So too was their final exchange: Charity was scanning for the exit, and an unaccountable sense of abandonment, of unfinished business, descended over Margo. *Tell me another,* she wanted to implore, although she knew there was only this one story worth telling, and that Charity was already anxious about missing her ride. What she ended up saying seemed so woefully inadequate that she recognised that it represented an affront of sorts.

"I am grateful to you Charity, really I am. This story is really going to be a great contribution to my work."

"Yes, madam."

The formality and finality both stung, but eventually, back home a few weeks later, Margo came to understand that she had trespassed in some way just then, and that therefore she had deserved this.

Charity was now on her way through the tightly packed crowd seated at the other small tables in the courtyard, skilfully threading her bulk between the chairs and bodies and out onto the pavement outside. Margo let some minutes pass then signalled for the bill. She paid, gathered up her belongings, and made her own way out onto the now-busy street.

Halfway to her parked hire car she stopped, removed the tape from the machine and threw it – unspooling slightly – into a trash can, then walked the short distance back to the café to present the little tape recorder to the surprised waitress. Standing in the midst of the afternoon shoppers streaming by her, she opened her notebook with some difficulty, scratched out all the notes that she had made that afternoon, and wrote underneath them the single thing worth remembering, before it escaped her mind.

The words that she said and the story that I heard and the sounds on the tape and the message I was supposed to understand. None of these can ever be the same thing.

Double-barrelled

The woman's voice on the other end of the line was talking all manner of nonsense in words scrambled and strung together in a language Ronney didn't really understand – Oshiwambo probably. He had grabbed the cellphone off the floor by his bed in the dark and answered it in a panic without checking the caller ID, just in case it was urgent news about his father from the hospital, or his stepdaughter's credit was just about to run out. But now it was turning out to be something else entirely, and his initial addled alarm was turning to weary resignation as he surmised it was yet another bloody end-of-the-month wrong number.

One night this had turned out to be a disappointed, belligerent businessman with an overdeveloped sense of entitlement who had decided to drunk dial his kamboroto to insist on his non-conjugal rights. Another time it had been a discarded sugar mummy who had obviously concluded that the early hours would be the time that her ex-boyfriend would be most receptive to talk of a remunerated reconciliation. The minute these people realised that you were not just *pretending* to be someone other than the stray lover they wished to speak with, but that actually they were haranguing a perfect stranger, they would summarily hang up without another word. This was a tendency Ronney compared with an observation from his truncated time studying overseas, where people dialling wrong numbers normally at least apologised after a fashion before ending the call.

But it's never anything less than nerve-wracking when a ringing phone summons you from deep sleep at 2 a.m. Especially when you have a father busy dying in hospital and a stepdaughter who is not serious in life studying far away from home. So even once he had determined, with blessed relief, that he was dealing with someone he didn't know, Ronney was aware that his heart was not returning to its regular rhythm just yet. Something about the desperation he detected in the shrill pleading on the other end of the line was keeping his attention stretched taut. And he recognised that it would therefore be a while, alas, before he would be restored to sleep after the call eventually ended, if he was able to slip back into slumber at all before the alarm on his phone went off at 6 a.m. Until his father passed, heart-thumping dread would continue to be his reaction whenever the phone rang at an unexpected time. Before he had recently started to accumulate doctors' and pharmacy bills, Ronney's father had been voluntarily estranged from him for many years, and the old man's recent peremptory, demanding calls from the state hospital aroused in Ronney a complex mixture of resentment, a deep and guilty pity, and impatience.

For some reason this lady was not giving up however, even though by now she must have understood, through Ronney's occasional brief interjections, that she was addressing a man unknown to her. The way that she gulped and swallowed her words made Ronney wish that God had not placed him in the centre of this drama, whatever it was, and however far removed from the hectic events of his own life it would inevitably turn out to be. She was weeping, that much he could tell, but also trying to talk to at least one other person besides Ronney: he could just about hear the necessarily indistinct sound of someone murmuring in a low but authoritative voice in the background.

He hazarded a guess and tried in English, to establish once and for all that she had called the wrong number and that he was not going to be able to assist. Then he could try to go back to what was left of his sleep.

"Madam. Stop now and listen, neh? You are calling the wrong person, and I do not know how I can help you. Maybe check the number you have just dialled, hey? Just go check."

Now there was a soft keening at the end of the line, not quite muffling the noise of a tired infant wailing desultorily and some scraping and scuffling, too. As well as what sounded like a metal door clanging on its hinges? And then more rapid-fire Oshi-whateveritwas.

"Please 'vrou. Stop now. Stop now and explain to me what is happening with you. In Afrikaans asseblief."

For some reason, though he spoke English perfectly well, he was slipping into a vernacular, stilted way of expressing himself in his desire to communicate quickly and have done with.

The line went dead. Something in the desperate way the caller had been crying and chasing words compelled him to begin the process of returning the call before he was even truly aware of what he was doing. An instinct kicking in, perhaps, but also a habit arising from long years of being the go-to guy for people, even strangers, in distress. The number's ID on the illuminated screen came up, to his very great surprise, as an address book entry he vaguely recalled.

And then the penny dropped.

Still Ronney didn't know what he was supposed to do next, though clearly the distraught Ms Hango-Johnson – as he now knew her to be – was expecting him to respond to her call in some practical manner. That much was clear from the unmistakable urgency of her incoherent tumble of words. Realising that one way or another he would now have to get up and get dressed, he pulled on tracksuit bottoms, worn white slops, and a cheap branded polo shirt from a workshop on HIV and the youth that he had recently attended. Of course, it was obvious to him now that all along she had been needing his personal assistance, but still, he didn't know where to physically locate her. Ronney acknowledged, with a dull fatalism, that it was going to be a long Sunday night now because – naturally – when he had tried to call her back, the number was unreachable.

⁓

Six months previously, he had been coaching the girls' soccer teams after school. The young women – ranging in age between 12 and 15 – were keen, skilled and ebulliently vocal, and he always enjoyed this part of his day very much. One of the distinct advantages of having secured a sought-after job in a private school was that the extramural activities were well attended as kids strove to pad out their CVs before applying for college. Sporting events were similarly popular, the bleachers filled with animated spectators often even more competitive than their children, especially the ex-pats.

The early afternoon temperature had been uncomfortable, even by the standards of the season, and the gusts of grit-filled, super-heated dry air were sapping everyone's strength and patience. A dust devil sprang up in the veld on the other side of the school's razor fence and tore a messy path through the low bushes and the sere, brittle grasses before it finally wore itself out near the bypass. Despite the considerable resources at their disposal, the best efforts of the three dedicated ground staff could not maintain the soccer pitch in good condition by this time of year, when the last decent rains of March were many months in the past. The automatic sprinkler system was always clogging up, leaving some patches of turf as hard, desiccated tufts and others like treacherous, miniature swamps. He had been coaching the A team – gratifyingly aggressive and athletic black Namibians, mostly, with a few equally competitive American girls from the NGO and diplomatic communities. His new deputy PE teacher, Salomon, had been coaching the B team, young ladies with slightly more mixed abilities and physiques. The pair had to stop the drills every ten minutes or so in order for all the players to jostle around the water fountains for a noisy slurp or two, or to get a bottle of luridly coloured energy drink out of their sports bags.

Ronney was just about to declare the outdoor session over and suggest that they repair indoors to talk tactics in the sports hall when he saw that one of the smaller girls, whom he had noticed earlier making her way to the side lines to sit out the dribbling practice, was now bent double on the bench with her neat braids falling in thick curtains that obscured her face. As she pitched forward onto her knees with a low grunt, Ronney ambled over. Salomon was closer, but Ronney was the one with advanced first aid training. He was sure that what they were dealing with was more a case of overdramatisation than a real medical emergency, hence his less-than-urgent, energy-conserving trot to the girl's side. If he knew one thing thanks to almost a decade of teaching sports to teenagers, it was that the boys liked to preen, boast and show off, regardless of their natural aptitudes, but the girls also manufactured their own moments in the limelight. This might be a celebration of genuine physical prowess or, failing that, through the engineering of some small-scale, reality-TV-mimicking histrionics.

But as he neared the child – whom he vaguely knew as Cecilia something-or-other – he was compelled to re-evaluate the situation, to admit to himself that she was not going to get up and race off once she had had her few minutes at the centre of attention. Her face was grey with pain, and he thought he also detected some embarrassment in the way that she held herself close, as if guarding a giveaway symptom that would cause her embarrassment. He hoped, then felt some shame in hoping, that this was not another situation where he was going to have to deal with a messy menstruation problem, since the female school nurse would have already left the premises for the day. He located Salomon, who was busy gathering the other girls around him some distance away. Cecilia's close friends had assembled to fuss gently around her, but all the others had cleared that part of the field, as they had been instructed to do when someone needed medical attention. Ronney then used hand signals to indicate that his deputy should lead the pack of girls away and off towards the changing rooms.

"Do any of you know if Cecilia has been sick? That's her name, right, Cecilia?" Ronney addressed the little cohort of girls who, touchingly, seemed intent on staying and who were now staring down in silence and frank curiosity at their friend's distress.

"No, Mr Christiaans," several of them mumbled, as Cecilia slid off the bench and into a squat on the grass.

"Is she on her period, do you know?"

The girls were sophisticated enough not to be fazed by this question, especially as Ronney also filled in with teaching health topics from time to time. But again, their few replies were in the negative.

"Okay, one of you go to the office and get Theresia or Mrs Kimble to call an ambulance. Actually, you know what, on second thoughts I am going to take care of her myself. Tell Mrs Kimble that we are going straight to the hospital in my car, and I will call her from there."

"Can we come with?" One of the girls was crying now and appeared to be speaking for the whole gang of seven or eight.

"No. It's better if you go change and get home rather. But one of you get the office to call her mother or her auntie for me and tell them to meet me at the hospital? Can you organise to do that between you?"

He had only briefly thought that they could also try calling the father – assuming that Cecilia had one present in her life, which was not necessarily the case based on his experience. Ronney knew that the kind of man who sent his kids to this prestigious, expensive school would not welcome a summons to the hospital mid-afternoon, if he could in fact be reached at all. Dealing with such family matters was strictly the business of womenfolk, no matter how westernised the family, and despite the fact that the mother was often just as successful, busy and important as the father.

He bent and scooped up the little girl. She had been moaning and rocking gently on her haunches in the dirt, her soccer shorts bunched up under her and her dust-reddened socks concertinaed down to her expensive trainers. This was the first chance he had had to really take a look at this girl, and now that he could focus his attention on her, he quickly cycled through all the potential causes of her collapse but nonetheless drew a blank. A heat was emanating from her, unconnected, he suspected, with either the sun beating down on them all or with her exertions on the pitch. When she sighed in his face and her eyes rolled to the side a little, he thought he detected an odd, sweet chemical scent on her breath – one he knew he should be able to identify but could not place. He checked over his shoulder to make sure that her friends were heading off in the direction of the office. One was concentrating on her cellphone, and the others were clustered tightly round her in a trotting phalanx, offering instructions as they went.

He loaded his burden carefully into the passenger seat of his bakkie in the staff car park behind the wire fence, only a few metres away. She was one of the smaller players and was easy to manoeuvre as he adjusted the seat to a reclining position for her. However, when he attempted to fasten her seatbelt, she unexpectedly arched her back in a spasm of pain, and it was with some difficulty that he eventually managed to secure it around her. She then drew her knees up to her chest once she was settled, and he thought to himself again, with a pinch of bitterness, that he was probably just dealing with women's problems. If only he had remembered to put a blanket on the cloth seat first, like he did when he had to transport kids he thought might throw up. But still, a colleague at another school had been sued by the parents of a learner when this teacher had failed to deal with a scorpion sting quickly enough, and the child had suffered an allergic reaction that almost killed him. So, it was best to take any kind of symptoms seriously until they were diagnosed and dealt with by the professionals.

Fortunately, this late in the day, the staff parking lot was almost empty, and a fast exit would be straightforward. Salomon raced over on foot as Ronney was reversing out, and they confirmed together that everyone who needed to be alerted had been told what was happening or was in the process of being contacted. Unfortunately, when Salomon handed Ronney his blue plastic drinking bottle, which he had left behind on the soccer pitch, it was almost empty.

At the A&E entrance of the nearby private hospital, where all learners who had an accident or health crisis at the school were taken initially, Cecilia – who still had not said a word and was still rolled up in a tight curl – was lifted gently into a wheelchair by two calm orderlies. Ronney was directed to wait in a brightly lit reception area decorated in too many pastel colours, the clashing tones of which, along with a strong paint smell and the low hum from the many overhead strips of fluorescent lights, had the effect of making him feel slightly headachy. Then the woman who had been sitting talking at a counter through a glass partition with the male admissions officer vacated her chair, and Ronney swiftly moved to take her place before anyone else could. He was still hoping to finish this girl's period business quickly and get home by late afternoon.

"Before you start handing me forms, I need to tell you I am not related to this girl. I am just her teacher. Man, I don't know her at all, actually."

"We can't treat her if we don't know her medical aid number, sir. Someone has to sign for her to be responsible for her costs. Or you must take her to the other hospital."

This would be one of the two government-run facilities situated across town, an altogether different kind of establishment where he anticipated that the child would still be waiting to be seen – in some godforsaken, dilapidated and overcrowded holding area – until around midnight. And he would be waiting there with her too, if Cecilia's mother was out of town, or unavailable. One of these hospitals was also where his father was seeing out his final days, so Ronney was keen on avoiding them altogether.

"Let me see if I can get some more information. Can I do that and stay here quickly?"

The admissions officer checked behind Ronney to make sure no one else was waiting to be attended to, then gave him the go-ahead with an understanding nod. Ronney used his cellphone to speed-dial the school reception desk, and in less than two minutes Theresia had pulled up Cecilia's file on the computer. She read out the relevant details, including her medical insurance number and the information that the child's surname was Eises, all of which he transcribed onto the square of paper the officer pushed towards him under the glass partitioning. Theresia also told him that they had already called the mother, and she had been apprised of the situation and had his contact number. Thank goodness the school nurse was on a mission when it came to keeping learners' records current.

He then began to fill in all the admissions paperwork as the officer checked on his computer screen that the details on the scrap of paper tallied with those for Cecilia's medical scheme and that the insurance policy was active, so that the process of finding out what was wrong with the girl could finally begin. Ronney's headache, doubtless exacerbated by mild dehydration at this point, he thought, was now occupying a wide panel down the centre of his face, causing it to tense and twitch in response to a throbbing ache.

Less than a minute later, Ronney's phone rang and a bored-sounding woman on the other end introduced herself in good English as Cecilia's mother's PA. She made no effort to hide her resentment at having her afternoon disrupted or at being made to wait briefly while Ronney retrieved the scrap of paper to note down more details. She curtly announced that her boss was in a meeting but she would join him as soon as she could, then asked if he needed anything else from her. Once he had ascertained that the incoming number belonged not to the PA but to Cecilia's parent, he asked her to spell out the mother's name in order to save it in his phone's contact list. Philadelphia Hango-Johnson. Ronney's annoyance that this mother with the ridiculous name was unlikely to be arriving in the near future added to his rising indignation at being there in the first place. He knew these types of people, always the last to collect their kids from any school function, if they even bothered to do so at all. All the staff members, at some time or another, had had to drive a little boy or girl home because the adults nominally responsible for them had not shown up, even hours after an event was over. This was another reason the school nurse sent out regular requests for personal details to be updated on the database, though generally, the parents or guardians most likely to misplace a child were hardly the ones likely to be fastidious about communicating their ever-changing personal circumstances to the school.

And also, he asked himself with yet more irritation, where did these three names suddenly come from? He had two names given to him as a baby, as did everyone else he knew, but recently people had started to insist that a third name be inserted between the ones they had previously been known by. It made learning the names of the children at the school doubly difficult since the extra name tended to change according to which singer or sportsman was currently in vogue.

He confirmed with the admissions officer that a Ms Hango-Johnson would be along soon-ish and that she would be taking responsibility for Cecilia's billing. Then Ronney stepped away from the reception desk to wait on one of the chairs arranged in rows by the soft-drinks machines. The headache came along with him.

✧

While he was recalling all of this with some residual exasperation, Ronney was searching through the drawers of the desk in the home-office corner of his flat for the most recent printed copy of all the learners' personal details. Paging through the thick file of papers – risk-assessment guidelines, dietary and religious proscriptions, and a whole pile of other such information that staff were supposed to have at their fingertips these days, and which got more unwieldy every year – it was a while before he found the database details for Cecilia. Tired and befuddled, he'd forgotten she did not share a surname with her mother. Under her records, unusually, the first parent's details to be listed were for a man – the father he assumed, though again the surname was different from Cecilia's – and it was a landline. The address was in a complex of new, three-storey luxury townhouses, a ten-minute drive from his own miniscule rented flat. He called, and to his slight surprise, the phone rang, and then to his even greater surprise, someone picked up.

"Hello. Is that Meneer Van Wyk's home?" he asked without much expectation of a positive reply.

There then followed a circuitous conversation with a foreign-sounding young woman during which he eventually established that he was talking to Telma, the new wife of Mr Van Wyk; that Mr Van Wyk was away in Angola on business; and that trying to extract any information regarding Cecilia's mother was going to be a trial of epic proportions. This lady did seem chatty and friendly enough, flirta-tious even, when the stilted talk was not about her husband's complex domestic arrangements. Indeed, he gained the distinct impression that not only was Telma still not in bed at 2.20 a.m. on a Monday, but that she was also keen for someone, preferably male, to talk to. Her evident reluctance to share the details of Ms Hango-Johnson's new address did not seem to arise out of any animosity between the incoming wife and the ex, but was maybe instead a case of her having sound reasons to be suspicious of anyone wanting personal details to do with the elusive Mr Van Wyk, especially a stranger calling in the early hours of the morning.

Ronney had deliberately not gone into details concerning who he was, nor furnished this new wife with the reasons for his call because he was unsure of them, really, himself. He definitely didn't want to get into a "he said, she said" between the ladies, with their patently complicated love lives, tonight or in the future. Now he lit upon a way to maybe focus Telma's attention on the need to supply him with the information he sought.

"It's about one of the cars of Meneer van Wyk?"

This – said in a way that he hoped conveyed some authority and concern, maybe even police-related seriousness – appeared to have the desired effect. Whatever reservations Telma had about involving herself in the affairs of her husband's previous partner, the thought that one of his cars could be in some sort of trouble, prompted her to give up the address he requested instantly. She didn't even ask how the car could be connected with the ex, though doubtless she had her own suspicions.

He reversed his bakkie carefully out of the ridiculously tiny, awkward parking space in front of his home and manoeuvred it through the rumbling security gate. The route to the Hango-Johnson/Eises residence was taking him to a new subdivision on the outskirts of town that he didn't know at all well, one of the many that Chinese builders had covered – almost, it seemed, overnight – with blocky, ash-coloured dwellings, surrounded by waist-high chain-link fences and desolate yards.

The denouement of Cecilia's hospital story half a year back had actually been laughably mundane in the end, he recalled as he drove. Far sooner than he expected, a stunning, heavily pregnant woman he assumed to be the Hango-Johnson mother had eased her way with some difficulty through the revolving doors of the A&E waiting area. She'd nodded a greeting in his direction – she clearly knew him by sight, even though he could not say the same for her, despite her arresting looks. She had then gone straight to the admissions officer and spoken with him in a quiet voice through the glass partition while holding up for inspection her medical aid card. As she had her back to him, Ronney had taken the opportunity to examine her – a woman of substance evidently, she had on her narrow feet new-looking yellow suede shoes with silver, pointy toecaps and low stiletto heels, complemented by a long, black wrap-around skirt of some silky material, a discreetly billowing tunic also in yellow, and some tasteful – and most likely real – gold jewellery. To anyone familiar with the way Namibian society divided itself, these items of clothing alone would have been enough to identify Ms Hango-Johnson as a high-level functionary or thriving enterprise owner.

A stocky white nurse had then appeared from behind a double door, conferred with Cecilia's mother, and led her off with a gentle hand underneath the elbow. Ronney again approached the admissions officer, now occupied with his cellphone in the absence of any clients.

"Am I done here now then? That lady, the mother, she can take care of things now, hey?"

The officer had smiled and concurred without looking up from his device. Ronney then thought that he had better check something that had occurred to him, just in case.

"That young lady? It's nothing serious. She'll be okay, ja?"

"Sir, she is just now being examined by doctor. But in any case, I'm sorry, but that information is confidential."

He had driven back home from the hospital utterly drained. People simply didn't realise what an exhausting job it was being a teacher – he didn't know how his colleagues who taught the academic subjects, with their assessments and homework and syllabi, survived. By then it was early evening and he'd been so shattered that it was only when he'd stopped at Nandos for take-out peri-peri chicken that it had occurred to him that at no point during Cecilia's crisis had he deployed a single aspect of his first aid training. So much for that.

The following day he'd learned from the school that Cecilia had been suffering from a kidney infection, brought about by a failure to stay hydrated over a period of days. She was not the first child this had happened to, though certainly her illness had had the most dramatic consequences, and as a result she played no further soccer after school that term. Her mother had texted him a brief "Tnx 4 helping out the other day w/C", and although he was gratified for that small, unexpected acknowledgement, he'd quickly let the whole episode drop from his mind. Only now, on this Sunday night many months later, had he discovered that he'd forgotten to remove the mother's number from his list of phone contacts.

He was now in a part of town with no street signs or lighting, but the full moon was still extraordinarily bright, and he thought that somehow he would be able to identify the right house. Maybe the distressed mother or Cecilia herself would be waiting outside to let him in, or some sixth sense would tell him where to pull up? As he drove slowly past all the identical, unfinished-looking, squat and ugly houses, arranged in numerous looping streets, he thought about how he came to be here, yet again, running to the aid of someone in need that he barely knew.

ɷ

He was once more in this regrettable position because he belonged to everyone: the absolute epitome of the child that the whole village raised, alas. An orphan, though in truth neither of his parents was late; a boy symbolically taken up into the bosom of the whole community, whose members later weighed him down as an adult with their expectations and shameless demands for a piece of him.

He accepted that everyone knew his history – it was, after all, a small town – and that as a result of his (initially improbable) triumph over adversity and the lack of any common-knowledge evidence to the contrary, he was generally considered to be one of the few good guys. Which is to say, someone who almost anyone could turn to when all other options – financial or logistical, chief among them – had been exhausted. In cynical moments, he thought of himself as the fourth emergency service – though operating with more efficiency perhaps, and along strictly charitable lines.

Ronney was tall, handsome (if you overlooked the two darker patches of acne scars under his cheekbones), solvent and still resolutely single, though he was now in his mid-thirties. Hence the gay rumours, which no one really gave much credence to: they had been started, elaborated upon, and shared with no malicious intent. He made a polite point of avoiding the more flagrant approaches from women faculty, learners' mothers and female guardians, and from the bolder, older girls that he taught PE. As his work could easily be covered temporarily by an under-utilised history teacher furnished with a whistle, and because management wanted to do what it could to retain one of their few black staff members, he could regularly take time off to attend various health- and sports-related workshops around the country and even, from time to time, abroad. It was at these functions, two or three a year, that he was able to surrender to the less saintly side of his character. Though his drinking (a few beers that always went to his head) and sexual adventures (nearly always condomised) were certainly nowhere near as disgraceful as those of many of the other event participants, he was fastidious about maintaining a separate, wholesome persona when he went back to work.

His reprobate father, Festus, had been severely injured when Ronney was five, helping the old German farmer who employed him to put out a small veld fire next to the workshop – a blaze of modest proportions that had nevertheless been threatening to move across to the vast grazing lands to the east during a morning of unpredictable high winds. Festus had been badly burnt when the fire had flared up in his face without warning. He had reflexively put his arms up as protection and his sleeves, made of some cheap, synthetic material, had instantly caught fire.

It eventually transpired that the farmer, Herr Häupter, had accidentally started the fire himself by failing to extinguish his early morning cigarette as he made his turn of inspection around the yard. Soon, a few people worked out that Festus's own severe 8 a.m. intoxication had been a contributing factor to his partial immolation as well and Festus's subsequent year-long recuperation gave Ronney's mother an excuse to run off with a policeman who had come to investigate the cause of the accident. The Häupters, whom God had not blessed with children of their own, were then prompted by their slight and grudging contrition to support Ronney through primary school in the nearest large town. Other people learned of this benevolence, and soon Ronney had more toiletries and (used) clothes, shoes and toys than he had ever imagined one person could need in a lifetime.

Although they were not inclined to indulge their workers, the Häupters found that their small act of charity (the school and hostel fees cost them next to nothing, really) developed an unstoppable momentum. In the end they resigned themselves to paying for Ronney – who turned out to be both athletic and a bright boy – to go to high school and then to college in Windhoek. The story of the poor farm boy with the absent mother and the burnt father, who was a star sprinter and one of the region's top scholars, eventually made the national papers, and Ronney found himself a minor celebrity for a while. He was sponsored by various large companies and in receipt of all kinds of useful (and less useful) gifts from national organisations keen to capitalise on his small-scale fame. But young as he was, Ronney already had a sense that there would come a time when he would be expected to reciprocate this bounty in kind. Even at high school, his middle-class peers assumed him to be more fortunate in material things than they were, and he was taken aback by the number of times his more-privileged classmates demanded money, food, or small items from him. As he grew older, and the extortion became more blatant, Ronney felt himself developing a deeply jaundiced world view underneath his blandly amiable exterior.

The Häupters discovered that the pride they took in being congratulated by neighbours on their largesse developed, in time, into a genuine regard for Ronney's achievements and even, ultimately, a kind of affection for the boy. In his turn, Ronney grew to respect their generosity, regardless of what he now knew to be its original aim of assuaging their guilt. He had no hesitation in asking them to help him out with living expenses when he applied for, and obtained, a bursary to study further in Scotland, a country he had chosen as he knew that the Häupters had fond memories of visiting there as a young couple. He had hoped, in a now rare moment free of cynicism, that they would make the same journey again on his graduation.

In the middle of his second year in Aberdeen, a drab, damp city he hated as he hadn't thought it possible to hate a place, he got a confused call late one night from a friend of a friend in Windhoek, who asked him to phone right back. Though he really didn't have the cash for a long-distance conversation, he resigned himself to skipping a meal or two, quickly bought some phone credit at an all-night corner shop, and returned the call.

It turned out that the girl Ronney had decided to marry once he graduated, an ambitious, decent girl whom he had met at college back home, had been killed in a car accident. Not only had she not been where Ronney had supposed her to be that evening (in the college hostel), she had also been driving on a surprising errand in her cousin's car (Ronney was unaware that she had even been studying for her licence, and later on it turned out that in fact she hadn't). He'd been shocked to learn that she'd been on her way to her village to collect her four-year-old daughter – father unknown – from her sister. A daughter he'd had no knowledge of until that moment. This sister was supposed to be looking after Ndali but had grown bored of her unpaid assignment and had therefore told his fiancée recently that she had to come and get her kid now-now. This was a compelling set of details Rita had neglected ever to mention to him, despite their emailing back and forth daily. Abruptly, he found himself far from home and assailed by so many conflicting emotions that, not for the first time, he'd buried them in a shuttered compartment in his mind. He resolved to disinter the contents at some time in the future when he felt better equipped to deal with them, a moment that he had been deferring ever since.

After Rita's funeral, as he stood holding the impossibly tiny, hot hand of his sleepy, newly minted stepdaughter, well-wishers came up to him in the church hall and told him that his burden of grief was all part of God's plan for him. The jocular pastor had placed a hand on his shoulder, and with a mouth full of masticated pink cake, intoned the same sentiments. Rita's family wished him the best and told him, unconvincingly, to call if he needed anything. They appeared to be labouring under the delusion that he was Ndali's father and had made it clear they would not hear otherwise. In that moment, Ronney couldn't help but hope that God had had His turn with him now and would fix His attentions on someone else for a while.

And so just as his life had been taking off, just as he had allowed himself to envisage so many versions of their future waiting for him and Rita, he had been obliged to give up his studies and aspirations in order to take care of Ndali, just as the Häupters had stepped in to take care of him almost two decades before.

Now his stepdaughter was away at school at the coast, though proving not to have inherited her mother's conscientiousness with respect to studying. Already she was talking of leaving as soon as she could and becoming a cosmetologist, whatever that might be – something trifling Ronney was sure, since she appeared to need ludicrously few qualifications to enrol at the expensive private Cape Town "institute" for which she had sent him the promotional brochure. So it would inevitably begin, the cycle of long-distance needs and wants, favours and demands, money transfers and pledges that he knew so well from his experiences with other grown adults – random people who felt that he owed them, somehow, since he had overcome the circumstances of his birth and they had not. He wondered, in his bleaker moments, how long it would be before Ndali's own inevitable pregnancy and its associated expenses were sprung on him.

✧

He turned off the narrow road in front of a house that had a small crowd milling about outside the chain-link fence. With a deflating trepidation, he knew that this had to be the place, and that what he was about to walk into couldn't be good. A small figure inside the empty yard, Cecilia in her lilac fleece pyjamas, stepped forward and shielded her eyes until he extinguished the car headlights. Then, walking with what seemed to be the utmost deliberation, one bare foot carefully placed before the other in the dirt, she yanked the protesting metal gate back until there was just enough room to squeeze his car through. He eased in through the gap and cut the engine, observing that no other vehicle was parked in the yard – an unusual state of affairs as this was not the very poorest part of the city by any means. Ronney then stepped around the back of his twin cab to confront the child, but the gate was already pulled closed, and she had disappeared someplace.

All the lights inside were off, but he could make out the front door, the only door, square in the centre of the simple block that made up the dwelling – the kind of foursquare building a child draws when he first wants to depict a house. This door was ajar, and he let himself in after instinctively locking his car with his remote. A claustrophobic hallway, closed glass doors to either side – the moonlight was dimly illuminating the type of home that hundreds of thousands of his countrymen and women aspired to but that, he knew, represented a spectacular reversal in the fortunes of this particular family. As he approached the end of the hallway, he saw a third open doorway, through which he sensed rather than heard people moving about.

"Can I enter? Can I switch on the light? 'Vrou?"

Assuming that they had power, of course. Even this much was not a given in this part of town.

There was no reply, so he carefully worked his fingers around the inside of the doorframe, first to the left and then to the right, until he found the switch. He was already aware of the sweet, winey smell that permeates a room where cheap brandy was consumed daily. Something from his past.

"'Kay now. I am switching on the light."

A single bare light bulb hanging from the ceiling cast its rude brightness out into the front part of a long, narrow kitchen. Philadelphia was sitting facing him at a heavy, carved wooden table that almost completely filled the room, her head in her hands. She was wearing a sorry-looking dressing gown, a pair of pinkish-grey cotton knickers and a man's T-shirt that was far too big for her. Cecilia, standing behind, had a hand on one of her mother's thin, exposed shoulders and was balancing a fidgeting baby on her hip with the other. Only the half-naked infant – nubbing frantically on the dummy in her mouth and with a trickle of yellowish shit visible at the junction of buttock and leg – was looking at him.

Except that now he saw, with a cold jolt of shock, that this wasn't the case. The light bulb at the far end of the narrow room had blown or was missing, but beyond the tableau immediately before him he was starting to make out a still, bunched volume of darker shadow piled up on the floor. The mass lay silhouetted by the moonlight in front of an open door that gave access to the back yard from the rear of the house, a door protected on the inside by a closed, barred metal security gate. It was a man, and he, too, was staring in Ronney's direction.

Ronney asked Cecilia to fetch a candle and light it. He had to make several attempts to speak, his voice emerging eventually from the back of his tight throat as a dry, nasal rasp. She handed the baby to her mother, opened a wall cupboard above her head, and found a box of matches and the stump of a candle stuck into a saucer, all ready for the next power outage. She lit it expertly and handed it to Ronney. One step, two steps towards whatever it was that awaited him at the back end of the room. The light from the candle wobbled unsteadily so that at first, he didn't know what he was looking at and then, with his stomach swooping and flipping over madly, he did.

A man – no, a boy – was sitting awkwardly in a small black puddle, his back against the metal security door. He was gasping in a ragged rhythm, with a look of pleading anguish in his glittering eyes. Most of the ferrous-smelling pool of congealed blood was trapped between his oddly splayed legs although a little also spread out to either side of him. He was fully conscious, alert even, and apart from the confusion playing across his features, he appeared to be in no obvious discomfort.

Ronney considered the most credible explanation as best he could, given that this injured robber might be armed, and he therefore needed to remain on his guard: Philadelphia had shot a thief earlier in the night, and he, not the police nor a private armed-response company, was supposed to deal with this? Even within the wide parameters of the more outrageous favours and demands he was regularly obliged to fend off, this was really asking way too much. Time to shift some responsibility and get going.

"He's still alive look. Did you call the police? Are they on their way?"

After a long intake of breath, Philadelphia spoke in a whisper, though she did not move her hand away from the face it still partially covered. The baby in her lap had started to yank hard and intently on her mother's untidy, loose hair, but Philadelphia did not appear to notice.

"It is my son. It's Diego, my firstborn."

Ronney was slow on the uptake. "Your son was robbing you?" He supposed it wouldn't be the first time.

Only a defeated, impatient sigh came from Philadelphia as an exasperated rebuttal. He tried again, raising his voice a little and noticing the pettish tone as he became slightly shrill, his words ringing in the small and crowded space.

"He tried to kill himself? Is that what he did? Philadelphia?"

"My mum shot him."

This from Cecilia now, her words strong and confident, a small miracle. The same voice, he now understood, that he had heard murmuring in the background when Philadelphia had called him at home, what seemed like years ago now. For a moment the girl's self-possession granted him a grounding sense of relief. Despite the import of what she was telling him, a hope rose briefly in him that between the two of them they could figure out what to do next. But almost instantly this was replaced by something more uncertain – a suspicion that she was only performing this poise for as long as was necessary to convince him of the absurd fact that her mother had tried to kill her older brother. The peculiar sense of prevailing calm made him wonder how long Diego had been sitting there, too.

"She thought it was my dad. Diego is studying there in PE, and we didn't even think he knew our new address yet. My dad has been threatening my mum. She heard a noise and thought it was him coming to get us."

Had she practised this dispassionate explanation prior to his arrival, or was she simply showing unnerving, unnatural composure? Or the first manifestations of shock, even?

A soft groan from the boy. He tried to rise by supporting his weight on his hands, seeking to establish a grip on the slippery floor by pushing experimentally on his palms until he felt tiles underneath them and not a treacherous viscosity. A handsome boy, Ronney could see now as his sight adjusted to the dim candlelight, with candid green eyes, a carefully shaved head and very light, evenly toned skin. Probably the result of the relationship signified by the "Johnson" part of the mother's name, Ronney supposed, as Diego could even have passed for white in a different country, where the subtle signifiers of race were not so well recognised by all.

It was obvious now that Diego had lost the use of his legs. He kept his gaze fixed on those redundant limbs as if willing them to move, but they remained exactly where they had been when Ronney had first illuminated the boy in the small, uncertain spotlight of the candle's flame.

"Where did you shoot him Philadelphia? In the back? Is that where?"

He had, after all, been called there to use his first aid training on the young man, he assumed, though anyone with the capacity to think straight, anyone not panicked into the crazy miscalculations of desperation, would have known Ronney was totally out of his depth.

Ms. Hango-Johnson still had one hand covering her eyes, but a small movement in her neck gave him to understand that she was nodding faintly and mechanically. If he had had any notion to move the boy or examine his injuries, this information at least reassured Ronney that Diego was better off left where he sat until the emergency services arrived. This they must surely do at some point soon, given the interest of the crowd he had seen gathering outside on the street. Ronney's relief at avoiding yet more drama shamed him afresh, but the less he had to do with this family and their relentless descent into greater and greater misfortune, the better, so far as he was concerned.

Cecilia had in the meantime embarked upon a further detailed explanation in a now less-steady voice. Of how word must have somehow reached this older half-brother regarding the sinister threats of Mr Van Wyk – whom Cecilia called her father, though it seemed likely he was, in fact, only the father of the baby. Of how this ex-husband had summarily ejected his family from the home they had all shared in order to make room for his latest woman, the juicy Telma. Ronney found himself imagining the pristine new townhouse that used to be this family's home, with its imported marble floors and multiple flat-screen TVs, into which Mr Van Wyk had recently moved the biddable new wife. A lost girl very likely in need of citizenship through marriage and pragmatic enough to make the ugly concessions her position forced upon her. The discarded family had then apparently fetched up here as good as destitute. Whatever well-paid job or lucrative business it was that Philadelphia had been engaged in when Ronney last saw her at the private hospital, her domestic relegation seemed to have led to a rapid loss of economic status, too. Cecilia was even in possession of a letter from the school saying her fees were late and she could not continue to attend unless they were settled, the girl explained, in a detail that seemed beyond redundant, given the circumstances.

Cecilia continued in a dogged manner. Without forewarning them, Diego – the man of the house now by default – had come up on the Intercape through the night when he had discovered somehow that his sisters and mother were being threatened. *Why threats? Didn't Mr Van Wyk now have what he wanted in Telma and a newly child-free house? Unless he was a figure of some standing in the community and what he wanted was to avoid the kind of scandal that Ms Hango-Johnson was possibly planning to blackmail him with.*

Diego had called Cecilia when he eventually arrived at the house after a journey of almost two days, and she had quietly let him in. But then their mother – who had been drinking with determination since the reality of her situation had begun to sink in – had stumbled into the darkened kitchen as her two eldest children had been discussing her situation in whispers. In her confusion, their mother had started screaming that they were all about to be slaughtered.

While Diego had walked the few paces back down the room and turned to close the outer door before the neighbours heard the commotion, Philadelphia had produced from the pocket of her dressing gown a gun she must have recently acquired. In her drunken state she had not recognised her own flesh and blood and had shot him in the lower spine from across the room. It was Diego's singular misfortune that although Philadelphia was too inebriated to register who he was in the gloom, somehow the accuracy of her aim had not been impaired.

Ronney had a curious feeling that this unnecessarily painstaking exposition was not for his benefit alone.

"My mum is scared of living here. She doesn't like this place. She says it's full of botsotsos. She must have got the gun because she heard about all the break-ins. And also because of my dad."

All of this Ronney heard but only partially absorbed or even believed. It didn't concern him anymore: the approaching daybreak was about to deliver its own resolution, thank God, one that he would have no part in. The walls of the little kitchen were spinning now with blinding flashing lights, a siren started its inflected whoop then was abruptly cut off, and someone pushed the grinding front gate open to finally let in the police. Although he knew that the full story would never come out, Ronney had realised – almost from the moment that he stepped into the kitchen – that another person had been there before him but had left, and that this absent one was connected with certain of the background noises he had heard when he had answered his phone so long ago, at 2 a.m.

Perhaps Philadelphia had not been drinking alone, and maybe it had been her visitor – a new man? – who had shot at Diego, accidentally or deliberately, taken by surprise at the boy's arrival. Or perhaps this sinister Mr Van Wyk, for his own reasons, had indeed seen fit to terrorise his surplus family and had turned up that evening with violence in mind. Cecilia's too-longwinded explanation was well rehearsed and ostensibly believable but failed to take into account that Diego, though almost certainly paralysed, would probably live. The amount of blood pooled around him did not appear to derive from a mortal wound and he had been sitting there, silent but lucid, for some considerable time now with no loss of consciousness or other apparent change in his condition.

So apart from the tiny baby, Diego had actually been – in the scenario that Ronney's sense of self-preservation was now forcing him to piece together – the fourth witness to his own shooting. The boy should recover and would then be able to speak the truth about who really injured him, if he chose to reject the script Cecilia had prepared and was taking care to articulate for his benefit one more time. In the future, Diego might decide to deliver up his testimony or could, perhaps, be convinced to remain silent about the true gunman – for the right, very high, price.

Within the half-hour, Ronney had been able to assure the policeman who heard his account that he was just a friend of the family who had responded to a distressing phone call not long ago and who had arrived just before the police. This seemed the safest story for all concerned, as well as representing his best exit strategy, although Ronney worried a little that they might check Ms Hango-Johnson's cellphone log and see that a fair measure of time had passed between her making that call to him in the middle of the night, and the present moment. Hours that would have been time enough for concocting a plausible fictional narrative between them all.

Of other witnesses there were none. The crowd that had gathered outside the house an hour or more before had melted into the dark the instant the police pulled into the street. In another country it might have been possible to ascertain the time that had passed between Diego's injury and now – Ronney had seen those American forensics shows on TV. But such close examination of a crime scene was simply beyond the technical resources of the police here, and the uncomplicated tale of domestic drama and misidentification that the police were even now hearing from Cecilia was likely to remain the one that accompanied the brief investigation through to its closure.

The police didn't even need him to come back to the station in the morning and help them to make out a docket. It seemed to have all been an accident. Happens all the time with house guns. People must just learn to keep them locked up in the safe, especially if they have been drinking, or have youngsters at home.

Ronney was free to go.

He took a roundabout route back into town and then across to his own suburb via the still-quiet backstreets. He needed a chance to clear his head a little before he rang the school and left a message on the answering machine saying he would be off sick that day. A headache. He negotiated a long-enough detour to also arrive at the conclusion that no one would be better off if the truth, whatever it was, came out. It was almost certain that Diego, for the sake of his shattered family and his expensive recovery, would confirm the story and timeline that the women had put together and that Ronney had, through his own almost-accidental duplicity, cemented into place.

He beeped the car locked under the shade cloth of his parking bay as the first hint of faint ruby streaks appeared in the sky to the east. He contemplated the dawn, which he was usually too fast asleep or too rushed to appreciate, and wondered that his first aid skills had wholly deserted him – or rather, had proved surplus to requirements – on the past two occasions he had been called upon to use them.

He also abruptly remembered how it was that Cecilia's name was known to him when those of so many of her fellow learners were not. Talk in the staffroom recently had been that she was expected to score outstanding marks when she eventually sat her national examinations, and she might even gain entrance to a university overseas in a few years. He doubted though, given the events of the past evening and his own experience of the far-reaching fallout of sudden death, that this would be the path that God had chosen for her to follow now.

A Bed on Bricks

She had become a stranger to herself. Or, more accurately, a shadowy person had appeared recently in the margins of Aina's life, a spectral presence with an agenda and set of imperatives from which she shrank. Although this visitor and her unwelcome insinuations largely withdrew during the busy day, she would always re-emerge from the edge of consciousness in the night.

At her birth there had been a twin sister, so she was told – one who had been destined not to survive. Was this her now, reasserting herself and demanding to have her indecent say?

જ્જ

The creeping cold of early morning had eventually roused her from a fitful sleep, and when she looked around to retrieve the thick blanket that had worked its way down to her knees during the night, she had the momentary, disconcerting sensation that she had awoken in a hushed and frozen world. From the perch she shared with Kent on the vehicle's roof, a variegated landscape of dull mercury and silver shades surrounded their huddled, sleeping forms in all directions. The brilliant moonlight transformed the rocks and scrub of the open savanna and the distant cliffs into a spectacular, snow-encrusted vista, one she could see brightly illuminated for a good hundred metres all around the Kombi parked in a natural clearing, where the couple lay on a mattress wedged onto the roof-rack. The cocooned silence – after the daytime bird song, creaking branches and the murmurings of the dry grass – only served to reinforce the illusion further.

As she reached down to haul the cover back over their bodies, she blew a breath out of her pursed mouth and into the darkness, hoping – in a way that she recognised as childish – that it would show as a cloud of warm vapour in the rapidly chilling air. But the wintry conditions really were all in her imagination, and the cold that had awakened her was only relative. Before she retreated under the blanket's warmth, she balanced herself on one elbow, awkwardly repositioning her body; the space was quite narrow and Kent was a big man. The sight of the sharply defined monochrome scenery, each pallid detail picked out as if rimed with frost, enchanted her, snow or no snow, and put her in mind of a similar scene from the past.

One of the many casual jobs her mother, Dalene, had taken when Aina was young, was as the office cleaner for an architectural practice in the city. On the days when her shambolic childcare arrangements had fallen apart, Dalene would reluctantly take her young daughter to work with her and try to keep her entertained and therefore silent with the limited resources at her disposal. The men in the office did not really mind the child being there occasionally so very much, they said, but they did need an orderly and quiet environment in which to work, please.

Once Dalene's efforts to keep Aina quiet were exhausted, Meneer Gildenhuys or Meneer Hoffmann would encourage Aina to page through certain of the more tatty volumes they would employ to make a point in discussions with their clients. They reminded her kindly to treat these books with care, and Aina always did. The one she loved to browse through the most was a huge, unwieldy book on modernist architecture, lavishly illustrated with many full-page photographs. The house she liked the best, because she could picture it here in her own country, was a ranging, single-storey bungalow in Palm Springs. Among the floor plans and the four or five recent colour images of the restored house was a very much older black-and-white photograph of the property under a sunlit, spotless white quilting after a rare heavy snowfall. The spiky desert plants were softened by their rounded mantles; the large pillowed boulders ornamenting the courtyard threw contrasting shadows onto the pristine carpeting. In the background, the frosted peaks of distant mountains formed a glowing, continuous ridge high, high above the house. Something tamped down and muffled about the building under its fresh blanketing always made her breathe a little more softly, just as she found herself doing now.

Eventually, one of the architects asked his secretary to make Aina a photocopy of this page, and she had managed to keep hold of this treasured piece of paper through all the upheavals of her subsequent life. She still held out some small hope that one day Kent would take her to a place where she might see snow and frost and ice. And icicles – those best of all. But she had a growing suspicion that when he left Namibia it would be as he had arrived, free and alone.

Aina debated waking Kent to share her wonderment with him, then rapidly decided against it. He had doubtless experienced various unexpected phenomena in his long career as a field scientist, and she wanted to avoid presenting him with an opportunity, no matter how slight, to make her feel provincial and unsophisticated. He guarded against doing so these days, but it did still happen from time to time. The tendency had manifested itself early in their acquaintance, even before they had become romantically involved. At that time, he would stop by her desk to chat and would ask Aina about whatever part of her country he would be driving to next on one of his trips. Had she been there perhaps? Initially she would simply shake her head shyly by way of a response. Later, once they had become intimate, she felt obliged to confront him in a roundabout way with some cold, hard facts about her situation. It hadn't seemed to have occurred to him that going anywhere at all involved an expenditure of money that she simply didn't possess.

For people like her, ownership of a car was, of course, out of the question. Even renting one for a few days would cost more than she could afford. And anyway, learning to drive and acquiring a licence – whether legally or otherwise – would also involve costs that she couldn't countenance when she had more pressing needs. The few places she had gone to – the coast several times over the Christmas holidays as a guest of her rich cousin; the North, when an old boyfriend took her there to visit his brother; the farm of a school friend when she was a teenager – she had only been able to visit on the whim of someone else (and the boyfriend had demanded petrol money soon after they had set off). So, she had started to answer all such questions Kent addressed to her, enquiries that exposed her limited life experiences and finances, by simply saying, "With what money?"

Eventually, after they had been sleeping together for a few months, the penny did appear to drop with him, but not before he had asked her once, in far too casual a manner, how much her new weave had cost. The modest fight that followed was as close as they had got to splitting up, and since disingenuousness was not his style anyway, they were able to move on, Kent having learned to tread far more carefully around the topic of cash and how Aina spent it. On the scale of things, his now rare unthinking remarks – amounting, in sum, to an acknowledgement that her practical knowledge of the world was sadly circumscribed – counted for little when weighed against his many generous gestures. But still.

She was aware of a sound now moving towards the clearing, a soft soughing in the dry, rattling leaves in the stands of mopane trees some distance away, approaching swiftly through the clumps of stunted branches. She narrowed her eyes in anticipation of the wind's gritty onslaught. And then another enchantment – the early-morning breeze was lifting fine particles of dust before it and through her half-closed eyelids she watched specks of glittering mica dance in the air. The tiny particles spangled in the full moon's generous luminosity and made the fantasy of a snowy winter landscape complete. Surrendering herself to sleep again, muscles that had tightened against the chill relaxing, Aina thought to herself that this spot on Earth was the furthest she had ever been from anywhere else in her life.

When they woke up later that morning, on the day before they had to leave, she still felt that to mention the strange occurrence of the previous night would somehow diminish her in Kent's estimation, and also diminish the moment in her own. And so she kept it to herself, resolving to only share it with someone who would find a similar astonishment in it, when she had the chance.

∽

Kent had decided to take her on his latest fieldtrip out of a growing sense of pity and remorse, brought on – he admitted to himself – by his scheduled departure a few months hence. As a sign, he supposed, that he did think of them as a couple of sorts, despite the obvious challenges this notion presented to the world and the necessarily temporary nature of the arrangement. He was highly qualified, well-travelled, and in robust late middle-age, one of the mass of foreign experts still in-country many years after Independence. They continued to take up well-paid consultancies despite the growing objections, in social media and print, of new local graduates who felt that they could do the work just as well. Aina was in her early thirties, though her tiny size and girlish voice made her seem younger, with an attenuated education. Her mundane, dead-end dogsbody job was euphemistically titled "PA" as a sop to the project's donors, and she possessed no passport or reason to acquire one. White and black, big and small, old and young. And rich and poor. They both knew how this looked to other people. They even had some inkling of how it looked to each other.

Two things – one contrived to emerge out of the other – had happened recently that had compelled them both separately to examine the issue of what it was, exactly, that they were doing together. One morning just over a month before, Aina was collecting some folders from a manager's car in the parking lot at the back of the run-down, converted colonial house where Kent's NGO was currently based. She'd heard muffled, snorting laughter coming from a narrow window high up in the outside wall of the women's toilet, and checking that no one else was around, she'd manoeuvred herself to a position just under the pane that had been left wedged open and listened. Three of her female colleagues were chatting within, and the topic was the unlikely – or as they were explaining to each other actually highly predictable – relationship between Kent and herself, which it transpired that they had known about for some time.

Aina had taken care to insist, when they spent the night together, that Kent drive her to within a kilometre of their office. Then she silently accepted a ten-buck note from him for the taxi she took the rest of the way to work for appearances' sake. Nevertheless, she now had evidence that they had been busted, as he later phrased it.

The couple had been, she flushed to realise now, the topic of a great deal of ribald commentary and spiteful speculation for some time. Today's discussion concerned the likelihood that Aina would deliberately get pregnant soon in order to trap this foolish old man before his contract, and therefore stay in the country, came to an end – thus gaining access to his no doubt large bank balance for the next couple of decades while not having to deal with having him in her life in person.

This genuinely novel idea had since lodged itself in a malign occupancy, embedded and swelling in her thoughts just as a tick buried in the fur of a dog in the only place that he cannot reach will engorge itself at the expense of its reluctant host. Even as she hated how her acknowledgement of the logic behind the crude but undeniably effective plan was demeaning her, she found she could not rid herself of its tenacious hold. Aina had always been a modest girl, a polite, hardworking, churchgoing credit to her family. She was not like these shameless types who had their first baby before they were out of school uniform. But now it seemed as if everybody at work had weighed up her limited options and had cynically settled on a pregnancy – courtesy of the unsuspecting Kent – as the best route out of her dull and desperate life. And this knowledge had infected her, weakened her, and made her susceptible to its temptations – just like so many other women in her position before her. Aina told herself that *she* would be able resist – if for no other reason than pride at showing that she was not like those grasping girls who convinced themselves that a baby would ensure them financial security in the future. Yet she was also bitterly envious at the unthinking facility with which these girls fell for this promise, false though it almost inevitably turned out to be.

The evening after she had listened to her colleagues' jokes at her expense she had presented Kent with an edited version of what she had heard. She offered, with some mortification, an approximate translation of the more unsavoury Afrikaans terms that had been applied to her but reserved those used against him for another time. She had some idea that if she described the plan she had overheard out loud to someone – and specifically her own nominated role in it – the unsavoury scheme would be revealed to her in all its awfulness, and she would be able to dismiss it from her mind for good.

They were chatting in a wine bar near his apartment in the expensive part of the city, and she couldn't help but notice another couple, rather similar to them, seated in a quiet corner nearby. The balding European man was stooped in a slightly cowed fashion over his drink and was sporting a showy collection of metal bangles and leather strings of beads around his ropey wrists. He was wearing the default uniform of the middle-aged foreign professional – head-to-toe khaki with tan bush boots, his sunglasses secured on a bright braided cord draped around his neck, despite the late hour.

The young Damara girl who accompanied him was partially hidden by the partition of their booth, but nevertheless the contrast was clear enough. This girl was tapping out an agitated rhythm on the floor with the sole of a showy red stiletto shoe while noisily lecturing her boyfriend on some issue of food purchasing. As she then leant forward to make a point with a long, manicured fingernail, she caught Aina's eye and gave her an insolent yet conspiratorial look. Clearly this young lady was deploying the currency of calculation to full effect.

Kent could not seem to appreciate Aina's humiliation and her sense of disgust at the version of their future that had been presented to her with such clarity the previous morning and which she was now relating to him.

If he was affected in any way by her embittered, whispered outpouring, he gave no sign other than to say, in his penetrating voice, "Look, I have been called a few things in my time, but I don't imagine that I have been commonly thought to be a stereotype, *or* a cliché for that matter. So, you know, what's all the drama about? People are inclined to think what they want to, whatever the truth might be. Same the world over for that matter, Aina."

She shrugged silently into her misery and hoped the other woman in the corner had not heard. Too late she also realised that presented with the scheme her colleagues had outlined, it might occur to Kent to mentally tally up the likelihood of this possible "accidental" pregnancy – as she herself had done. She would just have to hope he was not that cynical, or believed her to be that conniving, though she couldn't help but notice that his response to her outpouring had really been about him and not her ...

"We know who we are, and we know what we're about. Who gives a shit what other people think? Not me, that's for sure. It is what it is."

Kent's frequent use of that single last phrase was the thing that irritated Aina more than pretty much anything else about him. In its maddening lack of specificity, it was a deliberate evasion, but at the same time it always seemed freighted with some subtext, as if he had an empowering, advantageous insight into any situation, one that was unavailable to her, with her less sophisticated understanding of the world. She changed the subject but resolved to teach him a lesson when she got a chance. If he thought, in all honesty, that he knew precisely who they were, then she would conceive of a way to disabuse him of this in a heartbeat – to use a new phrase she had discovered recently and was attached to. She took some comfort from the warmth of her uncharacteristic spite and from the sense that, for once, the skewed dynamics of their relationship could end up working in her favour. It was also a relief to be able to start hatching a practical little plot that would relieve her, for the time being, of having to pay attention to the persistent demands of that other, altogether more troubling scheme that would not stop playing out in her imagination. One in which somehow a woman could get pregnant by a man who always insisted on using newly purchased condoms whenever they had sex.

Over the next few weeks, she refined her course of action and she was grateful to the girl in the wine bar for gifting her a simple idea that gave concrete shape to her plans. She didn't look at her objective in terms of getting revenge on Kent for all the times he had uncovered her ignorance in some discussion, because she understood that – apart from the ill-advised, half-hearted dig about her Brazilian hair – it was all unintentional. It was more a question of creating a little parity between them. For once he would be the one unsettled, wrong-footed, and a little embarrassed, she hoped.

From the time that they had first started seeing each other, Kent would pick her up for their dates from her tiny outside room in the backyard of a bigger house in Khomasdal. The section of the city designated for Coloured people in the apartheid era, it was now a more mixed suburb of modest, one-storey brick homes – many with an additional single room on the bare plot, which was rented out to people on low incomes, such as Aina. She'd now accepted that they had not been as secretive as they had hoped, and that their affair had been common knowledge among their co-workers for a number of months. Still, until now she had remained resolved to avoid any contact between Kent and her family and friends; just the idea of trying to explain their situation to other people filled her with anxiety and distaste. As a result, Kent knew the numbers and names of her siblings and half-brothers and stepsister, and the ethnic groups to which they and their spouses all belonged. He had also heard about her lucky cousin who had managed to land a job in some government ministry and whose name occasionally appeared in the newspaper as a spokesperson for his boss lady. But that was the limit of his information regarding Aina, and he seemed in no especial hurry to discover more – something that either pleased or aggrieved her, depending on her mood.

On the Friday of the week that she had chosen to engineer his small-scale disillusionment, Aina had sent him a text message just before he was due to collect her for a meal out. She explained that she was still attending to her sick mother – this much was true – and would need collecting from an address he had not visited before, one well into the former black location and almost as far from his apartment as it was possible to go and still remain within the sprawling city limits. On her own way to her mother's place, after she had collected some dressings and iodine for the ulcers on the older woman's legs from the pharmacy, she made a turn by the open-air informal market and bought what she needed for her plan.

When she heard the horn of Kent's boxy new 4x4 outside her mother's pitiful dwelling, she sent him an SMS that she was not finished yet, and he must let himself in. He entered through the only door of the little square shack, which gave directly onto a cramped cooking space with a hotplate and tin bucket on the floor in the far corner. There he was confronted by a large, uncooked skinned sheep's head resting in a chipped enamel bowl on the only table. A thin layer of semi-translucent, ivory-coloured fat covered most of the muscle tissue, and the purple blood vessels showed their intricate tracery under the flickering fluorescent strip light. The protruding eyes were a dimpled, mottled grey and the lips were drawn back to reveal two ghastly rows of long, uneven yellow teeth. The whole grim arrangement sat in a pool of dried black gore, and a cloying greasy odour filled the entire tiny space.

As she knew he would, Kent avoided any audible expression of disgust – an old Africa hand by now, it would have been a point of honour for him to affect nonchalance in any unfamiliar situation, even when presented with this choice dish, known in her culture as a smiley. From the only other area of the room, her mother's sleeping alcove, Aina observed him edge his considerable bulk around the side of the table furthest from the gruesome still-life. Positioning himself to the other side of the curtained space, Kent could steal a glance into the improvised sickroom while at the same time preserving some semblance of concern for the privacy of her bedridden mother. His tact was unnecessary, however, since Dalene had drifted off to sleep some time ago, lulled by her favourite gospel station on the radio. Aina held up her palm to indicate that he should not speak and carefully moved away from the cubicle containing her mother. She made sure that she left the curtain between the two spaces open long enough for him to be able to observe the long, emaciated body under the heap of cheap, rough blankets. He could also see that each corner of the ancient metal bed base was secured by wire and raised on two old house bricks, bound one on top of the other with duct tape to increase their stability. Aina squeezed by him and made towards the door with a small, involuntary skip of triumph; she covered the smiley with a threadbare tea towel against the circling flies, switched off the buzzing light, and locked up the miserable excuse for a home behind her.

They set off for the Angolan restaurant where they had decided to eat that night, one unlikely to be frequented by their colleagues, though she had decided, by now, that she didn't care about keeping their clandestine accommodation a secret any longer. On the long drive back into the city centre from her mother's place, Kent seemed withdrawn and yet also solicitous. The affectless tones of his Canadian accent were, for the moment, replaced by something more deliberate, searching and personal. The atmosphere in the soft luxury of the car was pleasantly companionable and intimate. He asked the age of her mother and appeared genuinely shocked when she said her mother was not yet fifty. She explained various practical matters to do with life in the kambashu and how she had paid a neighbour to string up an electrical connection to the shack. No mention was made, however, of the grisly morsel set out to be prepared for lunch the next day, or of the bed hoisted up off the ground in an effort to protect its occupant from evil spirits, the tokoloshes that might swarm over Dalene's poor body in the night. His uncustomary introspection prompted her to try to re-animate the conversation once it stalled completely.

"My mother, she is very proud of me."

"I can see how she would be."

She had an almost physical sense that something was at last falling into its proper place, while at the same time revealing its natural fault lines; she even half-imagined that if she listened carefully, she would be able to hear the sound of that something shifting and settling with a sliding, shushing noise. It brought to mind the times that, as a child, she and her little friends had played on the heaps of building materials that had been dumped along the front of half-built houses or in open plots in the neighbourhood. They spent many hours piling up the dew-dampened gravel or sand into hills and valleys studded with their few old plastic dolls and toy cars, little landscapes that always eventually collapsed and reverted to their more natural shapes once the playmates had left for the day. And she was struck anew by Kent's ability to employ a harmless, even compassionate, phrase to unconsciously reaffirm their respective standings within their relationship.

Soon after, surprising the both of them, he proposed that Aina accompany him on his final field trip.

❧

They had allowed four days for him to complete his plant survey work, but Aina had proved to be far more adept at assisting him in recording his data than he had privately anticipated. So now, with a whole afternoon to spare before they needed to pack up, he suggested that they should explore the overhanging ledges of the low cliffs near their campsite for San rock paintings. The tumbling slabs of gun-metal- and russet-coloured rock formed massive natural stairways, and it was not long before they found themselves, out of breath, at a vantage point high above the plains, with a memorable view out to the haze of the horizon and the rushing skies of autumn above.

Under a huge projecting block, they found the faint images of a rhino and her calf, as well as an angular bird that could only have been an ostrich. Kent took flash photos while Aina held her hand up next to the designs to give an indication of their size. He had chastised her gently when she had initially placed her palm right against the rock next to the rhino calf. He explained that contact with human sweat had hastened the deterioration of similar art at other sites, and so they should take care not to touch any of the paint surface here. He had said all this in as undemonstrative a manner as he could, knowing even as he did so that she might nevertheless take quiet umbrage. Although Kent could think of no other way of imparting this information, he acknowledged to himself how patronising it sounded to lecture an African on her cultural heritage. She'd be within her rights to point out that it was unlikely that anyone else would come that way for many months, if not *years*, and that the pictures would not be irreparably harmed by contact with her one hand, this one time, for a second or two. For some reason, however, she said nothing but quietly withdrew the offending palm and then repositioned it with care to hover slightly to the left of its original placement, and a few centimetres clear of the rock face itself. Another side-swerve, another part of the minefield successfully circumnavigated with no evident harm done, he congratulated himself with relief.

They had forgotten to bring a drink up with them, and the slabs were still giving off a considerable amount of heat as the sun lowered and started to fill the shallow cave with light. They paused to take one last look at the view, and Aina squinted, blinked quickly several times behind the expensive shades Kent had bought her for her last birthday, and focused on something she had not noticed previously. Wordlessly, she pointed. Not very far from the base of the cliff – not far in fact from the route they had walked from the clearing where they had been camped for the past few days – was what appeared to be, at this distance, a primitive, makeshift dwelling. The whole time they had been working, eating, sleeping, washing and talking in the solitude of this vastness, it was possible that someone had been keeping a silent vigil not three hundred metres away. Kent seemed galvanised by this discovery, but Aina found herself casting her mind back over the past few days, trying to remember if they had said or done anything of an intimate nature that would cause her shame if it turned out that it had been witnessed by a stranger.

Kent confidently led the way back down the rock terracing and, though he said nothing, Aina could see he was veering off in a direction that would eventually take them on a course towards this hut, fashioned from worn green groundsheets, pieces of rigid black plastic piping, and long branchlets carefully woven together into beautifully constructed walls. In fact, the closer they got to the shelter, the more obvious it became that it was a permanent dwelling comprising a number of separate but interconnecting low rooms, ingeniously laid out to blend into the surroundings yet provide a large, comfortable home.

"I was wondering if you had spotted our house and if you would be paying us a call."

A gentle, slightly jesting voice came from the depths of one shelter's shadows. It was someone speaking courtly German, but nevertheless it was still a shock to see a well-dressed, tall and wiry white man emerge nimbly from the dimness within, a lopsided grin on his face. Tanned, neatly attired in smart brown cotton shorts and a clean white shirt, his salt-and-pepper beard carefully groomed, he looked no different from the countless commercial farmers or businessmen one might encounter on weekends in any large town. He had a number of tell-tale small sticking plasters on his forearms that showed he had recently had some potentially troublesome moles removed.

Aina greeted him as best she could; she had not spoken German for some years, but she knew the correct way to address an elder and a stranger. Kent looked from one to the other with amused bafflement, and she could see the corners of his gentle eyes crinkling behind his sunglasses.

"We have been camping here, sir. I hope we were not disturbing you. We thought we were alone."

Now it was the turn of the man from the hut to look a little perplexed, though he hid his surprise well. A young black girl talking to him in his mother tongue while the older white man stood dumbly by.

"You did not disturb us. It is a pleasure to see someone else enjoying our lovely part of the world."

"I am so sorry, but we didn't realise this is your land. We would have asked permission to come here if we had known …"

"Young lady, I do not own this wondrous place, alas. We just live here, freely and undisturbed. As you see …"

Although he gave every appearance of being relaxed and friendly, the German man had dug his fists down into the pockets of his shorts, spoiling the line of the careful crease pressed into their front. Kent gently touched Aina's arm with an insistent pressure. Appearing to understand this signal between them, the man from the hut nodded to her to indicate that she should translate their exchange in its entirety. They then resumed their conversation in German.

"So. My name is Kris Kuhn. I live here with my son, Helmut. Who we call Helly."

"Aina Shikongo is my name. This is my colleague, Dr Kent Willis Junior. He is coming from Canada. We are here doing a survey of the plants."

Aina wondered anew if Herr Kuhn had already realised that she and Kent were not just co-workers. She was weighing up the likelihood of this as she spoke, and this distraction compelled her to revert to Afrikaans for certain, elusive words. She and Kent had made love on the first night, this was true, but had done so inside the Kombi since there had been a sudden drop in temperature as dusk approached. And neither of them was a noisy lover, so she doubted that their sounds would have carried far and betrayed their activity. Still, something about this gentlemanly, old-fashioned character made her more than unusually bashful, and she did not always meet his eyes directly as she spoke.

Kent seemed about to jump into the conversation, probably to ask her to find out what Herr Kuhn was doing out here, so very far from any obvious means of employment or indeed sustenance, but a movement from within the funny, ramshackle house now attracted the attention of the trio.

❧

Herr Kuhn took a large, almost ceremonial pace to one side to allow his son to come out through the doorway. Looking back on this moment later, Aina remembered that as Helly emerged, Herr Kuhn was looking not at his child, which would perhaps have been natural, but was busy switching his appraising attention back and forth between her face and Kent's.

The person, and it clearly was a person, who crossed the threshold and took a couple of shuffling paces towards them was unlike anyone she had ever seen before, and it took all of her concentration not to turn and flee. Only Herr Kuhn's eyes, fixed on her in a kind of amiable challenge, prevented her from doing this. She was aware of a long intake of breath from Kent, who was standing a little way behind her, then a sharp exhalation. The child – or was it a tiny man? – who took those few hesitant steps onto the pathway of flattened dry grass was stooped forwards at an uncomfortable angle and was inclining his head oddly towards his father at his side, as if awaiting instruction. He had been watching them from inside his refuge all this time, she was now sure, and it appeared as if he

A Bed on Bricks

had been waiting to take his cue from the older man, uncertain of what his first move ought to be. All the boy's limbs seemed to be elongated to an unnatural degree. His neck, in particular, rose in a taut, stretched white column from his collared T-shirt to support a shorn head that seemed to belong to a different body altogether – narrow, slightly misshapen, and very small indeed, like that of an infant somehow transplanted onto a small adult form. At the side of his head that was turned towards her, a prominent blue blood vessel pulsed at the creature's scarred and freshly scratched temple – though the throbbing sound Aina could hear, she knew, was coming from within her. Herr Kuhn reached out to his son and bent slightly to take his slack hand in a tight grip, and this reassurance seemed to give Helly the confidence he needed to turn and face the visitors.

Herr Kuhn took pity on them at last. His English, it turned out, was really not so bad after all.

"This is my son Helly. He is seventeen but small for his age, as you can see. He understands most of what you say if you speak slowly, and if you wait a little while he might even respond in his own manner. Isn't that so, Helly?"

The boy waited a long beat, then as if in reply, lifted his pale, thin face up to the sky in a beatific, unselfconscious grin. Herr Kuhn gave a shrug then turned and beamed at his son in unalloyed joy.

Aina felt sure that although she could not imagine a single appropriate thing to say in this bewildering situation, Kent – with his wealth of experience and his dealings with so many different people in his long life – would surely have some idea of how to react. But their keen discomfort bloomed and billowed about them, their silence growing more uncomfortable by the moment. Yet after a few more seconds, Aina became aware once again of that odd but reassuring, familiar sense of things physically sliding into their correct place while simultaneously revealing their fractures – just like those piles of damp builders' sand so long ago.

And Herr Kuhn was not done trying to guide them out of their impasse.

"Yes, you see, the world battles to know how to deal with Helly, though it does not work the other way round so very much. We can be thankful for that, at least when I am here to protect him and look after him in a place where he doesn't have to upset himself with the unkindnesses of thoughtless people. When she was alive, my wife was able to convince me that Helly should live in town. That he should go out and be around the normal people. Ah, ja, maybe so. But when she died, I found I had not the patience that is necessary for this, and I took a little pension and a little, um, money that was left to me by an aunt and we came here and live in our own way. And as you can see, we are happy?"

The question at the end of the explanation was posed not in relation to the contentment of Herr Kuhn and his son, which was plain for anyone to see, but was rather intended to determine if Aina and Kent understood this father's dilemma. Were they able to comprehend why he had taken the drastic action of removing Helly entirely from a society that could not come to terms with the startling physical manifestations of his otherness?

Helly disengaged his hand from his father's and, looking candidly over at Aina in the same way that he had previously examined his parent's face for affirmation, he took a few steps towards Kent and held out his other, closed fist, which he then slowly opened. His upturned palm held some small nuggets of grey-brown rock, marbled through with glowing patches of deep blue and vivid, watermelon pink. Helly had evidently been clutching them hard for some time because many of the lighter fragments clung to his dirty, trembling fingers, held in place by his sweat, while in other places could be seen deep indentations where the larger stones had been pushed into the young man's flesh. Finally, he turned his full attention to Kent, who was still evidently struggling to find one un-contentious or kindly thing to say, and the boy's expression darkened and grew troubled as his proffered gift remained ignored. With a theatrical flourish and a curious, high-pitched mewling sound, he snatched back his hand, pivoted on his bare heel, and stalked off into the bush with quick strides of his extraordinary, long, bony legs. His birdlike twitters and clucks could still be heard long after he disappeared from view into a mopane thicket.

As soon as the boy had departed, Kent seemed to regain his faculties and now, released from his trance, he was forcefully reanimated.

He spoke in a voice too loud. "Do you mind my asking you, Mister Kuhn …?"

"Ah, now it seems that I must go and search for my little lost chick," the father recited apologetically in English in a singsong voice, as if he were repeating a familiar, amusing refrain. His intention – to deflect, without rudeness, any further questioning, and to bring the encounter to a close – was clear. Herr Kuhn then turned smartly and started off down the same track his son had taken seconds before. Just before he vanished from view entirely, he turned and – she wasn't wrong about this, she told herself later – gave Aina a handsome, fleeting wink.

Then he was gone.

❧

Kent was instantly livid and crude, exposing a side of himself that Aina had never guessed at. For some reason the German and his son had enraged him in a way that all the logistical frustrations, office politics, clashes of personalities, and cultural misunderstandings at his workplace had failed to do in all the time they had been acquainted. As he started off on his tirade, she debated, briefly, if his ostentatious, vulgar outrage was just for her benefit, but she discarded the thought almost immediately. Kent was genuinely, explosively, mad as hell.

"What kind of fucked-up, full-of-crap country is it that you people live in, anyhow?" he demanded, in a manner that strongly suggested he didn't mind if he was overheard, nor did he expect or want any answer. It was pointless to cast about for a reply anyway – at least one that would mollify him. Aina walked behind him in silence as they made their way slowly back to the Kombi, Kent stopping every few paces to turn and fulsomely berate her home and her countrymen and women (and by extension, she herself, she supposed). He cursed more in those five minutes than she had heard him do in the entire time they had known each other; spittle glistened in his three-day growth of beard. And Aina hated him, in a disinterested but disavowing way, more than she had imagined possible. She realised she had been drawing comfort and reassurance from his habit of seeking out commonalities between them, even forcing them into existence on the slimmest of pretexts at times. She thought back – with a tiny, involuntary shudder of distaste – to the moment soon after they met when he discovered that the proximity of their birthdays – some decades apart – meant that they shared a star sign, and the small "Yay" of triumph and attempted fist bump this had occasioned from him.

Meanwhile, how to explain to herself what else she was feeling: an overwhelming affection and sudden but fierce fealty towards these two dislocated strangers, a need to shield them from Kent's incandescent rage as he cycled through all the different options for rescuing poor, damaged, *at risk* Helly from his dangerously delusional, *criminally negligent*, parent.

What *was* Helly anyway, she asked herself against the diatribe continuing in the background? The opposite of a tokoloshe, if there was such a thing, she concluded. Instead of the embodiment of malice and mischief, the man-child was the personification of the sweetest of natures and an innocence that cannot grow stale or sullied. She sensed herself colouring as she remembered how she had wanted to run away when first she laid eyes on him. Now she knew that from him she had received some kind of second chance, a benediction bestowed in that moment when he had looked across to her and searched her face for mutual acceptance. Guileless and elemental, Helly had begun the process of returning Aina to a more humane version of herself and ridding her of that shadow girl's insidious suggestions for her future.

A Bed on Bricks

Goodness was not a concept she gave a great deal of thought to in the normal course of things, not even in those long Sunday mornings at her church when concrete examples of charitable behaviour were regularly called out for collective examination. Yet now she found herself contemplating what it truly meant to be good, with the same kind of attention that she usually directed only towards its many quotidian and corrosive opposites.

Whoever had placed a curse on this family long ago, one that Aina suspected had probably eventually led to the death of Frau Kuhn, had not been able to make the spell strong enough to overcome goodness entirely. It had failed to simply conjure up a monstrous child – shrunken and etiolated in some places, and strangely stretched in others – fated to be cursed and feared throughout his life, ostracised, stigmatised and probably even subject to physical attack. The witchcraft had instead produced both this enchanted spirit and a father's blood bond of unbreakable power. Doubtless Herr Kuhn had once owned a nice big house or two and several cars, and had a prosperous career and hopes of a dynasty of strapping, sporty sons. Now he had found happiness in a shack with a chirping bird-boy.

In Aina's culture such misshapen, blighted creatures were to be hidden away in shame and mistreated, eventually to death – not pitied and certainly not loved. The girl who had helped her mother place a bed on bricks found tears forming now, not out of despair at the fate of Helly and his father, but out of gratitude that this openhearted, limitless love had been revealed to her.

Still her boyfriend ranted and fumed at what he declared, with unassailable conviction, to be Herr Kuhn's cruel, selfish and *dangerous* behaviour. He demanded that Aina tell him the name of the schools in the city that took in "challenged" children. She informed him she didn't know, even though in fact she did. Kent was already outlining a strategy to come back at the earliest opportunity "with the child-welfare people" and expose Herr Kuhn for the monster that he was, so that Helly could be institutionalised someplace where he would get the evaluation and subsequent help that he needed. Aina didn't care. Even if Kent were able to pull off this unlikely plan, the boy and his father would be long gone by then.

☙

Very early the next morning she tugged on her trainers, clambered down off the mattress on top of the Kombi, and went in search of a place to relieve herself. The sky was growing paler by the minute, and in the moment before the sun made its first sly appearance, the strange light took on the colour of ripening green figs. Kent, her soon-to-be-ex boyfriend, was still asleep; in the night she had determined that there were just too many differences between them for their unorthodox relationship to continue until he left Namibia. His wholly disproportionate and insensitive verbal attack on Herr Kuhn had just revealed this to her rather sooner than she would have eventually figured it out of her own accord. The scent of sweet wood smoke, that most evocative of all African smells, still hung in the dawn air from their cooking fire of the night before. They had prepared a spartan supper from the perishable food that remained from their supplies and had eaten it in almost complete silence, both drained by the encounter of the late afternoon and its aftermath.

Aina found a spot behind a clump of astringent-smelling camphor bushes that suited her, dug a hole and then finished quickly. Even while they had been lovers, she had had a natural delicacy when it came to sharing other bodily functions with Kent – a sensitivity that had provided him with a great deal of amusement on this camping trip. Not anymore, my friend, she thought with satisfaction. She would quickly tell him that their affair was over once he dropped her back, at her request, by her mother's shack. She couldn't face a six-hour drive spent fending off his patronising, reasonable counterarguments should she make her announcement now, or at any point during their return journey.

She stood at a distance from the Kombi and contemplated the slumbering form on its roof, crushing between her fingers some leaves she had picked off the camphor bush and releasing their pleasant, medicinal odour. The trip had been, even before its surprising turn of events and downbeat conclusion, a new experience for her, and she wished to hold the images, sounds and smells of their final morning together as a couple in her mind a little longer. She would never have reason to come this way again.

And then a curious thing: there appeared to be an arrangement in the sand in front of the vehicle's sliding passenger door that she hadn't seen there yesterday evening. She drew nearer and recognised what it was even before she was standing over it in wonder – a single, evenly spaced circle of maybe thirty small, rough stones, rinsed free of their dirt and positioned so that the rising sun was even now starting to pick out the brilliant colours of the gemstones embedded deep in their folds. She gathered the little rocks quickly but with the utmost care, knowing her actions were being watched at a distance. After she placed them in a plastic bag that she found in the passenger door and put this gently into her handbag, she began to collect the last bits of detritus from their stay, in order to leave the little patch of ground exactly as they had found it: a plastic fork half buried in the sand, a fluttering piece of yellow tissue paper pierced on a low thorn bush, and an unopened packet of firelighters. She wanted everything ready for when Kent awoke so that she could suggest that they quickly make a small fire, have their coffee, break camp, and hit the road before seven.

Progress

I was going to say that Progress and I grew up together, but actually, we didn't. How would that have been possible, in the end?

When I visited town with my father and his workers on payday at the end of each month as a child, patriarchs of the local settler families would cross the wide street to greet Dad as he parked his battered truck in the shade of a massive dusty tree. The burly men would enquire, in an overly hearty manner, after his general wellbeing. Then – if he did not make his excuses fast enough – they would look away at some distant object, squinting against the sun and their own disquiet, and ask casually when he was going to get around to sending me away to school.

Having watched me scramble down from the back of the pick-up, where I had been unselfconsciously wedged between the Africans who made up the small contingent of staff that worked for my father, they would stare down at my scabby knees and fraying, hiked-up skirt hem, and say things like: "Man, you don't want her running wild like a munt now, John."

My father would reassure them – in a distracted way, since conversations like this made him eager to get his chores done quickly and be off – that my education was being taken care of at home right now, that I was still young, and that when the time came, I would join my cousins at the boarding school for girls in a distant province. When the time came.

My father had met my mother in the early 1950s when he had stood on a rusty piece of wire at a building site in the Cape, where he was working as a foreman. Mum was a nurse at the hospital that he had reluctantly visited once a stinking infection that was impossible to ignore had set in. Estelle had been horrified at the thought of a grown Rhodesian man unable to locate a pair of shoes with intact soles before going to work in the morning. Horrified and enchanted. Following their marriage, the idea (her idea?) had been that Estelle would run a guesthouse at our new home in the highlands of John's homeland, and my jack-of-all-trades father would do small-scale engineering projects for the local farmers. The newly built bungalow on the steep, east-facing slope, with a view out over misty green-and-grey hillsides towards the border, was duly decorated with souvenirs of their honeymoon in Italy. Black wirework armatures depicting the Coliseum and the Leaning Tower of Pisa were mounted on one of the dining room walls, and an abstract collage Mum made out of wine labels and corks was hung in the reception area.

Then, soon after my second birthday, my mother, the engine room of their unlikely partnership, died of malaria and, in an instant, Dad's world shrank and its landscape became exhausting to negotiate. Regularly he was presented with a new set of ordinary social pitfalls to add to the occasional, more worrying, financial sinkholes he was forced to navigate alone. On certain days his longing for the refuge of the swift African dusk would fill the wide, echoing rooms like a tangible presence. Whatever impetus he had started to summon in order to contemplate attempting an everyday task would be overtaken by inevitable, welcome inertia once the cicadas set up their strident calling.

We did still occasionally have visitors at the guesthouse: local couples wanting to celebrate an anniversary with a night away from home, or unconventional overseas acquaintances of Estelle's vast circle of liberal Johannesburg friends looking for a novel holiday destination. This type was keen that their photographs of Africa would not depict the usual elephants, giraffe and flat-topped acacias, but moorlands, cascades disappearing into rain-forest gorges, trout streams, and balancing rocks. And when he drove into town my father's few remaining farmer pals would casually ask if he couldn't come out to their place and take a look at the broken water pump or their recalcitrant paraffin refrigerator – though these were repairs they could undertake themselves, and they only asked him out of charity and pity. Somehow, he contrived to make enough to keep our lives ticking over, and I think my mother's family sent him money from time to time in the hope that they would be invited to visit us. But my father could never have roused himself over an extended period of days to entertain visitors in the manner that he believed his sophisticated in-laws might have expected. It also emerged, when I took to visiting them myself from my mid-teens onwards, that he had believed Estelle's parents to be more observant than they actually were – the necessary provision of a kosher table, or something approaching it, having been the excuse he usually gave me for not inviting them when I was little.

When tourists wrote to us to book accommodation at the guest-house, John left all the practical arrangements to Thoko and Beauty. In those days the roads were well maintained, and the duration of journeys thus easy to predict, even with rest stops along the way. John would shower an hour before he expected to hear the visitors' car start to grind up the track to the house, then open a welcoming drink for them on their arrival (always Lion beers still in the bottles since he was wholly unaware that they might wish for something different). He would recite the attractions of the walks up to the open, heath-covered mountainsides behind the house and then give the bemused guests a stout stick in case they encountered a snake during their stay. Finally, John introduced them to the staff before he escaped back to his workshop and his protective desolation. If the guests had been expecting to spend their evenings in the sociable golden glow of a hurricane lamp, listening to tales of hunters and their prey, of native ways and sudden violent death, then they were destined to be disappointed. Few booked a return visit.

He must have been a dynamic man once, in his self-effacing way. My mother would never have settled on him and seduced him if he had been a genuine no-hoper, someone who – in her most pejorative phrase apparently – was "just a dabbler". As I grew older, I would take to looking at the Italian ornaments and wonder that she ever persuaded him to visit a place where the food was so very unfamiliar and the language utterly incomprehensible to him. I slowly came to see that he must have been a different proposition entirely back when they had married, but that at the same time, Estelle had probably been the only woman in the world capable of leading him up such unexpected pathways. Love mattered.

I also learned later that physically, I resembled Estelle far more than I did John. Where he was sandy, freckled and stringy, his movements and his voice deliberate and his brow often corrugated in concentration, she had been dark, buxom, mercurial and quick-witted, and always on the move. Gay, in a word that had a single, simpler meaning back then. In my teens I once absentmindedly coiled a pencil I had been using into my corkscrew curls to stash it briefly and free both my hands for some task. Auntie Mimi, upon entering the dimly lit drawing room of the rambling house she shared with her ageing parents in Parktown, backed out of the doorway with a ragged intake of breath, both her deeply dimpled hands covering her mouth in evident dismay. It turned out that I had replicated exactly some idiosyncrasy of my mother's that everyone close to her had forgotten about until I conjured it back into the present.

The centre of my world, even when I was very small, was an old set of encyclopaedias from 1951, which had arrived containing a veritable museum's-worth of ghost insects and spiders flattened, desiccated and bleached between the thin pages. John had come across the books on sale in Salisbury one weekend when he had gone there to pick up various tools, cables and other mysterious items that he couldn't purchase locally. With rising excitement, Progress and I had raced to help John unload his own purchases from the back of the truck, my father having used the promise of a "big time surprise" as a bribe to get us to help him without complaint. It didn't remain a surprise for long, as we pestered him to tell us what he had brought back for me. Two against one. For a good few years it never failed.

Progress, who was two years older than me and who attended the local mission school a few miles away, had already taught me to read after a fashion, and the appearance of any new reading matter in the house was almost always a cause for celebration. We had fallen upon the heavy books piled under a tarp on the passenger seat and scattered in the footwell as John wandered off to add the drill bits and the heavy bottles of lubricants to the stuff already gathering rust and skeleton leaves in his tool shed sanctuary.

Left alone as usual, Progress and I noisily heaved the books into the dining room, where a deeply cracked but lovingly burnished, empty yellowwood bookshelf stood, polished just that morning as if waiting to receive them. Progress patiently showed me how to arrange the volumes alphabetically. Then we stood back and, sneezing wetly, swept the dust and bits of dead bugs from our bare arms. We were so pleased at the way the rows of books looked that it was several days before we could bring ourselves to spoil the arrangement, pull out a volume from the middle of the set, and start to read the entries aloud to each other. Seated cross-legged on badly stuffed cushions on the beeswax-scented wooden floor, Progress helped me with the trickier entries, selected at random based on which illustrations caught our attention. (It was several months before my amused father set about correcting the skewed pronunciations I had begun absorbing from my fellow scholar that first day.) In turn, I imparted to Progress scraps of my second-hand knowledge, gleaned from conversations with John – how something that looked as odd as a penguin could still be a bird, for example.

Not long afterwards, and with evident regret, my father decided that I needed a more structured form of education. To start the day,

I would eat my bowl of gritty, dun-coloured cereal, standing in the lean-to that overlooked the staff quarters down the hill. This kitchen – a rickety construction smelling pleasantly of yeast, vegetable oil and sooty smoke – was where all the family meals were prepared when we didn't have guests staying. My breakfast looked (and, I suspected, tasted) like the dry, pungent preparation that I once saw in a bin at my cousins' stables, on a long-ago visit to their ranch near Bulawayo. From the twins' lexicon of privilege, I learned that they called this horse feed "bran mash". During the course of that one-off vacation, I also quickly figured out that even if I had been inclined to accept their parents' half-hearted invitation to join them permanently at Green Pastures, Caro and Fi would only ever have tolerated me as an irritating arriviste. Welcoming a newcomer into their self-contained world, with its abstruse rituals and routines, was simply inconceivable.

If she were not in one of her inexplicable sulky moods, Beauty would sometimes take pity on me and pour an entire tiny tin of condensed milk over my bowl of cereal instead of the thin, tasteless cow's milk I usually had. Then we would all look out together over the vegetable garden off to the side of the house as Job, Progress' widowed father, described in his patient low voice all the work he was going to undertake that day in the orderly rows of beans and maize and tomatoes. He would point out the separate beds in question as he spoke but sometimes, instead of following the direction of his index finger with my gaze, I would use the opportunity to contrast the difference between his hand and my own, between the warm brown, deeply incised knuckles of his long hands and my own stubby, warty, grubby digits. Beauty would then run a clean, damp dishcloth around my mouth, and I would join my father at the dining room table as he outlined the "schoolwork" we would do together until lunch.

I became a conscientious, avid learner. I wanted so much to please John in those mornings, to make his face light up as he saw that understanding was passing between an encyclopaedia's grease-spotted pages and his daughter's unordered mind. I now suppose that, in addition, I must have had a subconscious notion that if I didn't engage him fully with my attention and my curiosity, he would leave me as my mother had already done.

The life cycle of the tapeworm or the order of succession of the English royal dynasties were learnt, perfunctorily tested, and patchily consigned to memory before we moved on to the next haphazardly chosen subject. A small collection of compressed bugs was also extracted from the pages and by-and-by arranged and labelled in a neat display, improvised from a wooden fruit crate, on top of the bookcase. At around midday, John's own interest waning and his need for solitude suddenly pressing, we would share in silence a tin of luncheon meat and a salad of vegetables Job had picked and Beauty had washed, the two of them standing giggling together and decorously flirting at the huge chipped sink that dominated the outside kitchen. Then I would be left to my own devices for the rest of the day.

I was going to say that what we did was the same as children do everywhere: a universal rite of passage from Paraguay to Poland. But actually, that couldn't be true, under the circumstances.

The back of the main property – our home and guesthouse combined – led onto a deep stoep that ran the full length of the building. From this terrace our occasional guests would admire the expansive views out across to Portuguese East Africa, the colours of the msasa trees in spring, the rising and falling skeins of mist, and the garrulous, darting bird life. The thickly wooded gully immediately below was so steep that it was barely possible to see beneath its dense canopy towards the bottom. The wide ravine dropped for almost two hundred feet, becoming more and more overgrown and narrow, until it fetched up against a clear, slightly brown rill of water. Midges looped lazily in the still air above "our" stream, which spangled in a pretty glade at the foot of the incline.

It had been my mother's ambition, apparently, to turn this patch of rampant forest, with its moist soil as rich and fragrant as fruitcake mix, into a real garden. This was to have been roughly (very roughly) styled after a picture she saw in a magazine of a property in the Italian lakes that had terraces arranged down a hillside so thickly planted with geraniums and palms, lavenders and citrus trees in pots, that the winding paths were in constant civilised shade. My father often told me that at dawn, and still in her dressing gown, Estelle would allocate tasks to the staff (actually, he called them "servants"). Drinking her first cup of extra-strong coffee, with me tucked under her arm, she would inform Job almost daily that they must "wage war against the creeping gourmets". The slope below the terrace was so persistently damp and alive with small creatures – whatever the season – that to walk down it was to sink into spongy mounds of softest moss and risk squeezing a sheltering slug or thin-shelled snail underfoot. This world of caterpillars, centipedes, beetles and grubs – goggas as we knew them – was the kingdom against which she and Job had fought an ongoing battle of attrition until the week that she fell sick and, absurdly, died.

She had grown up in a grand home in northern Johannesburg, where a band of skilled garden boys would daily tend and prune the altogether more decorous European plantings. That she wished to wrestle the intractable, jungly, rock-filled valley into the same temperate submission with just Job to help her was an indulgence my father granted her – to make up for all the other pleasures she had had to forfeit once they moved out to their new home, I would imagine. Had she lived, she might only have ever won a frustrating partial respite from the insidious re-growth of the wild vegetation and the depredations of its voracious pests. Just as John would never have been able to persuade her, in his gentle way, of the impropriety of addressing the servants in her gaping robe.

Job, in Mum's memory, I suspect, tried to maintain the roses and cannas that she had started to establish in a small clearing directly under the stoep – so far as he could without knowing the right chemicals to ask my father to purchase in town to help this sickly foreign stock to survive. But the lily leaves were constantly patch-worked with mould, their edges nightly crenelated by the hungry insects and sliding things that emerged after the sun went down. The few raspberry-and-cream-coloured roses were bruised-looking and flaccid, but could still startle you with their sad, mocking fragrance when you brushed by.

Towards the bottom of this slope, tunnelled with arching, flapping greenery, stood the collapsing remains of a tin-roofed hut that my father had built Estelle for storing garden implements and various pest poisons, a good distance away from the house and the family they hoped to raise in it. It was so well hidden that it could only be seen from the barely discernible track immediately outside its lopsided door. From the house above, it was fully concealed by the ferns and the head-high, leggy shrubs that we named "nettles". These possessed hairs on their leaves that caused an immediate, angry irritation if you touched them and they smelled deliciously bitter and sappy whenever Progress stomped back their growth in order for the pathway to remain clear for a week or two. In the heat of the day the sheets of corrugated metal that constituted the still-sturdy roof pinged and banged in a regular percussion as they expanded, or drowned out our joyful shouts with a soft rattle and then a deafening clatter on the rare occasions when Progress and I got caught out down there during a storm.

I was forbidden to go down to the hut of course, inasmuch as my father had the energy or will to dictate anything to me. The striped shadows of the interior hid once-sharp, pointed and bladed tools, sticky brown bottles of pungent insecticides with the labels torn or missing, and the occasional dry rustle of a shy snake departing under the slatted floor. Yet Dad must have been aware that at some point we had grown old enough to descend the gorge in secret by ourselves in the hours of his afternoon torpor – tumbling over the hidden slimy rocks and whacking our way through the undergrowth with sticks (and later a broken machete that Progress had found in a ditch) without coming to much harm. Only occasionally we'd alert him to some minor accident with soft wails or panicked screams, depending on what had befallen us: an embedded splinter from an innocent-looking palm tree trunk or the burning stings of an aggressive swarm of paper wasps.

The truth is that there was little he could do to prevent our clandestine wanderings, even if he'd been more disposed to do so. I'd often heard him sharing his casual attitude regarding my welfare with the shocked wives of his friends – ladies who would come to visit with gifts of second-hand pinafore dresses and scuffed T-bar shoes for me. If his wife could die from a mosquito bite in an area which was supposedly too high in altitude for malaria, and if he could lose a little toe to a bit of discarded wire in the so-called civilised Cape, it was always going to be a matter more of luck than judgment if the children, black and white, of the small community he had created at Hillside View lived to see adulthood.

For all his overlapping layers of sadness, he did not have the tendencies of a bitter man. Neither was he unappreciative of the concern and kindnesses shown to us. He would therefore wink at me, if the opportunity arose, while he expounded his philosophy to Joanie or Bunty or Belinda, all of whom continued to pay dutiful calls on us despite, no doubt, a valid suspicion that they were being gently mocked for at least some of their troubles.

☙

It was late October, and the rains were predicted to soon start in earnest. The daily build-up of heat was still so unrelenting, and the humidity so enervating, that Progress and I were spending our afternoons deep within the cooler shadows of the gully. Lately, we'd been trying out a new game of our own invention that roughly mimicked the way we understood scientific experiments to be carried out – because it was scientists that we both now aspired to be. That day, we were trying to discover if it was hotter and clammier inside the depths of the sweltering, suffocating little hut or outside, under the green vaults made by the trees and bushes growing in unchecked abandon above our heads. We even had a new lined exercise book and sharpened pencil so that we could write out our methods, results and conclusions, as taught to me recently by John.

Our efforts required us to concentrate in a way that was both exciting but also a little tiring. We were growing up – Progress more quickly than me – and our games were coming to mirror real life more and more as a consequence. Until recently, our chief diversion had been to pretend that our secret world was an undersea kingdom, and the hut was a cave of treasures. I always had naming rights and had declared this game to be known as "Marine Children". We had navigated our aquatic realm by doing an approximation of the standing breaststroke. We could, of course, breathe underwater in this fantasy, pointing out to each other the fish, giant clams, corals and other forms of sea life that dwelt there in our imagination and that formed the basis of our stories of perils faced and gristly deaths narrowly escaped. Only many years later, when I thought back fondly on this particular game, did it occur to me, with a cold startle, that Progress could have had very little idea indeed of anything related to the ocean. To the best of my knowledge, he had never travelled more than a few miles beyond his home village and local school. Certainly, he had never learned to swim. Yet even at so young an age, he was evidently learning the advisability of following where a white person led and asking few questions.

We had spent several weeks postponing playing our new game – simply called "Scientists", at my behest – in much the same way that we had revelled in the anticipation of reading the encyclopaedias over several days before we ventured to open any of them. Of the various characteristics that we still had in common back then a keen appreciation of the pleasures of expectancy was one that Progress and I shared and regularly worked together to engineer.

On this occasion, "Scientists" was to involve each of us carefully drying a patch of flesh with a threadbare towel borrowed from the laundry, then seeing whether my olive-skinned, hairless thigh, prickling under the high ceiling of furling leaves outside the hut or Progress' leg – shiny chestnut and endearingly fuzzy, deep within the cabin's gloomy shadows – would produce a visible beading of sweat first. Progress had magically produced a battered but functional watch face, given to him by one of his many older brothers a few days earlier, for timing our experiment. But we were both so excited that we could not bring ourselves to actually begin the game proper – going over and over, instead, our detailed written plans and expectations. Once our prevarications were ended, the research was concluded, and our observations had been duly recorded, we then intended to scramble up the hillside and raid the ice box for a homemade lime lolly each. The day is so clear still in my memory: I was almost ten and Progress had recently turned twelve.

Just as we were at long last agreeing to begin the experiment, a series of sudden echoing, tearing crashes to the east of the hills announced that an afternoon storm had arrived. We had been so absorbed in planning our game, so cloistered within the green forest walls, that we hadn't noticed its approach. Strangely, we had not been forewarned by the usual low, almost imperceptible rumbles that you could feel up through the soles of your feet even before you could really hear them. We knew better than to run out into the open with the threat of lightning so close now. The mother of a girl at Progress' school had been struck and killed higher up the mountain the previous rainy season – "Looking like a stupid moth caught in a lamp!" as he put it, though secretly I doubted he had actually viewed the body.

In order to reach the house quickly via the precipitous gradient beneath it, we would have had to negotiate three longish flights of friable brick steps, without any handrail, that Job had built into the top of the hillside. These were always kept clear of surrounding vegetation in case a guest wanted to venture down them from the stoep to the edge of the cloud-forest below. None, however, ever went any further, for it was an unexpectedly sinister, depressing place once you were in its shadows, even at its margins. As with so much in my young life, these crumbling red steps represented a stopgap measure that had become a permanent fixture once my mother died. The builders who were supposed to use them to access the slope as they constructed her Italianate terraces were quietly relieved of their duties once she became sick. The curtain material she had ordered to furnish my bedroom remained uncollected at the post office and was eventually returned to the Salisbury store by the kind postmistress.

"The lightning will hit us if we run out in the open. We'll stay here until it's over, no Progress?"

It was actually more a command than a question. Although I was younger than Progress, and a little girl to boot, our social dynamics – dictated by our respective skin colours – had started to develop when we were still small and were by now established, understood and immutable, if unspoken.

"For sure, Phil. Your father would beat me if I let you get all burned up like that lady in the village."

Progress was giggling as he pulled my leg because my father had never raised a hand to anyone in his life – another personal shortcoming as far as his farmer friends were concerned. They knew – *everyone* knew – that a thrashing was the only way to preserve the fragile balance between their (increasingly illusionary) white dominance and the patient subservience of their workers. The model upon which the country's precarious status quo was still predicated, was to regularly sjambok a random munt in a more or less perfunctory manner for some minor or presumed infraction. More serious crimes were, of course, handed over to the police – though these were such rare occurrences on the farms that most would struggle to recall the last time an African from their staff quarters had been arrested.

My real name is Beverly, although it's a name no one has used for a long time. One of the reasons that my father tolerated my unorthodox friendship with Progress, I guess, was that he knew a "sharp character" when he saw one and sensed that – up to a point – our rivalries and differences while we were still small brought out the best in each of us. One evening, when I was still small, John had been in a good mood and – revelling in company for once – hadn't yet sent Progress back to the staff lines for the night. He put on a record that had been popular when he and my mother first moved into the house on the hillside. Progress – painstakingly spelling out all the words on the fading LP sleeve – asked if I had been named for one of the "Beverly Brothers". Hence (in a roundabout way) my nickname, once the misunderstanding had been cleared up, and also my father's genuine respect for Progress, only five or six at the time, I'm told. In fact, his promise must have been evident even before then, because from my earliest recollections, he had been the only child of a member of staff who had been allowed to wander at will in our home until dusk. This must have originally happened at my mother's insistence, I can only suppose now, with the gift of hindsight.

Thunder rent the air a little close by, and we jumped together through the tilting doorway of the hut, bellowing and whooping. A tiny spring to the right of it, just a thimble-sized dome of water permeating up through the bronze leaf litter, meant that there was always a miniature clear pool a few feet from the hut's threshold. This would quickly swell to a tea-coloured rivulet, then a scummy stream, once the rain began in earnest. The insulating silence of expectancy that always descends just before a storm hits wrapped itself around the hut, standing there alone at the bottom of the echoing green well. We could just make out the hillside opposite, half a mile away, where sparkling wild banana leaves were already thrashing in the great gusts of wet wind. A minute before, there had been the bubbling conversations of birds, distant monkey shrieks, the drones and creaks of insects, and the back-and-forth of our soft voices. Around our shelter now, however, the only sounds were the minute gurglings of the tender spring at our feet and the background trickles and rushes of narrow cascades and watercourses, distant and unseen.

I turned from the doorway to see that Progress was now standing at the back of the hut, next to row of scythes and clippers hanging from bent nails on mouldy leather straps. He'd taken off his pale-blue school shirt, which had been clinging to his body in regular navy patches of clean sweat, and he nodded his head sharply upwards in my direction as if to indicate that I should do the same with my hand-me-down, red-and-white gingham dress. But whereas a year ago I would have done so without a second thought, I was suddenly hesitant. Confronted with my unexpected reticence, Progress looked swiftly and intently out of the tiny unglazed window with its bulging fly screen, searching for a new topic with which to start a conversation. He narrowed his eyes as he always did when he sensed he had overstepped some mark that delineated his world and mine. I could no longer see the many small, dark-amber blooms that already clouded the whites of his eyes, spoiling – at least for me – his otherwise even good looks. For the first time in our lives, an embarrassment fell over our company.

"Look here now, Beverly …"

For several moments we had been caught in a reverie, suspended between that first series of thundercracks and the gratifying thrill that the next set, surely much closer and more frightening when it finally arrived, would deliver. I was surprised by Progress's use of my real name and sensed myself being reluctantly pulled back out of the pleasant, dull stupor that lunch, the electric air, and the enveloping stillness had induced. With my thoughts thickened by indolence, it wasn't at all obvious to me what I was supposed to be looking at, but I felt only the mildest irritation at Progress's deliberate vagueness. His words implied that standing in the patchy sunlight of the doorway, I was handicapped by being unable to focus on the object of his attention. Maybe it was to be found outside the window through which he continued to gaze, or perhaps it was somewhere else entirely, for "look here now" was also an expression he routinely used whenever he wanted to try out a new idea on me.

I moved into the hut to stand opposite him in the constricted space, edging forward somewhat awkwardly into the crammed interior, with its metal jerry cans and ranks of brown glass bottles on a sagging shelf lining one wall. Now I truly did feel at a disadvantage as my eyes took their time adjusting to the gloom. I was wearing two-strap sandals that I had outgrown some time ago and was suddenly acutely conscious of the vulnerability of my little poking-out toes. The dangers of lockjaw had been explained to me in unnecessary detail by a stout Scottish nurse at the clinic in town, where I went every year for a check-up and de-worming. Before her fever had closed over her for the last time, Mum had apparently impressed upon my father the need for this small attention to my welfare, should she not survive.

Progress silently dropped his close-cropped head in what seemed like sudden bashfulness. I was not used to all this frankly un-playful behaviour from him, and a tiny itch of confusion or suspicion made itself felt on the periphery of my still-dulled perception. I followed his downwards gaze but discovered I could see nothing of interest to me on the shattered floorboards – no bat skull or curled carcass of a giant millipede – so I sucked my teeth in exasperation, like I had heard Thoko do so many times in moments of vexation. Progress could be infuriatingly uncommunicative when he wished to appear mysterious or knowing, and it was dawning on me that what I was supposed to be examining was not some curiosity of plant or animal origin at his feet, after all. This meant that instead it had to be an abstract, complex notion that had been growing in his mind for some time – one that he now wished to impart to me in a manner that would display his greater learning and maturity.

"No. Here. Look *here* at this, Beverly. Do you know these things?"

He was moving both his index fingers down the two shallow grooves that I could now just make out at either side of his belly, above the top of his school shorts. I had last seen his torso a year ago, when we walked all the way to the neighbours' dam to paddle on an afternoon of crushing heat, only to find it full of leeches, swaying up against the submerged weeds and looking for all the world like animated strings of liquorice. Then he had displayed thin arms with the usual burn marks and other puckered scars of a childhood in the village, and a pot belly with an unapologetic, bulging navel. Now I saw that his body had hardened and flattened. The two indentations I could see outlined with perspiration under his fingertips were a new and intriguing development. My father's own anatomy – when I spied on him undressing through his bedroom door, which would no longer close due to the swelling of the wooden frame – showed the usual brown, speckled forearms and calves of a farmer's tan, while the rest was pink and white, grown pouchy and somehow defeated, furred with erratic patches of swiftly greying hair.

"You see? Now I will soon look like a man. I will be a man. You see?"

Where had this sinew and meat come from? Progress was not like his peers, already working tending goats, fetching water and hacking a vegetable plot out of the soil in spurts of silky dust. His father had wanted for his youngest son the prospect of books and classrooms and study, so that he would not end up an illiterate garden boy like generations of Moyos before him. Were all the other black schoolboys in his grade built the same way? I didn't really know any white boys of my own age, indeed any other white children at all apart from the imperious cousins, so I had no basis for comparison.

The first strobe of lightning illuminated him, sharpening him into extreme focus for a split second as he turned his thumbs inside the elasticated waistband of his thin grey and patched shorts. His skin was lit up in that moment in shades of lilac and deepest violet. I was reminded of an illustration in a disintegrating children's book on gardening that I had bought with borrowed pennies at a church bazaar on my abortive trip to Bulawayo. The picture had a large Victoria-plum tree in the foreground, the fruits a blotched mauve lightly dusted over in places with a powdery white coating that somehow made them look more delicious and juicier than if they had been shiny and uniform in colour. A benign-looking wasp was depicted crawling on one of the fruits, working industriously to nibble away where the fruit's skin had already been bruised and breached.

As I clumsily shuffled another half-step closer and balanced forward to see properly what Progress was now regarding with a mixture of incredulity and pride, our heads gently bumped together. This should have been occasion for some hilarity, an opportunity for the tension to be broken at last. Instead, the spell held.

The lightning was becoming more regular now, the thunderclaps closer and more insistent. I wasn't surprised to have seen what he revealed as he continued to draw his shorts and too-big Y-fronts downwards with a slow, jerky movement. I had run enough errands to the staff lines to know what village boys sporting only grubby white vests looked like from the waist down. What actually transfixed me as I regarded Progress were his changed proportions, as well as the tiny bundles of sparse, clumped black curls that started just under his now less-extravagantly protruding bellybutton and extended to the tops of his long thighs. Having lowered his clothing to his knees, he then raised his bent arms above his head for effect. Again, I was perturbed to discover that his armpits were now pelted with long black hairs. I was aware, too, of a new sharp smell coming from him, so different from the comforting, slightly sour and milky aroma I was used to, under the creamy lemon scent of Sunlight soap that always accompanied him.

He watched me, his eyes still narrowed, as I absorbed all these changes in what I hoped was a blithe, indifferent manner, and as I tried to locate the familiar – some vestige of his earlier self that would bind me to him and our shared childhood for a little while longer. He turned slowly, slowly, as the first blast of wind shook the hut and the air within chilled swiftly. My father's buttocks, were deflated-looking, sorry and flat like those of an old man twice his age, but as Progress presented his back to me, I could see that his own stuck out almost at a right angle to his body, full and fleshy like those of a handsome Shona bride.

And this then was a further surprise, for even though John was hardly a dedicated trencherman, he ate well enough, spoilt by Beauty who had come to us after Estelle had died and who had learned to cook with an Afrikaans family that liked starch and rich sauces, good fatty meat and beer. But Progress – so far as I could tell from the way that he always finished every last morsel when invited on rare occasions to eat with John and me – was unlikely to know the deep satisfaction of a full stomach when he was at home with his large extended family.

In our home, Progress was polite and diffident, suspecting perhaps that he was only tolerated these days because John hadn't yet found the right moment to gently engineer an eviction that he could justify to me. I knew, nevertheless, that he was on a constant, furtive search for food of any description, his appetite never satiated by the meagre pickings he received at home as the last child in the family, or at our table. At least once a month I heard him muffle a yelp of protest as Beauty, having caught him looking for biscuits in the lean-to on his way from school to meet me, smacked him repeatedly round the head with her huge open hand. And my father had once gone out to the yard late one evening to shoot a jackal or stray dog that we had heard raiding there, only to find Progress upside down in a bin, looking for scraps.

He had now made almost a full rotation, and I was staring down again, more closely this time, at what would indeed soon be his manhood made flesh. By this stage I had dropped all pretence of nonchalance and had decided to give free rein to my curiosity and just gawp, in case the opportunity did not present itself again. I don't recall feeling embarrassed or ashamed, though perhaps I was still too young and immature for that. Nor do I know how long we stood there, letting our shallow racing breaths out into the dank, rapidly cooling space between us. No one had spoken for what seemed like a long time. Then a hidden gecko barked its remonstration, and the trance was over.

I want to say it was our secret. But evidently it wasn't.

Surely no one could have come down the slope once we were at the hut without us hearing them. Even the most stealthy, skilled tracker (or later, guerrilla) could not have come upon us unannounced. The ravine was an ever-changing obstacle course of rotting, fallen wood, rocks slicked with algae, and unexpected, fern-covered depressions that hid knotted creepers and permanent reservoirs of sucking mud. Only three people ever used the path that led down to the hut, the brook, and its encircling grove – and even for Progress and me, who walked it almost daily, it would have been impossible to negotiate the track without some tell-tale noise.

Had Job, instinctively aware of something different in his last-born's behaviour that day, followed close behind us unseen, using the loud sounds we made to obliterate those of his own descent? And then secreted himself in one of the thickets close by the hut and watched us? I didn't think so then, and I still don't today. For a start, the "nettles" that grew up around the outside walls were pretty unforgiving ... On the other hand, I had known him, Beauty, Thoko and the others most of my life, and yet I would have been hard pressed to tell you anything about their characters, abilities and activities beyond those that directly affected me – so maybe keeping a clandestine eye out for his most promising son was part and parcel of Job's daily tasks. The War, when it exploded soon afterwards, revealed all kinds of unsuspected, astonishing loyalties and resentments on both sides. Some white people I knew pronounced themselves genuinely perplexed, hurt even, by the realisation that people they had lived alongside all their lives had really been total strangers to them and not "like one of the family, almost" at all.

Or had Progress gone back to the staff village that evening and been unable to resist boasting to his friends and brothers that he had undressed in front of the boss's daughter? To this day, I find this hard to credit. He must surely have realised, in some inchoate way only perhaps, that had the information become widely known – around the evening cooking fires and on the pathways through the open heathlands above the village as people went to and from their work, and eventually even reaching the ears of one of the farmer bosses, perhaps – he would have found himself beaten hard if he were lucky and (far more likely) in dreadful, immediate danger, if he were not.

But someone, somewhere, knew what we had been up to that afternoon. Knew outright because, undetected, Job had peered at us through the fly screen as the indigo cloud hung low over the mountains and the hut stood alone in the bright emerald crease of the valley. Or knew in the more general, instinctive way that some people, especially Africans I think, do – because they have closely observed the way a person familiar to them has changed, become more secretive or withdrawn, let's say. Tiny clues, but telling nonetheless.

I have no doubt that John's staff did regard him with affection and wished to save him from any further humiliation – having to raise a daughter by himself being the first cause for shame in their estimation. Thus my father was probably given to understand by Beauty or Thoko that perhaps it was no longer quite right for a black boy not far from his teens and a little white girl (with no mother, of course) to be left to play alone together for such long periods of time unsupervised. The finer details he may have guessed for himself or possibly extracted from one of them, not by threats or force but by appealing to them as a father who had no way of knowing how to do the terrifyingly complex work of raising a child alone.

John never said a word to me. Progress was left, as I came to learn eventually, unpunished. This is how I know that it was not one of the other white farmers who told Dad what Progress had done – and my father was thus thankfully spared the necessity of visiting public retribution on a black munt who tried to molest his baby girl.

Even so, I never saw Progress after that day because suddenly, shockingly, halfway through the third term of the year, I was going to school.

❧

Abruptly, the house fizzed with energy, ringing with the hectoring, authoritative voices of the wives of the three neighbours as they clattered back and forth on the wooden floors in their silly, heeled shoes. They shone with gratification at the chance to decipher for my father the baffling, typed lists of uniforms (plural), stationery, religious paraphernalia and other obligatory items he would now have to purchase in order for me to finally become a real Catholic schoolgirl. Sensing his bewilderment and consequent indecision, worse even than usual, they then busily took over the role of purchasing the goods in town, and of delivering them up to the house in person. Soon, the hallway contained a large, tidy heap of parcels neatly wrapped in brown paper, each with a store's sales slip taped to the top.

Less than a week later, the sisters at the convent in a town I had only ever visited once before welcomed a very reluctant, unkempt girl into their school flock. They undressed me and examined me for ticks, then praised what they called my "surprising general knowledge" (which included conflicting, half-understood facts pertaining to human reproduction). They kept me in for long hours after regular class in order to try to address my chasmic ignorance in matters of rote learning. The other girls were already in long-established cliques, bound together by rules of affiliation that would take me many months to parse. They let me know that the large and small proofs of difference that I evidenced through my every word and deed made me an oddity not worthy of their scrutiny or interest. Their studied indifference thawed a little over time – most of them were fundamentally decent sorts – but for the first time in my life, and surrounded by my peers at last, I was lonely.

∽

I want to say that was a long time ago, because in terms of weeks and months and years, it was.

Progress is gone, dumped in a hastily dug, unmarked grave by his young comrades in the War was the rumour, one that I will confess, to my secret shame, I did little to follow up. My father is also gone, of course, lingering for a month in typically quiet good humour in the whitewashed ward of a hospital for Europeans in

Bulawayo after an accident in a tobacco-packing factory broke his back – and what was left of his will to live – when I was seventeen. Soon after this I went south to study, and I have not been back to my blighted, lovely homeland since the 1970s. I have no desire to visit, knowing that the only thing that will distress me more than the changes I encounter will be the things that have stubbornly stayed the same.

I bought a plane ticket, and I shed a skin, growing pale and bronchial in London and getting lost on the Tube regularly that first year. Evenings I would spend sitting with my new girlfriends on futons in a shabby, overheated bedsit that smelled faintly of gas, sharing wine (*not* South African wine in those days, *of course*) and disclosures. I quickly discovered that the horror of candid revelations that formed part of my upbringing was judged old-fashioned and un-sisterly. Confessional stories of early sexual exploits poured forth from the others until I was required to make my own contribution. I told the story of Progress just that once, the (slightly embellished) exotic but nonetheless tame details inevitably failing to serve up the shock so gleefully sought by my audience. But trying on the new personas of feminism was also part of the ritual, and it fell to a posh girl called Imogen to try to extract some message for us all from the tale.

"Yeah but, you know Phil, *really* that boy was really responsible for the end of your childhood, wasn't he? That was the first time that the patriarchy had that kind of power over you. Even if nothing much happened that time."

Which is why I told the story only once. That moment in the dripping hut was born out of a pair of solitary children, whose innocence was about to come under attack from the adults who desperately wanted to protect two unlikely friends from each other.

Like any exile – voluntary or otherwise – I find that there are unguarded moments when I am ambushed by an unlooked-for recollection. For me, it can be brought about by the sight of a roll of wax-print fabric in Camden market, or the sound of a *mbira* on a radio station that plays world music, as I have recently learned to call it. Or by the bracingly sharp, sappy smell of wet nettles crushed underfoot along the verge of an English country lane in late May, when the trees behind the uncut trimmed hedgerows grow tall enough to form an almost unbroken interlacing of striving branches and incipient buds above my head. I'm taken back to the waiting, crackling air before the arrival of the storm, two breaths held in the closeness of a decaying hut, and the sheen of a boy's purple flesh held in the photographic flashes of an afternoon's lightning.

The Copper Bowl

Two weeks before we were due to depart, we decided, on a whim (when did we start to do whims?), to use up our remaining annual leave and visit a part of England we had never been to before. Anita said that we had worked hard, we deserved it, and once we relocated to Cape Town, things were going to get a whole lot more stressful and "gritty" (as she had it) so it would be a good idea to recharge our batteries somewhere tranquil in preparation.

The cottage rental, even though we got it at a special rate due to a last-minute cancellation, cost more than our flights to South Africa, but in matters such as these I always deferred to my wife. She knew best, she really did, and no sarcasm intended. And Suffolk that summer was at its most glorious – flotillas of high clouds scooting across the endless skies, ridiculously overpriced "traditional" ice creams savoured along the crunching shingle at Aldeburgh, and Radio 3 in the car sending the song of the ascending lark into our hearts and leaving a piercing melancholy in its wake. In the evenings we would watch DVDs of the movies that we had meant to catch up with over the years, when we had been too busy to have a proper life. In retrospect, there was something valedictory about the whole week.

We visited a tourist-pretty, spick-and-span market town and ambled by the antique shops filled with ersatz Victorian bed-warmers and framed pictures of faded dried flowers – the past laid out prettily for the attention of the wealthy summer hordes. As was our habit, we used all the little catchphrases and secret, silly words that we had acquired during the course of our long relationship to critique the middle-class families in their GAP T-shirts and identical chinos, milling about self-importantly and calling out the names of their children in braying voices. We decided then that if we ever had a child (why only the one, I asked myself much later?) we would give it a name loaded with some symbolism that only the pair of us would ever understand.

In a backstreet we came across some stalls that were selling objects that could more justifiably be called junk; despite ourselves and the risk of being trapped into a sale, we slowed our pace so we could take a better look. And there she was – as Anita pantomimed it for friends later – my darling, the one thing I could not live without, even though I hadn't known up until that moment that she was my heart's desire. Sitting in the middle of a trestle table littered with tiny china jugs and random bits of chunky, cheap crystal-ware, her dull gleam like a modest but irresistible beacon in the shadows of the lane – a rounded, beaten copper vessel the size of a kitchen mixing-bowl on steroids.

"No. No ways," Anita said with mock authority when I pulled up sharply before my treasure. "We're moving to another continent, and you want to use up our freight allowance on that?"

But just as Anita got to make all the big decisions in our life – including taking a three-year sabbatical so that she could work on a vaccination programme in Africa – so I got to make the aesthetic choices and the everyday calls (ready-meal butter chicken or tikka masala from M&S?) As she paid for it – an early birthday gift, she conceded with cheerful resignation – I asked the stallholder if he knew what it was.

"Well, back in the day, in these big old houses hereabouts, they would cook up spectacular feasts from time to time, see? Shooting parties and hunt balls and so on, I'd imagine. And the chief cook, she would use a bowl like this big one, see, to make a special fancy cake or pudding for the occasion for all the guests. Not much call these days for cooking on that scale, though ..."

He tailed off, lost in thoughts of grand parties at the mansion, idly picking at a magnificent gold front tooth, one of only a few that he appeared to have left. We declined his offer to wrap my bowl in newspaper, and having laid it reverentially on the back seat of the car (I resisted the temptation to strap it in), made our way back to the cottage. Tired and lost in our own silent thoughts, we drove through the long shadows of the narrow, sunken country lanes, pheasants skittering across the road and the oblique bands of sunlight flashing and blinding us through gaps in the massive trees that lined the way.

When we got back to the cottage, I immediately started taking artistic shots of the bowl resting on different surfaces in the old-fashioned country kitchen. There seemed to be a million different ways to adjust its position so that the mellow golden light of the evening, pouring in through the small leaded windows, showed it to its best advantage. Repositioning it once again, I took a tentative lick of a finger and there it was – a taste from childhood: copper pennies in a hot fist. I was admiring the results on the camera's digital display when I caught sight of Anita reflected in the screen as it changed briefly to black. She was standing behind me with her arms crossed (nothing unusual in that) but I caught an expression I had never seen her send my way before on the smeared display. It was the unmistakable flickerings of a weary contempt.

სა

And then there was foresight too. I went to visit my mother on the day before we flew out, when Anita was busy reorganising our luggage one last time. Walking into Kim's little flat, high above the river and the streets of Brentford, I saw her pulling a heavy pan of my favourite soda bread from the ancient cooker. She didn't even turn to acknowledge me as I let myself in, and I guessed she was finding a way to compose herself for what would be our last visit together in what she doubtlessly considered a long time.

"It's actually cool that you are going there, you know?" she puffed in her fugitive Irish lilt. "Getting in touch with the other half of the family perhaps at last."

She plonked the hot tray down onto a wooden chopping block with a flourish and turning to regard me with her jaded, seen-it-all look, fired up a fag.

"Mam, I'm not even going to look up Pa's folk there. Why would I? You are my family, and Anita, and that's all."

"Yes, well, while we're on that subject. Will you two be bringing a little grandchild back with you, do you think? It's time you gave it some thought, my boy, before you two maybe start to drift apart a bit, I would say. Nothing like a child to bring a couple back together, now."

This struck me as a singularly uncharitable and incautious thing to ask me, today of all days, especially in view of the fact that it had been my birth, as Kim told it, that had caused the irreparable rift between she and my father. Neither Anita nor I had any desire to start thinking about a family just yet, and my mother would normally be more discreet than to raise a personal topic like this. For all she knew, perhaps we *had* been trying, or had some other sound reason why she had not yet been given the opportunity to be a grandmother.

Though that wasn't what pulled me up short and made me spill water everywhere as I ran a drink from the tap after the long climb up to the ninth floor. Could it really be that she had just suggested there was a possibility that my Anita and I would cease to be joined at the hip, with identical goals as a couple and on parallel tracks, as we had been since we'd become an item at 6th-form college? We were used to people remarking that we were like two halves of a whole, two peas in a pod, finishing each other's sentences, soul mates, all the clichés … Couples told us they envied our mutual understanding, our ability to read each other's thoughts, our bond. The way the shortcoming of one (my antipathy to decision-making) was balanced by the strength of the other – for example, Anita's need to control every last logistical detail of our recent travel arrangements.

It always pleased Anita to hear this kind of thing, to be reminded of our tag-team dynamic, but it disconcerted me from time to time. It appeared to be shorthand for saying there was no obvious erotic connection between us, that we were together because we comprised a sort of mutually dependent double act.

Kim skilfully sliced the hot bread and buttered a thick, crumbling chunk for me. We ate in silence, standing at the kitchen counter as jets coming in to land at Heathrow boomed overhead. I sensed that she wanted to press me further by insisting that I try to find my father, wherever he might be in South Africa. My mam was slyly using me to try to re-establish the link that he must have thought he had severed forever when he walked out one morning when I was two. She had harboured an inkling, even before I was born, though, that he had one foot out the door, and so she had insisted that I be given his surname and had found a way for me to be issued with a green passport from his homeland to add to my red British one.

But tact prevailed (and only once Anita and I were in Cape Town did I discover the reason why). Mam and I chatted about the work Anita would be doing, helping to design immunisation programmes in townships across the country. And my work helping to set up and run a small community arts project – unpaid and part-time at this point, though there had been hints that if my paperwork was in order, I might apply for a paid position eventually.

I took my leave and reminded her that I was only a night flight away and would be back at Easter the following year. I searched her worn, prematurely old face for the tears I half expected, but in her vagabond life she had already said too many goodbyes. We simply hugged and parted in silence, the pockets of my jeans stuffed with the little packets of bread she had made up for my wife.

∞

It was on our first day in Cape Town, I decided as I looked back later, that my wife and I had started to part ways. Anita drove the hired car in the mad traffic from the airport, gesturing with both hands off the wheel at every vehicle that ran a red. Although my phone battery was dead, she kept asking me to navigate – as if somehow, I ought to know in my genes which streets were one way and which led us in exasperating loops in the opposite direction to our destination. We arrived flustered and undone by our argument. The first serious one we'd had since the day when we'd first met.

Once inside our rented flat in a small, modern block, I started to hum out of sheer, shocked embarrassment as I unpacked my precious camera gear – a childish gesture to show that I wasn't fazed by what had happened in the car. That unprecedented event had made me feel so faint and sick that I headed back out of the door as soon as I reasonably could, throwing over my shoulder as I went the explanation that I needed some air and wanted to orientate myself in our new neighbourhood. I also wanted to examine my complicated feelings regarding the green passport that I'd noticed Anita had secreted in a zipped compartment of my suitcase. The two women in my life had been in cahoots all along.

When I returned, having taken just a few photos for the sake of bolstering my excuse for leaving so gracelessly, my wife was sitting on the little balcony cradling a cup of chai tea, made from the supplies of "things-we-can't-live-without" that she had bought with her. She had showered and changed into a midnight-blue shalwar kameez that she liked to wear when she was relaxing. Like my humming earlier, her choice of clothing seemed to be designed to signal a serenity she wasn't truly feeling. Anita accused me of being stupid, wandering about by myself with expensive camera equipment in a country that was notorious for muggings and violent crime. She asked me yet again if I had dosed myself with the expired anti-malarial drugs she had told me I didn't need but that I bought anyway from a mate in the pub who had some to spare. Then she asked me if I was all right. "Are you *all right* Sean?" but the way she said it made me feel as if she was probing some aspect of my sanity, rather than expressing any concern for my physical wellbeing.

When our small shipment of household belongings arrived a few weeks later and I began to unpack the cardboard carton that held my copper bowl, Anita announced that she would make a turn by the nearest shopping centre to buy something for our supper. In our little apartment there was no free surface large enough to hold the bowl comfortably, so until something better occurred to me, I upended it and placed it over the top of a freestanding coat rack, where it wobbled very slightly in the sea breeze from the open balcony door. When Anita came back, she glanced at it so briefly I wasn't sure it had even registered.

However, later in the day, as the sun dropped and paillettes of light reflecting from the pitted surface of the bowl started to play on all the walls, she looked up from her reading and said mildly, "Sean it's like a fucking gay disco in here. Find somewhere else to put that stupid bowl of yours or in a cupboard or something, or else it's going to drive me totally bonkers."

∞

When did you become ours?

Anita had been working so many hours at the programme that, mindful of burnout, she had scheduled a few days' midweek leave at my suggestion, and we had planned to take off and drive wherever the road north took us. We had meant to go in the direction of Lambert's Bay – we liked the name since it reminded us of an actor whom we both admired. Unfortunately, somewhere in all the confusion of Cape Town's early morning traffic, unexpected roadworks, and a one-way system that defeated us time after time, we missed the turn-off entirely and found ourselves heading in the opposite direction that brilliant morning. I ventured that it didn't really matter: east was as good as north when the aim was to spend time together exploring beyond our immediate surroundings in the city. At the time, I remember being touched when Anita agreed to my proposal that we improvise our plans, as I knew it was most unlike her to do anything impromptu. In fact, perhaps I should have been worried at this uncharacteristic demurral on her part. Her gaiety on that day off was infectious though, and she didn't even take a dig at me for getting us lost once again. I thought nothing of it all, really, until later.

On our way out of the city we picked up some salads, cool-drinks, and cooked frikkadels at a Woolworths and put them into the coolbox that Anita had reminded me to place in the boot of the little Suzuki. Then we took the swinging coast road until we came upon a pretty seaside town laid out high on the cliffs and falling to a dramatic rocky bay below, complete with a second-hand book shop where we retreated from the underpowered air con and sticky seats of the car. We went our separate ways in the narrow aisles of the shop – dark, cool and smelling pleasantly of lavender polish – while the colossal, bearded young shopkeeper took us in from behind his manual cash till. In this seemingly bohemian little enclave, with its crystal shop and organic health-food store, it could not have been unusual for him to have seen a mixed couple like us, I thought, but he nevertheless scrutinised us as if we were something of a novelty.

For form's sake, maybe out of British embarrassment at the idea of leaving empty-handed when we had been in there for some time, I bought a new-ish handbook on the wildlife of the coast. We were hoping to spot a whale or two, or even some dolphins or sharks, though it was really too early in the year, I had been informed by my colleagues at the arts project. As I was counting out the money for my purchase, Anita asked the titan at the counter where we could stay locally, and where we could spend the day once we had checked in to a suitable B&B. This was her department – making plans and establishing objectives for the trip – so I was, today as on all days, happy for her to choose our destination and our activities. I was along for the ride, as I had been since the moment I had first set eyes on her at our local independent cinema, more than a decade ago now.

In the thickest of Afrikaans accents, the amiable giant directed us to drive a short distance partway up the slope out of town, and there we found a guesthouse of exquisite kitschiness where we could stay at a reasonable rate. Our room was a homely magazine spread of marine-themed blue-and-white textiles, DIY shell-encrusted mirrors, plaster lighthouse lamps and faux stained-glass dolphins hanging at all the windows. It could not, we smugly agreed, have been more perfect, and before we headed out for the day's sightseeing, we made sure to capture the more tasteless highlights on Anita's phone.

We liberated the coolbox from the now stifling car parked alongside the B&B and walked across to the cliff path that we could see on the opposite side of the narrow road. We set off, with the intention of finding a spot in the scrubby heathland of a nearby promontory where we could settle for the day, struggling slightly awkwardly to carry one side of the large container each by its rigid handle as it bumped painfully against our shins.

Anita was tired out from long shifts, and we both thought, without saying as much, that the nicest thing to do would be nothing at all. We had purchased a large navy-and-turquoise rug made of plaited rags in the same town en route where we had bought our picnic. This we now spread out on a concrete bench that overlooked a limitless expanse of gently undulating deep green sea. Twenty metres or so in front of our seat the short cliff fell away in tumbles of broken boulders until it met a series of wide rocky shelves at its foot, over the seaward side of which the slow waves broke with some force. Standing at a distance from each other on two of these enormous platforms were a pair of Coloured fishermen, wearing nothing but white wellington boots and silky soccer shorts. They were casting lines deep beyond the surf while racing back and forth with considerable skill to avoid the waves' more penetrating incursions. We sat in contented silence and tried to train our eyes to distinguish between the creamy lines formed by long crests of wavelets out at sea and the wakes and washes of the sea animals we hoped to spot.

"Is there not very much a sense in which, surely, if he is French, he should be called *Michel* Lonsdale and not Michael?"

There was no need to ask Anita to explain: our renowned psychic communication was at work, and I knew instantly what she was doing. In her lethargy, Anita had lapsed into a game that we played when we hadn't the energy to tackle issues of greater import. It was a way of exploring our mutual love of films through the adopted personas of a pair of intellectuals on a late-night TV show. I accepted the bait, always pleased to do anything that reinforced our clique of two and that, in addition, allowed us to be childish – a state into which we fell less and less often these days.

"One might equally well say, might one not, that Lambert Wilson has a strange name for a French actor?"

It must have been early on in our relationship when we began this game of ours, maybe even before we started sleeping together, and I don't recall precisely what its original purpose had been. Perhaps I was still trying to show off at that stage (did I ever really give up showing off for her?), and I suspect that, conversely, she was trying to wear her far-greater learning more lightly. Perhaps now we played it occasionally so that we could be transported back to simpler times.

We had been eating an early lunch – the salads, though a little warm now, were fresh and tasty, as were the meatballs and slices of Parma-style ham. The sun was circling behind us, and I felt the back of my neck becoming uncomfortably tight and prickly – a fair Celt in Africa is always going to be at the sun's mercy. Nevertheless, I was enjoying our semi-serious discussion as it progressed. We had not had much of a chance to watch any movies since we had arrived, and it was good to be back on familiar territory. I looked out over the ocean, spreading to a thick band of surprising mint-green water at the horizon, and thought about how seeing the Atlantic like this was an immersive experience in a way that going to the seaside in England was not.

Keeping up the affected, pretentious tone, I started in on a monologue about Michael Lonsdale's greatest performances, happy (I see now) to have had the opportunity of pulling back together a seam in our relationship that had seemed to be under strain recently. Then I looked across at Anita to see that her head was bouncing forwards and then jerking upright as she fought sleep. She had consumed a single-serving bottle of sparkling rosé while I had stuck to juice.

"Let's find a less exposed spot, and I'll read my book if you want to doze."

She peered up at the sky, with its scattered puffs of clouds that looked as if the sun should dissolve them away like clumps of candy-floss in a hot mouth, then down at the rolling, empty ocean and only sighed by way of agreement. I picked up the now empty coolbox and followed her slow ascent further up the cliff path to the top of the headland, which seemed to offer the promise of better shade.

Little animals that looked like giant sandy guinea pigs raced from the cover of the undergrowth as we passed them, giving out an eerie shrieking whistle. I stopped to consult my new guidebook and told Anita that these were dassies, remarkably the closest living relative of the elephant. She feigned interest and scanned the path ahead for a spot where we could retire unseen for a few hours. The main path had now gained the open cliff top, but various side routes wound down through dense brush into areas of shade below, where the cliff gradient to the sea was not as steep as before. We selected one that was clearly rarely used and pushed past the scratchy evergreen bushes until we found a large patch of short grass and sand almost entirely surrounded by overhanging branches. And there on the rug my wife slept on her side while I looked through the book and tried to keep awake and keep watch.

After an hour Anita awoke with a start; it caused a palpable pricking in the region of my heart to see how momentarily vulnerable she looked, gazing up at me in bleary confusion while she established her surroundings. She didn't do weak or unguarded, so if I wanted to locate these in her I had to come across them by stealth. I noticed with simple adoration how the kohl she always wore had smudged around her green eyes as she slept and made her look like a beautiful child acolyte in a temple. I didn't mention this though – she would have called me soft.

The hidden clearing in which we had rested had a gap in the bushes on its far side. We got up, a little unsteadily since the rag rug was not padded, and we had some muscle aches by now, then both moved off towards the sounds of voices we could now hear coming from the direction of the opening. Once we cleared the break in the shoulder-high scrub, we could see that a path led on, via a series of gentle winding turns down the slope, to a large flat concrete platform that had been constructed at a place where the cliffs encircled a small natural cove. Ten or so people were sitting or lying on this, and a number more were visible in a pool of seawater just below that was accessed by metal steps such as you get at the side of a swimming pool. This bathing area had been constructed by closing part of the mouth of the cove with a seawall, over which the waves beyond were just about trickling. A kind of manmade rock pool, it even seemed to have sea life attached to the bottom at the place where it was shallowest. At the other end, three small children were hurling themselves into the deep end, launching into the dark water in side somersaults while screeching with pleasure. A couple sat with their backs to them, chatting animatedly and occasionally looking over to check that their charges were okay.

What struck me immediately about the dozen or so bathers was that they were all black, and it seemed, all poor. None of them had on proper swimsuits. The women were mostly in bras and knickers, and the men had rolled up their jeans or were in boxer shorts. They all, so far as I could tell, had a passing acquaintance with each other, and the whole scene was as pleasant as it was unexpected. The photographer in me wished I had brought along my camera kit because here was an aspect of the local community that I doubted had been captured often before. One for the portfolio, if only my security-conscious mind hadn't stymied the impulse to bring along my equipment today.

"Where do you suppose these people have come from, Sean?"

"Today's not a public holiday is it? There was too much commuter traffic this morning."

"Nope, I think they are just people enjoying a nice end to a lovely day. I could do with a paddle myself …"

Anita, always so much more self-assured, had apparently already decided to join the bathers, so we tottered with shuffling sideways steps down the sandy path until we both stopped at another empty concrete bench on a natural ledge a few metres above the bathing platform. Once there, however, it seemed as if we were both gripped by an inhibition about joining the others, whose numbers had now swollen to about thirty men, women and children. And since our perch on the bench made us almost instantly self-conscious, without consulting each other we each took two corners of the rug, spread it out on the turf to one side of the seat, and sat down. From there it was possible to see that the crowd had come up along a path in the dunes below that met the main tarmac road about half a kilometre distant, off in the haze of the late afternoon.

"My guess would be that this posh place has an informal settlement hidden away some place, just like everywhere else. Because it wouldn't do for the tourists from overseas to see how the other half lives."

Anita was surely correct. Every town we had passed through on that day had had, on its outskirts, a sprawling collection of run-down shacks and mean, improvised dwellings. After four months' stay, we knew that these were occupied by the blacks who laboured in local houses, gardens, factories and warehouses. This seaside village, swanky though it was, could be no exception.

I asked permission to take forty winks. I felt a little irresponsible leaving Anita to mount guard duty, but she could take care of things and would wake me if she had to. I did a quick inventory – apart from our two cheap mobile phones, designer sunglasses we had treated ourselves to at Gatwick, and the car keys, we had no valuables to speak of. Instantly, I felt ashamed of my assumptions and rueful at how quickly I had learned one of the rules of living in this country: never take to a public place anything you can't afford to lose. Within days of our arrival, I'd been disabused by colleagues of my misguided belief that since Anita is not white, perhaps we would be less likely to be targeted by an opportunistic thief when out together as a couple

It was deeply pleasurable to hear the light lapping of the waves, the uninhibited laughter, the splashes, the murmurs of conversations, to be part of a group having fun, even if we were only on the periphery.

ભ

When did you become mine?

I drifted in and out of sleep, then through the lassitude, I became aware of a voice – a girl was talking to Anita. I stifled an instinct to immediately snap into protective male mode, which my wife would surely not have appreciated, and forced myself to remain as if asleep, to listen to her and take my cue from the pitch of her voice. She was talking softly and gently, with an undercurrent of concern in her words, which to my frustration the breeze was snatching away. I opened my eyes just enough to assess the situation, then found myself unable to make a pretence of sleeping any longer.

Lying full stretch on her side on the grass next to Anita was an almost-naked girl breastfeeding a tiny baby who was swaddled in multiple layers of thick, home-knitted clothes under a dirty white waffle blanket. The mother had slipped one pathetically flattened breast from her torn tangerine lacy bra and was nursing the child as it lay facing her on a corner of our rug. The young woman, whose only other attire was a pair of miniscule denim shorts, was resting her head comfortably on one palm and with her upper arm was gesticulating and explaining something in lisping English. Anita was quietly murmuring in agreement with her, and I felt very much like an interloper on the intimate scene. I tried to meet Anita's eye, but she was looking intently at the mother while asking a series of short questions. The child was apparently sleeping while still suckling, and this was why, I now realised, Anita was talking in a whisper.

Back and forth the conversation went. The girl deftly used her toes, with their pitiful chipped polish, to push scratchy blades of grass away from her bare legs. Her side of the discussion appeared animated and aggrieved – from what words in English I could make out – while Anita's was reassuring and calm. Then the woman used an index finger to ease the baby's pouting mouth away from a long nipple, pushed the exposed, formless breast back inside her bra, and stood.

I tried again to attract Anita's attention, but she was still engaged in conversation, more loudly now since the girl – I saw now she was only in her teens – was moving away. Anita was still lying on her side on the rug, resting a hand on the bundled-up, immobile form left there like the grub of a massive insect. Some instinct was telling me not to speak until I received a sign from my wife, but only once the young mother had set off along the path to the road and was out of earshot, did Anita turn to me and began filling me in.

The mother, a schoolgirl called Thembi, had come to the swimming place to meet with the father of the child, a married man and a skelm. He was supposed to be giving her some money because since the child's birth she had not received a cent from him. Now he was late for their rendezvous, but her brother was in a car at the parking lot by the main road with some of his friends, waiting to take her back home after her appointment. She would use his phone to call the errant boyfriend, then come back up and collect the child – who had been sick and fretful and whom she therefore did not wish to wake.

As the slow minutes passed, we started to joke about how we would tell the little girl (the way the baby was dressed under the blanket gave away the gender) that we had found her on the cliffs one day and had decided to take her home, like a foundling in a fairy tale. The child, in her handmade ribboned bonnet and yellow mittens, snuffling gently in her cocoon, slept on. We debated how long it would take Thembi to reach the car park; whether her brother might not have gone off to run an errand while he waited for her return; if the brother might have no phone credit, or no battery charge, or no signal. Neither of us wanted to be the first to state our growing fears.

The crowd below us started to drift away as the air swiftly chilled and the wind picked up, and we continued to argue against reason a little longer. Maybe Thembi was having to negotiate the money out of her sugar daddy; perhaps they had sought some quiet spot in which to have a brief reconciliation. And still we would not say what we were both now starting to understand. That we had been left, quite literally, holding the damned baby.

ↀ

The baby awoke with a sleepy wet yawn and started to thrash her limbs about inside the blanket, as if in slow motion, and make a peevish mewing sound. The time to blame Anita was long past. Even asking her why she had agreed to mind the child seemed irrelevant, given the seriousness of our unfolding situation. But, really, our position was not so desperate, we agreed. There were local agencies, no doubt, that must deal with abandoned children all the time, and all we had to do was make contact with one as soon as possible.

An unsettling thought came to me, though, and in my resentment at Anita's lack of common sense (though what would I have done differently in her position?) I used my vague suspicions to score a point against her. It was an unkind thing to do – but a larger, admittedly bigoted, thought lay behind it since our brief time here had already armed me with a set of mean-spirited assumptions about the different sectors of South African society.

"You know, this could be a shakedown, couldn't it? We get up and leave with the baby – 'cos we have no choice – and then later today the police show up and accuse us of kidnapping it. Then we have to pay off the mother in order for us to stay out of the courts. Could be, you know?"

I was expecting Anita to slap this down with contempt, to accuse me of cynicism or worse. But she simply scooped up the infant from the rug and looked about her, as if the swell of the pewter sea or the small clouds turning to mother-of-pearl in the falling light would give her inspiration. She could have been on the other side of the world right then, and in a sense she was, as it turned out.

It was too far for us to walk back over the cliffs to town now that the sun was setting so rapidly, and I was still not convinced that my interpretation of the mother's intentions might not turn out to be true. I certainly didn't want to meet this Thembi, with a blackmailing boyfriend or brother in tow, at dusk on the long trek back to our accommodation, now that the route was sure to be deserted.

I found the number of the B&B on my phone, called them, and asked them to send a car to meet us at the still-busy parking area where the path through the dunes met the main road below us. I had to briefly summarise for the woman who took the call why we suddenly needed a car to collect us, and she didn't seem as astonished as I supposed she might. Another nasty thought – had this happened here before? Was this town a hotspot for baby-dumping? Anita meanwhile continued to scout about, the now-sobbing baby tucked expertly over one shoulder. Its head was safely cradled in a delicate brown hand as she bent and looked around our rug and bench as if she had mislaid something. My patience at her composure was wearing a little thin by now.

"What have you lost?"

"Nothing. I just thought that if it had been her idea all along to leave the baby with a stranger, she might have bought along some clothes, or bottles or something. Even just a toy, you know?"

Naturally, there was nothing to find. We walked down the easy path among the high hummocks, hoping even now that we would find Thembi and some sly explanation. Anita carried the baby, and I hauled the coolbox. I was already rehearsing how I would relate this incredible story to people in the future – *TIA, what can you do, man?*

Slowed by our burden, when we finally arrived at the parking area, we found that it was empty, apart from broken bottles and a pile of fast-food wrappers being snuffled by a rangy stray dog that loped off as we approached. We stood and waited and told each other how angry we were at the length of time the B&B was taking organising us a ride, when really, we were cross at each other, and ourselves. We came to the conclusion that the schoolgirl had made a spur-of-the-moment decision to leave her baby with us, two well-off strangers. Surely this was not something she could have planned for, and it might still be that she would have a change of heart?

What was left of the day was taken up with explanations and logistics. It turned out that the guesthouse had already alerted the police, and it was they who eventually pulled into the parking lot and drove us away. We stopped on the way to the police station in a bigger town nearby to pick up nappies, milk formula and bottles, which the middle-aged officer kindly paid for since we had no money on us. While I helped this policeman complete his preliminary report at the station, Anita called the numbers of the local child-welfare offices he had supplied, jiggling from foot to foot in an effort to quiet the baby, who was now hiccupping and squalling in a tiny voice. The social workers she reached were all backed up and could only come out tomorrow at the earliest, Anita eventually reported back to me.

Then she took the infant away to the women's toilet to attend to the nappy that everyone could smell, for all the world as if she had been surrounded by babies all her life. The capable, impersonal, *professional* way that she handled her noisy bundle – so similar to the ease with which she helped with the children of her cousins and sisters – was her way of telling me, I now believe, that maternal behaviour was part of her job's skill set but not something she intended to adopt in a private capacity.

"Has this happened before do you know? A mother pretending to give a stranger her child to mind and then disappearing?" I asked, hoping for a comforting answer in the affirmative.

The policeman admitted that he couldn't think of such an occurrence happening before in the area, but some of these young girls were desperate, you know? The baby's father won't take them back until they get rid of the problem of the baby. Or they couldn't get themselves a new boyfriend until the baby nuisance was taken care of. To the grandmother, or a sister. Or whoever.

Anita returned from the toilet looking even more bemused than when it had dawned on us that the baby had been abandoned into our care.

"It's a boy. We thought by the way she was dressed that it was a girl, but it's *definitely* a boy."

Another revelation in a day of surprises, with another following close on its heels: we were gobsmacked to discover that in the absence of any other contingency plans, we were to be allowed to take the little boy with us back to the B&B for the night. The healthcare worker in Anita wanted to nip this idea in the bud and began to articulate, in a practised, even voice, her very natural objections to this plan. It was *beyond* inappropriate, in her professional opinion, and just plain wrong – given we knew nothing about this specific child or about caring for babies' needs more generally. Not to say probably borderline illegal and, in effect, a paedophile's dream come true.

But the policeman patiently explained that there was no one at the station willing or able to take responsibility for the baby, and none of the local child-protection units or orphanages (and there were quite a few it seemed) could raise anyone until the following day. With tomorrow being a public holiday, this might mean they didn't come that day either, as they were chronically understaffed at the best of times, as well as lacking vehicles.

The officer assured us that the mother was extremely unlikely to emerge at that late time of the day and lodge any charges against us, and so the police were happy, delighted actually, for us to take the child into our temporary care. We could be one-hundred percent certain that there would be no negative repercussions as a result of our Good Samaritan act. This he went to great pains to repeat, though he did say that the police would need us to return quickly the following day to complete more paperwork, with our ID or passports and the money for the baby equipment too, please, if we didn't mind.

As a policewoman drove us back to the B&B, Anita went over once again all the strong reservations she had about the arrangements we were now compelled to comply with. She reiterated them a final time for my benefit, to show me how she was disentangling herself from my helpless engagement. She knew me that well.

You slept between us that night. With the help of Elize, the B&B owner's daughter, who had a toddler and lived in the next street, we had worked out how to sterilise your bottles in their kitchen and feed you. She also lent us a battered but clean baby's car-seat so that we could drive you, if necessary, to an orphanage the next day. Because neither of us was invested in you emotionally, and because we knew we were going to hand you over to someone capable the next day, we were more relaxed than we might otherwise have been. No one was watching to see how we did things; no one more experienced was going to chastise us for not bathing you correctly or for feeding you at the wrong time. It was as if someone had given us a small, uncomplaining puppy to look after just for the night. Anita and I laughed together more than I could remember us having done in a long time.

My wife put on her one-piece swimsuit and got into the massive corner bath, filled with tepid water. I undressed you, cleaned your bottom with a baby wipe, and passed you over to her.

"Next time someone tries to present us with a baby while they run an errand, let's agree to hand it straight back?"

"Yeah, but Sean, look at his tiny hands. Look at the way he's looking at Daddy," she mocked.

"That's not even funny, Anita."

But it was a test, and I knew it – and I failed the moment I began to imagine how the copper bowl would make a perfect bath for you.

෴

As we half expected, when we returned to the police station the next day following a surprisingly good night's rest, and the officer on the front desk made the necessary calls, all the relevant institutions that might have come to collect you pleaded lack of staff and vehicles due to the holiday – National Women's Day (of course it was). We took all the details of the nearest "place of safety" that had agreed to keep accommodation open for you and drove off. You slept throughout the whole journey.

You won't remember the orphanage, so I want to tell you about your second home. It was a wonderfully happy place, newly painted by volunteers in primary colours with funny, wonky murals, charmingly lacking perspective or scale. Recently, it had received a large donation of new bunk beds, cots and playground equipment from a furniture warehouse store, too. Even the gardens and the small vegetable beds were lovingly tended and neat. The staff members who greeted us were friendly and considerate, if also clearly harried and overworked. Our story, though they claimed not to have heard of anyone else being given a child under similar circumstances, did not seem to unsettle them in the slightest.

One of them took you from my arms with the gentlest of care, murmuring in isiXhosa as she spirited you away for your initial examination. I thought she would then bring you back to say goodbye, but she didn't. After everything else that had happened, this seemed at the time like just one more surreal turn in a sequence of disorienting events. *Life isn't cheap here*, I found myself thinking, *but it is very harsh*.

My wife kept exclaiming what a lovely place it was, how satisfied she was that we had done all we could for you, and how she could now leave knowing that you would be well cared for. Some of the older children who'd been playing outside looked on gravely through the office window as we completed the formalities and a photocopy of the police docket was made, along with those of our passports. We handed over your bottles and the rest of the milk powder and left. In the car on the way home we didn't say anything to each other, except to figure out the arrangements for returning the car seat we had borrowed from Elize before heading back home.

Anita was back at work the next morning as if nothing at all odd had happened during our break, but I was out of sorts and so decided to take the day off. I found my way back to the orphanage, where the polite, jolly lady in charge greeted me most warmly then explained that since I had made the trip out specially, she would allow me to see you. Ordinarily, however, they did not recommend such contact visits unless I was seriously thinking about initiating the process of adopting you.

"It raises up the hopes of the children, you see, Mr Maritz? They think someone is coming to take them home. I know you bought a little baby to us but soon he will recognise you and get upset when you leave. We try to discourage any events in the lives of these children that will cause them further distress. I know you will understand."

On the way there I had purchased a small blue towelling teddy bear at a pharmacy. I handed this over to a younger staff member, who seemed to be in charge of the cheerfully decorated nursery for infants, then I peered at you in your cot as you slept. Someone had dressed you in a forest-green onesie, and you looked much darker than you had before, out in the sunlight on the cliff. I thought to myself how easy it would be to take care of a baby that hardly seemed to spend any time awake.

"He sleeps a lot, doesn't he? I don't know much about babies, but I didn't think they slept *that* much."

"Some do, some don't, Meneer. We think this baby has not been getting enough nourishment and that might be why he sleeps. Or he could be sick."

The girl shot me a quick, meaningful look. "He will be tested tomorrow when the nurse is back. We may not place babies with new parents until we know their status."

When I got back to our flat, I threw the crumpled receipt for the teddy into the cardboard box we kept under the kitchen sink for collecting paper to be recycled. Anita was already home for some reason and immediately retrieved it – she liked to keep a tally of every purchase we made, and so kept bills and receipts until she'd entered their details into her accounts' spreadsheets.

She smoothed it out and read it absentmindedly, then took a deep breath and asked me outright. I wasn't seriously thinking about keeping in touch with this child, was I? I knew she was trying to broach the subject of the sheer impossibility of adoption without letting the freighted word itself out into the room, where the idea in all its clarity might reveal itself to me for the first time and captivate me. She had a simplistic view of my thought processes, I decided; convinced that I would always be easy to manipulate and lead, waiting for adult guidance from her. I didn't say anything, knowing that if I kept silent then her own opinions on the matter, as well as her evaluation of my intentions, would emerge.

"This is crazy, Sean. We haven't even discussed having children of our own yet because, duh? – we are still too young. I'm not even sure that I want them, actually. Have you given *me* any thought in all of this, in your crazy fucking parenting fantasy?"

"We don't always get to choose when to have children. No time is really the right time. I've heard that from my mam."

"You're mad, Sean. And my answer is no, we're not doing this. Forget it."

In one dizzying, delirious moment, I knew I had nothing left to lose, and this realisation intoxicated and emboldened me. So I told my love, my wife, my Anita, *my better half*, that she had been taking me and my easy-going nature for granted for years, with my own career nothing but a minor inconvenience for her. That she had needed me and depended on me in a practical sense, that we made (of course) a good team, but that was not a partnership of equals, a marriage. Which meant it wasn't any kind of basis for a family, *if* she got round to deciding she had room for such a thing in her busy life in the future.

As I tried out the idea for the first time, I told her that she didn't love me as I wanted – no, *deserved* – to be loved and had never in fact loved me that way. The bright wonder of this truth spurred me on, and I was laughing now as I paced around the little kitchen space. I said that for a long time I had known this subconsciously though I had never allowed myself to fully acknowledge it until today. But now it was over. (Had I really said that? It was over?)

"It's over because you've come to me with an insane fucking idea to adopt a baby we met for a matter of hours, and somehow my common-sense response to that idiocy means I don't love you?" She snorted in derision at the end of that question.

We slept that night in different rooms, for the first time since we had started living together at university. In the morning it was her turn to set out her store. There were mulberry-coloured patches under her eyes, and I acknowledged my secret satisfaction that my announcement of the previous evening had left her sleepless and tearful. I watched as she flailed away, her bare feet slapping on the tiles, her ceaseless hands orchestrating, organising, her arguments. She was abject. She would do anything to stop me feeling the way I evidently did. She'd had no idea that those were my feelings (neither had I, up until yesterday). Everything I had said had been just totally correct; she could not fault my characterisation of our life together up to this point in time. But, could she just say? She thought I had been content with this and had been in agreement with the way our roles were divided up currently. We had never really discussed it, but that was what she had assumed. And for this she was sorry.

And, you know, my time would come. It was just a case of making more effort to scope the right opportunity for me. She would help … And there was no one else in her life. I was wrong if I thought she was on the lookout for some tyro medic who would mentor her and boost her career.

Where had that interesting idea come from, I wondered?

All of this. I was hearing but not really listening because I was thinking: *If you love someone, and they don't love you back, is the love that you give them wasted?* I looked up at the copper bowl, which Anita had placed high out of reach on top of a kitchen cupboard one night when I had been at the arts project. I imagined filling it with water one evening in the sink or the bath and easing in a fat little brown body, safe in my big hands. A body with soft creases at the tender places where joints were learning to work, one that caught gently for just a moment when the puckered flesh of the tiny bottom stuck against the shimmering amber of the bowl's side before sliding down into the welcoming warmth of the water.

I imagined a love that could not go to waste and knew I hadn't a moment to lose. My green passport, the only thing my father had ever given me, apart from my surname, would be a good place to start.

They Took to Boats

Yves had been gone some months now, and Hermine knew he could not return to her very often. They were worried that if he kept on appearing several times a year, flying into the country on a tourist visa, some official at the international airport would start to get suspicious and cause trouble for them. It could even be that he would be refused entry altogether – it had been known to happen. No one could give either of them a straight answer concerning travel protocol for people like him who would pop in and out as his freelance work demanded.

He would be back when he could get away. This was all he wrote, and Hermine didn't dare pressurise him further. He didn't want his wife to know about his plans to abandon her until he had had a chance to speak officially with an immigration consultant and make sure that his getaway would go without a hitch.

Yves could only send her messages when he was sure that his wife would not have a chance to check his phone – two men at the publishing company he worked with sometimes had had their covers blown in this fashion. To make matters worse, he and Hermine could only communicate when there was an internet connection working at the camp where she was currently employed, which was frustratingly seldom in certain weeks – as the guests who had booked a wilderness safari in this isolated region often complained.

Mainly, the lovers attempted to contact each other at night, once her duties for the day were over and he was making a run to get cigarettes or groceries in the neighbourhood where he lived in Saint-Étienne.

In the evenings, Hermine would make her way to the office – where the internet connection was most reliable – and search online for photos and information about Saint-Étienne. Steve, the boss, sometimes allowed senior staff access to the room at night when it wasn't being used for camp business, well aware that retaining experienced, useful personnel at such an out-of-the-way spot depended on keeping them happy and entertained.

Son Ettyan, Eve Arkoon – Hermine practised saying the names when she waited for a message from her lover. She practised *Parry Son Sherman*, his soccer team.

∽

The camp was situated on a sharp inside bend of the river, a few kilometres upstream from the start of its wide, shallow estuary, where its jade-green flow became braided with shifting sand bars. By any measure, it was far, far away from anywhere else. Yves had told her that he had looked up the distance between them, and it was around six thousand kilometres, although that took no account of how difficult it was to access the remote area. He was an hour behind her also, sometimes two, though it took her a while and a few roundabout enquiries to finally figure out what this cryptic phrase meant.

It had been a year and a half now since they had first met, and Hermine was sensing Yves drifting away from her little by little. She believed that the bonds that held him to her were being tested and frayed throughout the course of every day he spent at the beautiful apartment that he shared with his wife.

Yves had taken a snap of the main room of his home, then WhatsApped her the photo. She didn't know why he would do this

– it made her feel provincial, like the village girl she was, and even more far away from him than usual. The glare from the flash had bounced off a large, ornate and foxed mirror above a fireplace and had spoilt at least a third of the image – the portion that ought to have shown Yves taking the shot. Even so, she could tell that these were rich people with taste – European taste. This was all a bit of a mystery to her, though she was trying to educate herself by looking at interior-design websites, which tended to show old, scruffy furniture alongside abstract artworks and uncomfortable-looking modern chairs. The juxtaposition baffled her.

Yves was a photographer by trade – how odd that he had taken this dreadful picture. Even she could have done better. Hermine jiggled the story of the photo around in her imagination so that it didn't discomfort her so: the poor quality of the picture was the result of Yves having to snatch the opportunity to take it while Michelle was briefly out of the room. It was actually sweet that he wanted her to see where he lived when he wasn't with her.

Despite this, and for reasons she didn't wish to examine too closely, this was the one picture that she deleted from her phone very soon after it arrived. She retained, however, the habit of reconstituting fuzzy bits of information derived from their chats into narratives that were a better fit for her interpretation of their love story.

Their communications had been intimate and protracted the first few times that Yves had returned home after filming in the area. The lovers messaged each other back and forth every night to start with, and more often if he could grab time at work as well. She blushed at some of the personal things he had written, and she took her time replying. She couldn't summon the shamelessness necessary to type words about his body that were as explicit as those he used about her own. *Yes, me 2* was as far as she could allow herself to express what she felt when he reminded her of the details of the nights they had spent in his canvas-and-thatched room. She never let anyone observe her when these messages arrived nor when she revisited them: she was convinced that her reactions to the short descriptions of her wantonness would be reflected in her face for everyone to see.

Hermine archived their chat and read the messages back at night, especially at times when the internet was down and she couldn't explore his neighbourhood in France on Google Earth, or scrutinise obsessively some other aspect of his life away from her online. He had told her that women tended to over-analyse what men wrote in texts and that a great many of the ones he wrote were really spur-of-the-moment thoughts composed in a hurry that he then just sent (then deleted his end, of course). Yves was amazed at some of the messages she reminded him about many months after he had sent, then forgotten, them. *Wow! I do not remember telling u that lol.* He had gently explained more than once that his English wasn't the greatest, and maybe sometimes he might not mean exactly what he wrote. Or understand exactly what she was trying to say, either.

He had saved her contact details as "Henry Kunene" and sometimes he sent her an impersonal message about logistics or a forthcoming travel schedule, just to keep up the pretence. Yves did not delete messages like this, as they were part of an unsophisticated scheme to keep Michelle off his trail. There was a lot to remember, being an adulterer.

Over recent months, Hermine had started to maintain a detailed breakdown on a thumb drive of how many times he initiated a conversation; how many times in total he wrote messages to her during each of their chats; how many times he rudely left her hanging with no explanation. She assessed each individual comment from him for its degree of intimacy, scoring those that were general observations about the weather or his job as a zero and those that spoke of his longing for her and his distress at not being able to end things with Michelle as a ten. The scores were inexorably going down over time, and it made her feel quite sick to have to acknowledge that their communications were getting more pedestrian and perfunctory.

The exceptions to this trend were the chats where he elaborated on his latest difficulties in trying to establish from various so-called experts how he could set up home in Namibia legally – these explanations seemed to grow more confusing and filled with extraneous detail over time. Conversely, he had stopped talking to his second-best friend from school, a family lawyer, about divorce arrangements, or at least he had ceased mentioning to her any such discussions the pair of men might be having far away in France.

In these and many other ways, Hermine felt she was losing him: to time or to distance or to the lovely Michelle – the photos of her glowing, giggling rival that she had searched for and found online she *did* keep in a dedicated folder on her phone, in order to masochistically torment herself when her spirits were especially low.

Would the chats just gradually dry up, so that she was expected to take the hint, like a big girl? Or would Yves grab the initiative one day and come right out and tell her it was over? She kept a draft email on her phone that she would send him if that happened, articulating her feelings as she had never been able to do during the course of their chats. (He had avoided hints that he should furnish her with his email address – Hermine had found his business card in the old cigar box where Steve stored such things in the office.)

She crafted and then reworked each draft compulsively, polishing the words until they shone with the truth of her feelings. She tried to make sure that if it was the one thing from their time together that Yves kept, it would be a reminder of how clever, strong and brave she was. If he did indeed desert her for the time being, he would perhaps one day read that email through again and miss her too much to maintain the distance between them for a moment longer. Like in a romantic film, she thought: he would just drop whatever he was doing as the realisation hit him, grab his coat and his passport, and race up to the airline check-in desk closest to wherever he might be to grab the last seat on the last flight out to her.

She was meticulous about removing from successive drafts any expressions that made her seem abject or desperate, or that would confirm to him that he had made the correct choice by staying with Michelle. But then he would write something that made her glow with warm joy, and the latest iteration of her email would be deleted and also removed from the trash folder on her phone, only for her to begin developing a revised version when something he wrote, or omitted to write, tipped her back into misery.

Her mother had disapproved of their relationship from the start. Hermine had mentioned Yves's name during an evening meal on a visit home, and even though she frequently entertained her mother with stories about guests at the camp, Ottilie had immediately discerned that this particular tourist meant something important to her daughter. She had objected to him for reasons diametrically different from those she voiced when she critiqued one of Hermine's local suitors. Ottilie had reservations about Yves's race, his age, his job – which entailed a great deal of travelling and therefore opportunities for him to stray, as all men will do given the chance. Then there was the fact of his being childless – what kind of man has no children whatsoever, despite the days of his youth being long gone?

Ottilie already had strong doubts when she had believed Yves to be white, and expressed even stronger ones when Hermine shyly showed her a photo, and his North African heritage became apparent. His long, dark ringlets and thick, black eyebrows; the heavy, slightly greying shadow on his chin and cheeks; and the deep wrinkles around his small, brown humorous eyes. Luckily, the discreet hoop of gold in one ear was hidden from view in this particular shot, as was the tattoo of a wolf on his left wrist. Ottilie made no comment but just nodded sagely: all her darkest suspicions had been confirmed by that one picture, the emphatic gesture seemed to say, and she knew her only daughter's sad abandonment was now a foregone conclusion.

Hermine thought it prudent not to mention that Yves also had a wife who believed she was still very much married to the man.

Wednesday evenings were when she and Yves could usually devote the most time to messaging. Friday nights were what he called "date nights" with Michelle, and the weekends were often taken up with trips to see his family or Michelle's father's family or to go and stay with friends. Many of these friends seemed to have several different homes, and Yves sent more pictures – of boats, chalets and villas and once, a small chateau. Was he implying that one day it would be the pair of them who would be going to stay at these places, rather than he and his wife? He never said.

His inability – or was it really a refusal? – to be more specific about their future was driving her quietly crazy, but she forced herself not to give in to the temptation to write anything that would be construed as nagging him or making demands. She simply didn't know the etiquette – if she had any right to ask questions about his plans, for example, or if a request for elucidation, no matter how it was phrased, might be received as an unacceptable transgression. She would rather not know the answers to the questions that were plaguing her than risk having her worst fears revealed in a final message from him. In this, she conceded, she was a coward and her own worst enemy, as well.

Hermine even started to dread these midweek nights in a way, because more and more the messages that appeared from him on her phone's screen seemed impersonal and distant. She would ask him if he was okay, and he would simply respond: *Yes. U know. Things r tricky 4 me right now.*

She didn't know what he meant, honestly, but she made sure to write back each time: *i understand Yves.*

Recently, he had begun just sending a sad-looking emoji, instead, when she asked. Some of the stuff they discussed was even boring to her – she didn't know what he meant when he started to write about the forthcoming elections there, or some problems with a local politician who hated Muslims. This was not why she was giving up her free time when she could be catching up on her sleep – to read his views on events that she knew barely anything about. Was he testing her? Was Yves using her replies to decide if he truly wanted to abandon the life he'd built with a woman he admitted was brighter and far more successful than he was? Checking Hermine's responses to assess if he really wished to start over again in a far-off country with a woman who had no experience of the world and who had a child, too?

She was panicking these days, and every chat seemed to just increase her anxiety: Yves was slipping away from her, he was moving on. She had no direct proof, but her scorecard showed her that his commitment to their exchanges was waning.

In his most recent messages, he had reiterated that he didn't know when he could come and visit again, and he avoided any mention of a timeline. Michelle had discovered a small lump in her breast, and although the doctor had told them it was probably nothing serious, Yves didn't feel that now was a good time to suggest he made another trip overseas. Not until the results and then some follow-up tests confirmed that all was well, and Michelle had calmed down and gone back to work. She was super highly strung, so the process of returning to normality could take a while.

No, that wasn't right, Hermine reminded herself with a terrible flush of jealousy. Yves had written that it had been *he* who had felt the lump initially. She had starred the message so she could find it easily and mull over its meanings at her leisure.

This was also the exchange during which she discovered that Michelle was older – quite a lot older – than Yves. Perhaps this explained their lack of children, although Hermine vaguely recollected a comment that he had made during one of his visits where he had implied, in a rather snide way, that having children would have been beneath them both – a bourgeois, retrograde step for a professional couple with full lives already. It seemed as if only a very few of their friends had children, a remarkable thing to Hermine. After that, she made a point not to mention again the son born while she was still at college, now in his last year at primary school and living with Ottilie many kilometres distant, and Yves made a point of not asking.

Michelle's advanced age ought to have made Hermine feel more confident in her ability to steal away the husband, but it had the opposite effect – of making her feel silly and superficial. What was the value of her own career, other than as a small, expendable and really quite unimportant cog in a service industry with a notoriously high turnover? Michelle ran a restaurant where famous people would come to eat. In fact, Yves let on one night during a chat when Hermine had conjectured that he might be drunk, her family had owned the establishment going back almost a century. Later that night, Hermine had searched for this place online and let out a little hiss of satisfaction when she was able to find it, despite not knowing how to spell the name properly. The photo made her spirits sink once again though, a common-enough sensation by now. It was not a restaurant like those she knew from her rare visits to Khorixas or the capital. It was in an old castle, lit up on a hill in the night in a golden halo of complacent prosperity handed down through the generations. She tried to translate the menu that she also found online and to convert the prices to a currency she understood, but at that point she was overcome with despair and couldn't continue her amateur sleuthing.

Yves could come to her out here and they could find things to share, but there would never be a chance that she could adapt to his true environment, to the things he knew and could afford and took for granted, despite his distant immigrant heritage. *Lowberje d la fourett*: she repeated the restaurant's name to herself in all the different variations that she could conjure up, even though she accepted that she would never set foot inside its doors.

Hermine had found a tiny, almost-unused notebook in a bin in a vacated room and began to keep a written list of topics they could discuss if she found a way to turn the conversation towards her home turf and where she could temporarily set aside her feelings of inadequacy to show him that she knew more than he did about certain things. Dramas that had happened around the camp that she thought would entertain him. Little reminders of their moments together that she hoped would pull him back into her little world. *The mozzys r getting bad now. Remember we used 2 jump under the net 2gether 2 escape from them in ur tent and ur hair wd get tangled up bcos u r so tall?*

It felt so mercenary, though, writing out these shopping lists of subjects they could safely cover without venturing onto matters that might make him feel guilty or ambivalent about their long-term plans. She forced herself to avoid tapping out the most obvious message of all: *When r u coming back Yves?*

☙

It was her third year now at the camp, and the forthcoming rains were predicted to be spectacular. She had been promoted to trainee assistant camp manager, and as such was expected to know the routine if the rising waters of the river threatened to overwhelm the site. It had not happened in many years, but drills were practised and procedures updated based on the company's safety policies, just in case. Hermine was from the desiccated mountains to the south, where the heavy storms part-filled the steep gullies with water for a few hours before heading off westwards to the coast. That place of flat-topped bergs and dramatic gorges was quite a contrast to the place she now called home, with its perspective-defying views across the huge sand drifts piled up alongside the start of the river mouth and out towards Angola on the other side. She never got tired of watching the motion of the emerald current in a real river that flowed every day without fail, one that was not just a gravel bed occasionally containing a puddle or two for a few hours.

It was to this place that Yves had come almost eighteen months ago to do some work on desert-adapted animals. Even now that she was doubting her ability to interpret what their relationship had been and what it seemed as if it was becoming, she knew her life had been changed irrevocably by meeting him. People talk about falling in love, but each time she tried to think of how she would characterise the effect of their relationship on her, it was in terms of elevation. Loving him, she had been lifted aloft and could experience – from the higher place where her heart had been tossed – hopes and emotions that she had never allowed herself to dream of back in her previous, ordinary life. His love had given her a vantage point from which to appraise her world and what she might ask of it. She often felt a physical lightness in his presence – the heady intoxication that let her know that together they could do almost anything they wished.

He used to look at her with such open adoration – he would not let his gaze move from her face so that she felt crushed under the weight of his scrutiny and had to look away. To call any of the short, unsatisfactory months she had shared with other, duller men a relationship was a travesty, she now realised, and Hermine was grateful that she had waited until this became apparent, instead of settling for some poor, half-formed notion of coupledom as her lot.

❧

Her tiny mauve notebook listing the things they could discuss became a precious talisman. Hermine felt that if she stuck to the events and ideas that it contained, she could keep their messaging on track towards the day when they could be together and accountable to no one. But the ongoing effort of pulling him in, of maintaining his interest, was enervating and often, by the conclusion of a chat, distressing. So many times, as the conversation unfolded, she felt that she was working too hard and that the effort required betrayed the fact that they were two mismatched people who had enjoyed a fling and couldn't let it go. There was nothing romantic about asking him what he had done with his day and reading back the pointless details of development meetings and office politics. The names of the people he worked with – so many of them women, it seemed – appeared on her screen too many times for comfort. This group of colleagues and acquaintances stood before her as a barrier, in her mind, to the resolution of their story – the happy ending that was her goal, the pursuit of which was now making her distinctly miserable.

❧

He had given her his old back-up iPhone at the end of that first visit, when they had already become intimate. He said that he was thinking of getting a new one anyway, but he would pretend that this one had been stolen out of his luggage at the airport and make a claim on his travel insurance, so it was a win all round.

Yves deleted all the photos off the phone, and all the personal information, and told her, several times, that he was donating it to her as a gift, and he didn't believe in telling people what they should do with presents. Hermine could even sell it if she wanted – but, certainly, they could use it to instant message each other, if she wished. It seemed an extraordinarily strange thing to say. She had assumed she had been given the phone specifically so that they could stay in touch now that they had become lovers.

She immediately started to use the phone to check up on him. He had given a few clues about the location of his apartment in France, and she spent many hours wandering around his town on Google Earth, looking at likely buildings until her eyes hurt. Steve, the senior camp manager, had a great deal of affection for Hermine, and it was when he realised that she had developed a painful obsession that he suggested she avail herself of the better connectivity in his office to slake her curiosity – the sooner to bring the inconvenient crush to an end, he fervently wished. Nevertheless, she was too embarrassed to spend more than a few hours there each week – she knew how foolish she appeared and how unprofessional such a relationship might look. "Khaki fever" it was called whenever a female guest fell for a male pilot or a tour guide, and she was ashamed to be swept up into that same category, albeit in reverse.

She looked up the website of the agency that Yves worked for as a freelancer – she checked the professional-looking portraits of the women staff whom he had mentioned as colleagues. Beautiful, thin, sophisticated and well-preserved – every one of them more of a catch than she could ever feel herself to be. She began to wonder: was she truly the reason why he was seeking to escape his current existence, or simply an excuse that would fall away soon enough once his freedom had been gained?

Quotidian enquiries had a way of turning into little traps, but she couldn't stop herself from setting them. The phone could show her what time it was in his country, and what the weather was like in his town too. He would contact her from his workplace to tell her that he would message her when he took the dog out for a walk in a couple of hours, and she replied the first time: *U take the dog out in the dark?* It seemed as if – she didn't really know how – he had slipped up in telling her about his schedule or his current location. If he was lying about that, then what else wasn't he telling her?

But he carefully explained later that night that where he lived the streets were totally safe at all hours, even the early morning, and many people did the same as he did – walked their dogs before bed so that they could smoke a cigarette in peace and get some fresh air. Maybe bump into someone he knew, even partake of a brandy at a café. Every time that she thought she'd caught him out in a shabby lie, it would eventually turn out that Hermine had been ignorant and wrong. Her snooping only served to make her feel more lonely, stranded and unworldly.

In those arid stretches of time when she felt like an unwitting victim of a drama unfolding far away, she would wait a little before she responded to a message from Yves, even if it arrived pretty much exactly at the appointed time. She didn't want to appear too eager: *I am not just here at your beck and call,* she thought, allowing four or five minutes to elapse before she replied. She was disgusted with herself, playing these tricks like a teenager when she had no grounds for thinking that he was engaged in any reciprocal mind games – but not disgusted enough to stop.

One night he said that he was going skiing over the coming weekend and, as soon as their conversation was over, she checked the weather where he lived, and did a search to look at the terrain. There were no mountains anywhere near his town, and mild weather had been reported in the forecast.

Then she reasoned with herself: why would he say something like that if it weren't true? What did he possibly have to gain from telling her this story, apart from justifying a couple of days out of contact with her when he could feasibly claim that he couldn't get a signal up in the mountains? Was he actually staying at home *but taking a holiday from her*? The idea made her feel chilled and slightly feverish simultaneously.

On the Monday night she could wait no longer. *How was the skeeing?* she asked after a short battle with the autocorrect.

Skiing was wonderful tnx. Luv Italy @ this time of year.

She was mortified – at her adolescent suspicions and at her complete lack of familiarity with the everyday logistics of his life: Yves could travel to a snowy resort in a different country in a matter of hours, apparently. She was relieved, but only temporarily. He continued: he had gone without Michelle, *She hates to ski*, it had been a boys' trip away. Hermine couldn't help but notice that, freed from the necessity of sneaking about and trying to find a way to get in touch with her for once, he had apparently forgotten about her for the whole three days.

And yet she frequently put her own phone in airplane mode now or pretended that the internet at the camp wasn't working. She would engage in this little subterfuge when she was too exhausted to try to make chit-chat or to anticipate how the conversation would snake away from her when she simply ran out of things to say. If she were very busy with work, she would just not have the mental acuity to try to decode his words' possible hidden meanings. She preferred to spend time looking back on how he had been in real life, the words she remembered seeing come out of his dry and lip-salved lips, and the touch of his experienced hands on her biddable body.

☙

She was becoming tearful, and insomnia was making her forgetful and therefore far from satisfactory at her job. She would give herself quiet pep talks in the shower, where she could be sure that no one passing her little room at the back of the site could hear her. Hermine reminded herself that all her wrong-headed misgivings about Yves to date had turned out to be unfounded: whenever she'd thought that he had been untruthful or evasive, it had always turned out to be simply a function of her patchy knowledge concerning his routine, his household, and his often spontaneous social arrangements. She would need a full-time detective on his trail to satisfy her curiosity about him, and even then, she would never know how Yves was in bed with his lovely wife, the things he might have shared about their affair with his worldly male friends, the thoughts about her that he could be having in his own private moments – or perhaps was failing to have.

All she seemed to do most days now was carry out her work tasks on autopilot and look forward to those hours of the night when she would have the freedom to rake over her memories of Yves and re-read those older archived messages that continued to reassure her. She found herself referring back to the ambiguously worded recent chats between them less and less often – they were corroding the foundation on which she had carefully erected their story and weren't to be trusted.

It took her a while to realise that when he was chatting with her, he could also be engaged in conversations with other people. This seemed like a small-scale betrayal. When she first got the phone, she had sent messages to him and him alone and stayed on the app, waiting for his replies. Recently, the flow of their messages would be broken up as he took off to respond to someone else. One night he wrote something she didn't understand:

Sais pas. La vie est compliquée en ce moment. Ça va pas, ma tête!

She sent him a question mark and he replied, after a few moments, that the message had been intended for someone else and things had got mixed up. He had to go. *Sorry.*

Worlds within worlds. The internet gave her access to layers of information and uncovered answers to questions she had barely formulated, but the process of investigating the byways of Yves's life was one that took up many, many hours of her time. She had already found out that she could translate the information in French on his agency's website by simply clicking on a little Union Jack flag – now she had to set about finding a way to decipher what Yves had typed to a stranger when she thought she had possessed his undivided attention. As was increasingly the case, what she uncovered did not salve her nagging unease. *I don't know. Life's complicated right now. It's doing my head in!*

During a different conversation, Yves had mentioned that he had been able to persuade Michelle to take on a new member of staff at the restaurant – a female sommelier from South Africa who was also black. Hermine briefly left their chat to look up the unfamiliar word and then returned to tell him *Well done!*

She appreciated that this news of his was a little affirmation of the effect she had had on him, a compliment even, and was meant to be interpreted that way. The boost to her ego from the testimonial was undermined by his next comment, however: *She is also v pretty.* Were his tastes since he had met Hermine changing? Was Mpho the wine girl a threat now?

Then one night a few months later, it seemed as if she had been right all along and that he was indeed leading a double life. She had mentioned in her chat that on the news it showed the whole of Europe in the grip of a disastrous heat wave.

Not where i am, he had written. Then after a few long minutes: *U will b surprised 2 know that actually i am not far from u. In Luanda on my way back home.*

She put the phone down carefully on her nightstand and walked unsteadily outside into the late evening's peace. She heard the soft chatter of staff washing up in the area behind the dining room and a distant jackal yelping rhythmically and then giving a single, panicky high bark in the dunes along the river. The movement of the water, still low and not yet visible from this part of the camp by day, could be made out from the occasional chop and gurgle that the breeze would carry across. The stars wheeled overhead as she swung her gaze across the whole sweep of the sky, with tears coming now, quick and welcome. At last, she had the evidence that she been right – that Yves away from her was an Yves who was a stranger to her. She felt relief that the anxieties that had been driving her quietly mad were not necessarily groundless but could have been justified all along. Yves had been carrying on with his life and his work and who knows what else, and she hadn't even known a fraction of anything. He was, at this moment, just a short flight away, like the hop to Italy where he had skied recently, and yet he hadn't even told her of his plans and had definitely not made arrangements to see her. He was becoming lost to her, if in fact she had ever held him at all.

The night-watchman spotted her from his rounds up on the path above the staff accommodation and came over. They had known each other for many years, and in fact Elias had been the one who had told her about the vacancy that had come up at the camp three years ago. They chatted awhile now, and Elias – also aware that something was disturbing Hermine's heart but unlike the boss, unsure what it could be – put a consoling arm around her and tried to draw her in for a kiss.

She pushed him away good-naturedly, knowing he would not be offended. Life at the camp was routine and boring, when all was said and done, and short-term attachments helped to while away the time. A different type of consolation was needed right now, though, and Elias wasn't so insensitive that he didn't recognise this. He handed her the little flat bottle of dark alcohol he had hidden in the pocket of his trousers, and she took an inexperienced swig.

When she went back inside after a few more minutes, Yves had disappeared offline. Neither ever mentioned his trip to Angola again.

She had far too many questions, and by now knew that any answer he might give, no matter how honest and complete, would only drive her a little closer to a kind of low-grade insanity. Their relationship had been reduced to a procession of words that Yves deleted from his phone the moment each of their chats was over. She was left the mad custodian of their exchanges, and yet the more she read them back, the less she understood how they bore any connection to the physical facts of their affair.

After one of his stays, he had accidentally left behind the bandanna he wore around his neck and lifted over his mouth on windy days to keep out the sand. The bandanna smelt of him, and she kept it under her pillow and would sniff it during the night when she couldn't sleep. Little by little the scent started to become fainter, and she asked him one day what perfume he wore: *Lol. Not perfume. That is 4 woman? It is cologne.*

Again, he seemed reluctant to give her the name of the brand, just as – so it seemed to Hermine – he was always reticent these days about telling her anything personal. She had seen his dark, hairy body naked in her moonlit room, had stroked every part of him and knelt in the shower to place her lips around him at his gentle instruction – something she had never done with any other man. Yet now he would not tell her what scent he wore. She found that she was struggling to breathe.

At the very end of the chat, he did give up the name, as a kind of flung-out afterthought. Maybe he'd harboured fears of his own, she considered – that she would mail him a bottle as a gift and he would have some awkward explaining to do? Perhaps he had then recalled that in fact he had taken care not to give her any clues to his address in Saint Étienne, thus ensuring that no suspicious mail of any sort of would ever be making its way to France from his African lover.

Not only was she now second-guessing his words, she was deep into imagining how he was interpreting her own.

The next week, she looked at her tiny book and found that she had three new and interesting things to tell Yves since last they were in contact, including the information that the annual floods originating in the interior of Angola, the efundja, would soon be arriving at their stretch of the river. She opened WhatsApp and saw that Yves's name had disappeared from the growing list of people she chatted to now. Her belly lurched as she absorbed the fact that he had taken some action to finally cut the one channel of communication open to her. Then she looked a little more carefully. So many people had been in touch with her since last she and Yves had chatted – good Lord, a full week ago now – that his name was way down the list and not immediately visible on the screen. She scrolled down and found him and sent a message: *aardwolf seen on the large sand bank below the camp!* but it was only much later that he responded with a single word: *Wow*, then disappeared. Where was he, awake at 4 a.m. her time?

***

Then it rained in the river's huge catchment, longer and harder than anyone could remember, and nothing else mattered. The little memo book stayed in the small olive-green canvas bag that Hermine always wore slung across her body, but the pages became damp and started to stick together. She didn't need it anyway. There was only one story, and that was the rapidly rising water level in the river and the need to evacuate the guests from their chalets along its banks.

The last big flood had been almost half a decade ago, and only the camp boss remained on the staff from that time. Their well-rehearsed drill for dealing with just this eventuality began to unravel as the more entitled guests made their feelings known. Having spent a fortune reaching this out-of-the-way place, they were reluctant now to be flown back to the safety of unexotic Windhoek.

Together she and Steve dug out photos that he had taken in the general vicinity of the camp the last time it had been flooded out and showed them at supper to the six remaining guests who were proving so difficult to dislodge. There were pictures of entire palm trees upended midstream; crocodiles stranded on the lawns and in the swimming pool once the waters had subsided; and the belongings of the staff floating sadly across the submerged pathways in a dirty tide. The very last one showed the bloated body of a cow in a puddle with its baby nestled dead next to it – except closer examination revealed that this was not a calf but the corpse of a little herdboy from a village higher up the valley. Like most people hereabouts, he could not swim and had been caught off-balance as he attempted to chivvy the cattle across a swollen tributary. This final and most pathetic piece of corroboration seemed to secure the argument, and the guests finally accepted that they had no choice but to leave. Hermine understood exactly why Steve had produced the photo, but if anything, it upset her even more than it had done the tourists. She had not known the boy, it had been well before her time, but she could not easily forget how it was only after Steve pointed out his miniature leg and foot and ear that the muddle of limbs had resolved itself into his pitiful human remains in the picture.

That night she had the worst nightmare she could ever recall, and awoke in a kind of numbed shock that stayed with her for the rest of the day. She dreamed that she was lying in a huge, beautiful four-poster bed on a sort of platform outside her room, surrounded by gauzy curtains in a high, billowing canopy through which she could see Yves, a little further down the hillside. He was naked but for an apron and had his back to her, standing at a camping table preparing fruit. Hermine understood that they were on their honeymoon, and the camp had been transformed for their benefit into a gloriously romantic setting, which they appeared to have all to themselves. She was wearing a gorgeous long, diaphanous nightgown, and as she left the platform and descended the hill to join her husband, it caught around her legs wetly, for she found that she was walking through scummy, knee-high water. Yves turned to greet her, and she was shocked to see that one corner of his mouth had been disfigured by an enormous stalked growth. It was the size and shape of a paper-wasps' nest, except that it was a dark amber colour and seemed to be glowing and pulsing from within. Yves was paring away at the tumour in a fury with a rusty razor blade and fat white grubs were falling to the ground from their hexagonal chambers within. Hermine felt sick with disgust and helpless with compassion – she was aware that somehow the malignancy was all her fault. Then she saw that Yves was brandishing an enormous kitchen knife in his other hand: he mouthed the word *sorry* as he lunged towards her, and she awoke in tears of grief.

~

The guests had all now evacuated the camp, and the boss had been discussing with Hermine which members of a skeleton staff would have to stay behind to try to secure the infrastructure if the waters overflowed their banks. There was no merit in everyone staying on, and the road out of the area would eventually become impassable for some of the vehicles. The more people who departed now using those cars, the better.

Hermine knew this was her chance to rise in Steve's estimation, which had been faltering of late as she let her preoccupations overwhelm her, and she was determined to stay onsite for as long as possible so that people with families could be sent away first. They also needed to confirm all the logistical details while they still had phone contact with the outside world, but after that flurry of activity, all they then had to do was sit and wait for the efundja to make its appearance.

By now, the river had begun to come to life – the murmuring swirl of the numerous sluggish dry-season channels had been replaced by a quiet rumbling, as the yellow tide picked up momentum, grew in volume, and pushed past the high bluff that held the now-quiet admin office and reception area. It looked as if it were only going to be a few more days before they could expect the lowest portions of the shoreline to be covered by the rising waters. Already, small bushes were occasionally seen sliding past.

And yet with the exception of Hermine, a feeling of joyful expectation was spreading among the few personnel who were now left behind. None had been working at the camp during the last flood except for Steve; there were no clients to worry about, staff valuables had been secured elsewhere, there were enough semi-amphibious 4x4 vehicles still available for them to make a speedy getaway if necessary. There was a growing excitement that soon they would be witness to perhaps a historically high water level, bringing with it the sort of sights that nature delivers only once in a lifetime.

Meanwhile, Hermine wondered why Yves had not made a special effort to come out and capture the event – she had told him that the predictions for rain were excellent, and it was only a matter of time before the river put on a show that would produce a portfolio of astonishing images. He had only replied that he would see what he could do, and that was where they had left things. Hermine hadn't the energy to pursue the matter – her constant state of misery was making her incapable of any greater effort than going through the motions required for work.

Partway through the morning, during which the last of the non-essential staff were preparing to leave, Steve came to find her. He had the mischievous look in his eye that sharing a new or exciting experience always produced in him. It was why he remained such an outstanding manager after decades on the job – his passions were genuine and infectious, and he could find astonishment in the smallest snail shell or pattern of lichen on a sun-cracked rock. He hailed her using a nickname he'd recently invented for her, with more than good reason.

"Come on Sad Sadie. There's something special happening."

With scant enthusiasm she followed his loping figure along the riverside path and deep into a large cluster of makalani palms at the western edge of the camp's grounds. A picnic bench had been set up in the swaying shadows so that clients could spend time here in comfort. The pair sat here now and looked upwards together in companionable contemplation, then Steve searched Hermine's face to see if she had noticed yet what was different about today.

When Hermine had found time to join guests in the grove in the past, she had always been struck by the contrast between the flat planes of the sunlit, open river landscape, and the shifting vertical patterns of shade within this dense, closed patch of trees. A small flicking motion overhead might give away the presence of a secretive bird that would call once faintly, sending a fragment of frond spiralling downwards as it built an unseen nest high above. Or the visitors would be startled by a sudden clattering when a breeze shook the leaves at the top of the giant palms, even as the air underneath remained still and almost silent, except for the droning of a few clouds of small flies. She always felt as if she had entered a holy shrine and observed that tourists who came there always lowered their voices to whispers, as if in observance of the sanctity of the space.

Hermine adjusted her senses now, focusing to try to hear or see what had changed, and within only a short moment she perceived what had piqued Steve's interest. The lowering gunmetal-coloured bases of the pinnacles of cumulonimbus sailing overhead had placed a sort of sonic lid over the plantation so that, for once, every sound within echoed and reverberated at high volume. The birds that she knew were maybe twenty metres above her in the flapping canopy sounded as if they were right next to her shoulder, so distinct and loud were their individual voices. In fact, the full songs and their echoes, where usually she would hear only a snatched note or two, and the chasing shadows of the clouds streaking above, lent to the thicket the atmosphere of a twilit chamber. Hermine shut her eyes and absorbed the clanging and whistling of the different species of birdlife, the unexpected, intimate claustrophobia that the gathering storm had created. She knew without looking that Steve was scanning her face and showing his tobacco-stained grin, so pleased to have been able to share this transformation with someone he knew would appreciate it.

"It's as if the whole world is waiting, Sad Sadie."

Yes, she thought, glad that the tear that was growing in the corner of her eye was on the side of her face not visible to him. *And I am waiting, and the waiting has become all that I am.*

Something else, too: when Hermine reluctantly opened her eyes at last, Steve was pointing through a gap in the smooth palm trunks at the far side of the grove to where the distant hills on the Angolan side of the river could usually be seen, clear and blue, guarding the horizon. A thick, unbroken roll of cloud was cascading down their sides now, incredibly fast, looking for all the world like an avalanche of unconscionable power, and Hermine was happy that her boss was not the sort of talkative person who needed to provide a running commentary at times when nature was putting on a show. His silence now was the moment's blessed grace note.

They sat in this way for many minutes, and she was glad of Steve's evident sympathy for her, as well as his delicacy in not delving into the source of her troubles. *Let me stay on here in the shadows forever*, she thought with paralysing self-pity.

❧

Steve now broke the spell by grabbing her arm roughly and meeting her eyes with a look of incomprehension, then the panic of horrified realisation. The constant monotonous rumble from the swollen river had just become much louder, and this could only mean that the flow had suddenly become exponentially more forceful for some reason. They both rushed across to the Land Rover parked on the bluff in front of the office and clambered up onto the roof to take a better look at the state of the river below them, just before it swung around its deep elbow bend. A massive moving island made up of entangled grasses, reeds, brush and trees, big and small, was cruising swiftly down the centre of the channel a few hundred metres distant, followed a little way behind by a towering wall of water that spanned the river. The mass of accumulated vegetation must have caught on the river's bottom at rapids a few kilometres higher up and obstructed the urgent rush for many hours, but eventually the dam it formed had given way under the relentless surge. It was now descending in a tumbling melee with the full spate, perhaps two metres tall, following up and tearing at the banks on either side, adding more and more palm fronds, slabs of mud, and broken boles to what was already a terrifying, living, growing force.

Where the banks dipped closest to the waterline, two companion waves were overtopping them, one on either side. These were forcing their way inland parallel to the central tide, although the water itself could not be seen underneath the stalks, uprooted plants and fist-sized rocks that were being lifted under the irresistible, rolling charge. It was this less-dramatic but somehow more surreal sight, a mirage of heaving foliage and dirt on either side of the churning river, which held Hermine's gaze. She couldn't look away from the undulating, unstable ground, and for the first time since the anticipated deluge had been announced weeks ago, she wondered if she might die there.

∽

After the last floods at the camp, the company had made a decision to replace the old, badly damaged wooden pontoon with a larger, much sturdier metal one. The pontoon had always been a popular attraction at the camp: it was used for ferrying vehicles and people on foot to interesting points on the river, and clients would also just sit there in the evening with a beverage to watch the world go by at the level of the wildlife that sometimes came down to drink. The new one had also been designed to be used as a kind of makeshift raft for holding stores or for some other extemporised purpose, as the need arose.

One outlier section of the tangled archipelago of debris had just detached itself entirely and now swung into the little backwater that held the pontoon. Steve and Hermine watched as it hit the structure broadside and snapped it loose from one of the pair of chains that secured it to two large pilings sunk into concrete blocks embedded in the bank. As the partly freed structure pivoted slowly out towards the main channel, the growing wedge of vegetation gathering underneath it forced its upstream edge to tilt skywards. This revealed a Himba man snagged on a thorn tree that had become pinned against the metal base slats by the force of the water behind. He was alive, just, and could be seen to be calling out, although his voice could not be heard above the thunderous sound now coming up to them from the oncoming wall of water to their right.

Without exchanging a word, Hermine and Steve tumbled back down off the car and started to scramble over the slippery lawns in front of the office to where a pathway descended the slope to what was usually a protected shore. From here guests could access the pontoon on foot or cool off sitting in safe shallow rock pools in the lee of the headland. They had both independently decided, in their desperation, that it might be possible to better assess the situation at the pontoon and perhaps even reach it on foot from this little beach, assuming it was not totally covered by the river by now.

As she ran, Hermine slid and fell heavily on the damp grass. By the time she had righted herself, Steve had already reached the lowest part of the track and had hopped up onto a substantial platform of rocky sand that projected some way out towards the main channel. In doing so, and directing his gaze downstream towards the pontoon using the binoculars he habitually wore around his neck, he had failed to see behind him a huge piece of part-submerged corrugated roofing that had been propelled around the river bend by the torrent and fetched up against this projecting piece of bank. The destabilised sand on either side of him was peeling away in the rising current and slipping noiselessly into the water as his space on the lookout got smaller and smaller. Then he staggered and fell. Rotating first in one direction then the next in the brown tide, he also came to rest some seconds later against the base of the pontoon alongside the other man, who was barely visible now under the sticks and other trash that was still piling up against him.

Clinging to the vertical underside of the pontoon – miraculously still attached to the other chain, which was holding for the time being – Steve looped an elbow under the other man's armpit and managed to raise his head and shoulders free of his prison of branches as the bore finally drew alongside them. The power of the water was concentrated in the middle of the river channel, where the furious swell was at its highest, but nevertheless Steve and the thrashing man were lifted so high that once the breaking front of the surge had continued on its journey downstream, they were both left clinging to the top edge of the pontoon, which remained hoisted up at a crazy angle by the mess of branches still firmly trapped beneath.

Steve was yelling at Hermine, but it was pointless trying to figure out what he was telling her above the groaning roar still coming from between the banks. She was going to have to devise a solution of her own to rescue the two men. Both seemed unharmed, and were now straddling the top edge of the metal structure, transfixed at the sight of the wall of water that was still pouring itself down the main course of the river. If they could hang on until all that water had passed beyond them and subsided a little, she thought, then getting them off would be much easier than trying to pluck them away now, with much of the force of the flood still to contend with.

The pontoon was swinging and bobbing madly as the seemingly endless wash continued to move past it. However, it appeared to be at least partially anchored in position by the tonnes of plant material still accumulating underneath. Although the bore behind the enormous island of flotsam had risen as one body, the beach and little lagoon sheltered behind the headland had collected far less water than the principal channel. The tide had risen almost to the level of the lawn only very briefly but then had fallen back almost immediately in the area behind the promontory. The giant cresting wave that almost spanned the river further out had thankfully only really clipped the pontoon and not engulfed it, although the force of the one-metre wave that smashed against it must nevertheless have been extraordinary. On the Angolan side – where the farthest section of the river, rather than following the course of the 90-degree bend was instead being thrown straight upwards by the bank in a sort of booming spout – the angry, visceral power of the flood could truly be appreciated.

Hermine was trying to remember where she had seen a coil of blue nylon rope recently when a new noise made itself heard above the roar of the river. Elias had appeared at her elbow while she still stood debating her best course of action at the edge of the lawn and had grabbed her arm as he pointed to the sheet of metal that was slicing into the spit of land where Steve had been standing moments before. It was being forced deeper and deeper edgeways into the bank by the weight of water pushing against its curling rim and was easing horizontally through the little patch of sand like a slow knife. Should it continue to undercut the bank here, the whole thing would give way shortly, and the twisted metal sheet, tonnes of rock, sand and earth, and a dead tree trunk would slam against the pontoon and the men on it a little further downstream. If this didn't tip the whole thing over completely, trapping them underneath, it would certainly knock them off and back into the boiling current. This is what Elias was probably trying to shout in her ear as he showed her the car keys he had dangling from his fingers.

She couldn't understand what he was saying, but it was clear that he felt the Land Rover to be their best means of saving the men, and indeed he was now getting into the car, as if to seal the matter. Her own mind was considering the beach and lagoon below, the latter now perhaps under only half a metre more water than usual. The car could not go down the footpath that Steve had just used, but there was a more substantial slipway around to their left which gave vehicles access to the pontoon. This is where they would have to go.

The interior of the car was a little quieter, but beyond using a sweeping gesture of his hand to indicate that Hermine should turn the car around and drive left, Elias gave no further indication of any plan of his own. Without stopping to evaluate either her route or the dangers her destination might hold, Hermine eased the car down in the direction of the landing stage and thus reached the part of the lagoon's shoreline where vehicles would normally proceed onto the pontoon. The pool was rapidly regaining its normal depth now that the main mass of water had passed on its way, and once they had inched alongside the pontoon's one remaining anchoring, the water level could be seen to reach only halfway up the front wheel. As she continued to edge the car forwards, Hermine kept checking on the two men through the passenger-side window and could see that Steve was helping the other man to shuffle along the top of their improvised gantry so that they could be closer to the car once she had positioned it as near to the structure as she dared. The half-drowned Himba was wearing only his short leather wrap; she could see now that he had a nasty gash on his thigh and was bleeding freely from deep thorn punctures all over his body. Yet he was using strong arms to haul himself along on his bottom and it was he who reached the corner of the pontoon nearest the vehicle's bonnet first and lifted himself up onto all fours on the guardrail, ready to escape.

Hermine didn't dare drive any closer to the corner rail on which the two men were now balancing. It was still entirely possible that a further strong surge of water into the lagoon could shunt the vehicle adrift against the pontoon or even tip the car right over, so she needed to be able to back out from the shore quickly. Nor would the vehicle be able to withstand the mass of the sand bar should this be dislodged by the tin sheet and swept downstream. Steve was gesturing wildly at her to approach closer, but he had no awareness of the enormous roof panel that she believed now probably presented their gravest danger.

The distance between the front of the car and the near edge of the pontoon was maybe five metres, so it was too far for either man to attempt to jump. Neither, evidently, were they going to risk immersing themselves in the wildly churning channel to try and swim or wade across the gap. As if to reinforce the point, just then a knot of fencing material – the heavy black droppers tangled up in thick wire – catapulted into this gap with a dead dog entangled in its midst. The man squatting next to Steve suddenly released his grip and sat down heavily on the rail. It looked as if he was close to fainting, and Steve threw Hermine another desperate look, accompanied by another round of frantic beckoning, as he tried to balance the collapsed man in place between his knees.

At that moment, two of the newest members of staff – boys taken on to keep the grounds tidy who had not yet gone back to the local settlement – appeared at the top of the slipway. Each carried one of two long lengths of ladder, balanced at its centre point on the top of his head. Behind them trotted the stout figure of Mumbuu, the cook, with the heavy coil of sapphire-blue nylon rope similarly balanced, and a blanket under each arm. The appearance of more bodies to help gave Hermine renewed hope and energy. Between them they could still figure this out before who-knows-what further peril appeared from around the bend in the river. She revved the car's engine in encouragement to Steve as each of the two young boys used the ladder he carried to hoist himself up onto the vehicle's roof and then pulled it up behind him.

Mumbuu laboriously hauled himself onto the roof of the car via its small fixed ladder, and Hermine heard the three of them slide the end of one ladder under the roof rack's rear rail to wedge it in place. Then she leaned out of her window and watched as Mumbuu and Elias, also now aloft, helped the boys secure the second length to the end of the first, passing a length of the rope around and around the overlapping rungs until some ten, wobbling, clanking metres extended along the top of the car and out over the whirlpooling race beyond the bonnet.

Mumbuu now sat on top of the roped-together ladders' junction for extra counterbalance, his legs dangling down over the windscreen. As his feet touched against the glass, Hermine saw that his shoes both had large holes in the soles. *If we all make it out of this mess, Mumbuu, I think you will deserve a new pair of boots.*

The far end of the second ladder was now projecting out over the gap between the car and the pontoon, and through the windscreen she could see the younger garden boy bravely start to edge out along it and extend his small hand in encouragement to the Himba, whom she suspected he knew. Though he couldn't reach him, this gesture seemed to electrify the injured man, who a moment or so ago looked so very close to collapse. He rose from his slump and quickly and easily grasped the first rung and then, as the ladder bowed alarmingly downwards but held, he belly-crawled along until he gained the safety of the roof rack, and Mumbuu presumably bundled him into a waiting blanket.

Steve paused for a moment, crouching on all fours on the pontoon's guardrail and gazing downstream in a sort of trance. Hermine wondered if he had lost his nerve and frozen and what they would do if this were the case. He had been a camp boss for more than twenty years and had seen many wondrous things – maybe he just wanted to capture this sight in his memory because, with retirement only a few years away, it might be that he would never see something quite so spectacular again. She remembered the huge panel of tin that might be launched in their direction at any moment, and involuntarily glanced back to the shrinking spit of land where the river made its turn. The sheet of roofing was hidden by the angle from her view, while the projecting platform of sand and rocks still gave the impression of being intact for the time being, thank goodness. Though it was now maybe only a third of the size it had been when Steve had used it to scan the pontoon with his binoculars.

By the time she glanced back at him through the first tentative drops of rain, Steve was on his way, cat-crawling along the last few centimetres of metal rail until he, too, could seize the rung of the ladder nearest to him and begin the short journey to the sanctuary of the vehicle's roof. Clearly, though, the six people up there felt less than secure because they were all soon clambering down using the short integral ladder by the back door, Steve and the Himba man practically carried to the ground by the two older men. As a dripping Elias got back into the vehicle, Hermine watched the others slowly filing up the slipway through the now-steady downpour, as if in exhausted slow motion, the rescued men almost completely covered by their thick grey blankets. She was feeling suddenly very drained herself and disinclined to make a move just yet, until from the back seat, Elias tapped her on the shoulder and pointed back at the bend in the river, where the water seemed to be gathering itself for the next onslaught.

Hermine began to swing the rear end of the Land Rover back along the beach so that she could drive forward away from the rising lagoon. She didn't want to try to reverse up the slipway in the torrential rain with the men as good as invisible through the rear window. Aware that her feet were becoming damp, she saw that somehow the strap from her bag had become trapped in the car door, leaving a gap in the seal though which a trickle of river water was now oozing. Without really thinking, she cracked the door open to release the obstruction but once the door was freed from its catch, the pressure of the water rushing inside made it impossible to shut it again. Indeed, the door was being pushed open wider and wider by the brownish silty current sluicing into the footwell and then around her knees. As Elias leaned forward from behind her to add his manpower to her jerky attempts to pull the door closed, Hermine saw that the men had made their escape just in time: the base of the slipway was totally covered over again with the thick creamy scum and swirling eddies of a fresh flood.

A hole the size of a garage door opened up right in the centre of the bank that still held the roof panel on its far side, and the water cascaded through for a brief moment before the whole thing collapsed in on itself with an infernal sucking sound, just as the engine of the Land Rover died.

In an instant the horizon disappeared, and the view through her open doorway turned the colour of chocolate milk. The door, which was still stubbornly resisting their panicked, illogical efforts to close it, now slammed back violently and crashed into her crown, compressing her head onto her shoulders with violent force. The searing pain as her scalp split open and her neck was jammed back at an unnatural angle were the last things Hermine remembered of that day.

∽

It hurt too much to open her eyes against the brilliant light, but when Hermine recovered consciousness some days later, she knew that she was in a hospital from the beeping sounds of the equipment that she was apparently attached to, accompanied by the sharp pine smell of disinfectant. At least three people were consulting quietly in the room, but a thick bandage right around her head made it difficult to distinguish the voices. It was so peaceful in that room, and so cosy and clean under the covers, that Hermine pretended to be asleep for a while longer. Her immediate welfare hadn't really been anyone else's concern for a very long time, not since she had been a small child, really, and she found herself wanting to make the most of this opportunity to take drowsy, fitful rest and be helpless and demanding even, if necessary. It felt good to have no choice but to be on the receiving end of solicitude.

Time stretched and bunched in an erratic rhythm over the next week or so as Hermine gradually recovered. Some days seemed to last only a few short hours and others – filled with questions and tests and trips to other parts of the big, modern facility for diagnostic procedures – seemed to go on forever. Her mother and son were there often, whispering conspiratorially in a corner and going through Seun's schoolwork, and they were on hand the day that the dose of painkillers was reduced and the heavy bandage removed, so that she could finally make sense of what she was seeing and hearing, and where she was. Wanting desperately to embrace her frightened son, Hermine found that she could raise her head from the pillow for a kiss without feeling too dizzy and nauseous.

The company had helped out a great deal finding Ottilie and Seun accommodation nearby so that they could visit every day, but now Hermine was improving fast, with no life-changing damage detected, her mother wished to return to the village with the boy until her daughter could be released and transported home to recuperate. Elias would accompany them northwards to resume his work, having only been hospitalised for observation for two nights after the accident. He had been resting up with one of his girlfriends in town ever since, making the most of the attention that she lavished on her brave hero.

Hermine listened to the radio and slept and slept. Despite her injuries, which really didn't hurt a great deal, a kind of bright bliss descended on her, aided no doubt by the cocktail of drugs she was still taking. Late one evening, however, she experienced a moment of shattering, dry-mouthed panic as she realised that she had totally lost track of time and that it had probably been many days since she had been in contact with Yves, if not weeks. Did he even know or care that she had narrowly escaped death, and that the only thing that had saved her from being ripped in two by the freed roof panel had been the car door slamming shut with concussive force against her head just before the corrugated sheet tore into the vehicle?

Tipping sideways to open her bedside locker brought on a fresh attack of giddiness, but Hermine managed to find her iPhone on the shelf within by feel, her eyes tightly closed against the lurching room, only to find that the device was dead and its charger was missing. So was the little mauve notebook of prompts for messages to Yves that she always kept tucked inside the phone's cover.

The following day she surfaced from the fourteen-hour sleep brought on by the exertions of finding her phone with an awareness that there was someone in the room with her, in all likelihood comfortably ensconced in the easy chair where visitors sat playing with their phones while they waited for her to wake. She opened her eyes just enough to make out who it was so that she could prepare herself for the conversation to come, then shut them again while she processed what she had seen. Steve – who she had assumed was taking care of things at the camp – was slouched in the chair, with one ankle balanced on the knee of his other leg. At his feet was an overstuffed overnight bag, suggesting that he had popped in to see her on his way somewhere else.

He looked very at home and was out of uniform – something of a novel sight, although not one that Hermine paid special attention to right then. Through the slits she made with her still-swollen eyes, she saw with shock that he was holding her little purple book open in one hand and was at work stroking his goatee with the other as he read in silence.

She gave an involuntary moan of distress at being exposed in this manner, her embarrassment an almost tangible pain in her tight throat. Steve moved quickly to tuck the notepad under him in a back pocket of his jeans as she gave him to understand by some more whimpers that she was emerging from her sleep. She was pretty sure her deceit had been successful, and they chatted in a desultory way about her progress, how the company was dealing with her medical bills, and the fact that she would be forced to remain on leave for some time while the damage to her spine and scalp healed. Perhaps she would like to think about doing a little bit of light studying while she was off work – brush up on some skills so that she could take on a different position, one that would make fewer physical demands on her, if she returned, he gently suggested.

"Are you telling me that my old job might not be waiting for me once I am better, Steve? And are you giving me this information as a messenger of the company, or as a friend?"

"Neither. You are wasted in the position you hold at the camp, and I put you forward for promotion a while ago, if you really want to know. But then you – how shall I put it? – got distracted by your personal life, and I could no longer justify extolling your many virtues when your mind was clearly not on your work anymore."

"Thanks … I guess. For thinking of promoting me back then, I mean. But guess what. I *can* have a personal life and a career. Plenty of people do. You used to."

That was something of a low blow, since Steve was suspected to be still reeling from the departure of his much-younger fiancée a few years back, when she left the camp they were managing together in the south with a tooth abscess that needed urgent attention, only to fall like a schoolgirl for the blasé pilot who medevaced her out.

"You can indeed. No doubt 'bout that. But you can't be a Sad Sadie moping around the camp, forgetting important stuff and messing up the running of the place by being bloody unprofessional because your heart got broken. That's just not how it works."

He rose to retrieve the carrier bag he had brought containing magazines and sweets, and Hermine realised that he was doing this because the combative tenor of their conversation was not conducive to the direction he had wished his visit to take. But there was one more thing she thought they could thrash out, since they were being candid with each other today.

"Steve, I need you to try to find out what's happened with my belongings, please. My phone is here, so I suppose that someone brought that down for me from the camp, but other stuff is missing. The charger for the phone. And a little notepad?"

The last item she added as casually as she could, but nonetheless, Steve looked up too quickly from sorting through the presents he had brought. These included, she noted, some comics and action-figure toys for Seun. Hermine had never seen him nonplussed before, but now he coloured, reached into his back pocket, and handed the notepad over in silence. He then placed the plastic bag of gifts on the bed and turned to start gathering his stuff together before spinning round to face her with a new, hard look.

"Some advice for free, since we're not doing any pretending any more. If you really have to work at it, put in huge amounts of effort and tie yourself up in knots, and spend every day in misery, then really, it can't be love, can it? With me, I promise, you truly would not have had to work your butt off to keep my attention."

౪

Just then, one of the youngest nun nurses stuck her head around the door with a wide smile. She glanced at Steve, who was gathering up his ancient tweed jacket and a folder of company paperwork from the floor, and then beamed at Hermine, rolling her "r" proudly as she announced, "Someone I think you will be verrry pleased to see is here. Can I show him in? It's not officially visiting time anymore, but he told me he has come indeed a long way."

Steve slipped out behind the nurse without saying goodbye and appeared to spend a moment or two in quiet conversation with someone directly outside her door. There was no need for Hermine to wonder who this person might be: the cadences of his phrasing – even though she couldn't make out the words individually – were a giveaway.

Once again, she slipped down the pillow and faked sleep. She wanted to have a little time to process her confusion of emotions now that the one thing she had wanted above all else, that she had stopped even allowing herself to think about out of sheer self-preservation, was seemingly about to happen. She would be the discarded lover no longer maybe, but what would she end up being instead? She needed to prepare herself for any possibility, but the fact that Yves was here at least meant that he had not forgotten her, not at all.

For one appalled instant, she thought that he had entered the room with another visitor and her mind, aghast, told her that it could only be Michelle. Then she caught the peppery, fresh scent of some flower that she didn't recognise – everyone else had brought roses and carnations – and relaxed as she made out the sounds of the nurse, who had come in with Yves, placing the vase of his flowers next to the others, which were by now over a week old and sorry-looking brown specimens mostly.

Then the door shut, and she heard the noises of someone settling into the low chair. Across the small room, Yves gave an enormous sigh, and then she thought she heard him stifle a sob, and then a second one.

Yves, it seemed, was impatient for her to wake. He rose from the chair now, she could hear this clearly, and with a faint scraping sound moved his vase of flowers along the shelf where the nurse had left it. Then he seemed to take his lighter and – she guessed – his cigarettes out of his leather jacket (she could smell this too), think better of it, and then return them with another sigh. Hermine made an effort to open her eyes as narrowly as she could, just as she had done with Steve not long before. She still wasn't ready yet to handle all the emotions of their reunion. She needed to see him, gather him in, without him knowing that he was being observed. It had been six whole months now.

Yves was standing in half-profile, facing the almost-closed venetian blinds at the window with his hands clasped behind him.

He had lost a great deal of weight, even though he had been of slender build to begin with. The seat of his jeans sagged, and his bomber jacket looked as if it belonged on another man entirely. Hermine's heart could hardly bear to acknowledge what their months apart had done to him, to note the first appearance of a few coarse white hairs stark among the blue-black gloss at his temples, and his shaggy beard only grey and silver, with no dark bristles at all. She realised that he was approaching middle age, and her heart contracted sharply with tenderness for this man who had given up so much to be with her now.

There would be time, once they had re-established their relationship, for her to go back over all the archived messages on her phone and identify which of them had led her off onto the treacherous, meandering paths that had caused her so much grief. The harmless expressions he had used, not realising how much they had caught her up, helpless, in a steel trap of her fears, and the too-short exchanges that she had misinterpreted as signs of growing apathy. She had not just been a sad girl, as Steve had reminded her regularly and with what she had mistakenly taken to be only paternalistic concern, but she had been a silly, *silly*, girl, too.

But all that would change now. Yves had left a woman of beauty, quality and wealth for her, and she would prove to him, in a million ways every day, that he had made the right, the *only*, decision. There could be no doubt that her entire life had been leading up to this point: for ever more there would be her dull life before Yves and her real life, beginning now that they were together.

Yves finally turned, and Hermine could keep up the pretence no longer. She opened her eyes fully so that her life, Part Two, could begin.

Yves had put one finger between two of the slats of the blind, and it remained there, letting a beam of late-afternoon sunlight rake the space between them as he scrutinised her from across the room. She had asked for a mirror as soon as her bandages had been removed, so she had some idea of what he saw now: the small bronze head, shaved for an operation on her skull; the fading bruising still visible around both bloodshot eyes; the torn and sutured place on her scalp where the hair was already growing back a lighter shade than the rest. He must also have observed that some damage to a nerve was making a little area of skin pinch and twitch rhythmically at the corner of one eye.

In a quavering voice he appeared to be trying to locate the words he needed to reassure her. He held up his left hand, with the puckered band of paler skin encircling the ring finger, so that she could be in no doubt of the choice he had made, while he haltingly explained that his decision was final now and could not be reversed.

"I have an alert on my phone that lets me know any news of the area? I knew about the possibility to flood, because of course, you told me. And so I was checking all the news reports, but they were all contradicting each other. One said all the people of the camp were safe. Another, that staff people had been hurt. I couldn't decide what to do, not hearing from you and not being sure, you know what I'm saying, Hermine?"

She nodded too encouragingly and winced as the stitches in her scalp pulled.

"So I called through to the main office in South Africa and spoke to some young company guy who didn't know what was going on, it was obvious to me. He tried to discourage me to make a visit. When he said that all the staff had taken to boats, those are the words he used, then I knew it was crap because there are no boats that I remember, and I know that place very well by now. And yes, I came, no excuses to Michelle, and when I was on the plane just now, I told myself, Yves, accept. Coming to find Hermine, that's the sign. You belong with each other. That's the truth."

His expression was loving and open, just as she remembered. His eyes shone with certainty, and relief was making him sob, very softly, one more time. Yves stood back there against the window blinds as if he was waiting for her to say that he could approach her, that he had passed through some sacred rite and now they could start their life together openly as a couple. He looked like a little boy, a bit pleased with himself but still unsure, for the moment, if he had made the grade.

A buzzer sounded at the door beyond the nurses' station outside. Urgent footsteps passed by.

"Ouf. My English hey …?" he said, as if he had to make the anxious silence somehow productive.

He started to apologise again as still she said nothing. When she closed her eyes and sought her familiar refuge behind her prickling lids, he said that of course she was *très* tired and he had been too selfish, too eager to begin their life together at last and had spoken too much. All those stupid messages when neither of them could say what they really wanted to – this had made him too impatient now to express his true feelings and he had overwhelmed her. *Pardon*. He would leave her to gather her strength; he had not, of course, realised how sick she was until now. But he would be back first thing the next morning.

There was a faint, regular clicking sound. Hermine had been disconnected some days ago from the machines that had monitored her progress, and at first, she couldn't work out what the noise could be. Then Yves began to sing softly, and she understood that he had been snapping his fingers. She didn't recognise the song, so it was probably from before her time.

"Once I left you took a part of me. Is that so hard to believe? Come here baby because we belong together."

He excused himself and left.

Hermine relaxed the clenched fists that had been gripping the soft blanket that Steve had given her less than an hour ago. She still didn't possess a suitable cable for her phone, but once she had it charged again, she would have to begin looking back over all the messages she and Yves had shared. She had meant to say so much to him in the months when they had been apart, to pour out her feelings so that he could never claim he didn't know the depths of her affection for him. But always she had been constrained, fearful that Michelle would one day chance upon a declaration that would leave the lovers exposed. It was such a cliché but also very true. It did happen, no matter how careful people were. Her natural bashfulness, too, played a role – she was simply not used to forming and using sentences describing the state of her desires. It wasn't Namibian or African perhaps? It certainly wasn't her …

When Yves had turned to speak to her, partly silhouetted against the glare of the setting sun behind the blinds, she had held her breath for a long time. She did not want hysteria to be the response that he remembered from this moment, the minute when all their plans and hopes finally came together. Yes, for a moment only, she had allowed herself to weep, very gently, with relief. The horrific belief – yes, that was the correct word, it was real horror – that he may have cold-heartedly abandoned her had not turned out to be warranted after all. But otherwise, she had kept things under control. She had been determined not to be silly. That was of great importance to her.

Hermine had waited for the honey flow of love to start anew. She had searched Yves's face for traces of the man she adored – he was the same person, there was no doubt, if looking fraught and much older.

Nothing. She felt quite literally nothing. Not from shock, not from surprise. She felt nothing because the messages, the anticipation, the detective work, the infatuation, *the waiting*, had indeed been all that there was. Even the agony of uncertainly had been a welcome distraction of sorts. Now that she could have him, was actually trapped by the reckless burning of all his bridges, she sensed that she had already left him behind, far away on the banks of the green river where her feelings for him had flowed sweetly for a while, and then curdled into something bitter and punishing – though she hadn't had the experience or perspective to know this at the time.

There would be a lot of explaining to do, many recriminations. She knew that she could cite her messages as evidence that she had never, not even once, asked him to leave Michelle. Their conversations when they had been together had revolved around hypotheticals – what if he managed to get an investment visa? How about if they tried to strike out for Angola? Nothing concrete had been asked, and nothing definite had been decided. This was her guilty conscience now twisting history.

In fact, all the time that they had been sending messages to each other these past six months, she had been carefully cultivating a hurt, not a passion, and it was into this that she had poured all her energies. As the tone of his later messages led her to believe that he was easing his way out of her future, she had not been able to hold back the resentment. Yves *owed* her something tangible in return for her patience, and he therefore had a responsibility to come back to her. Now the positions were reversed. Incredibly, so incredibly, Yves had not let her down, even though – the irony was making her laugh now – she had been depending on him to do so.

Were there words that she could say that would put everyone back where they should be, where they all were at the beginning? Of course not, although if Steve returned (and she found herself very much hoping that he would) he could maybe help her to find a compassionate way to explain things to Yves. Steve knew the score, after all. Maybe it wasn't too late.

She wished she could just leave the hospital and disappear, right away, but since she could barely balance herself upright yet, let alone walk, this was not a practical way out of her dilemma (and it definitely would have been silly of her, anyway). Maybe she *would* even have to go through the motions of being Yves's girlfriend for a while until things fell apart naturally, of their own accord, due to their basic incompatibility. Due to the fact that lust had been all there was. He was still an attractive man – could she convince herself to fake it for a while to spare his feelings?

But no, although she knew that this compromise could turn out to be far less messy for her, she had to face facts. Tomorrow morning, she would have to tell Yves that things had changed, she had moved on, it had been fun while it lasted. No hard feelings? Maybe it had been the near-death experience of the accident, or the way that Steve had taken on a different role in her life …?

One way or another, they were going to have to talk to each other face to face and end it.

Ticks, Even

Dina had texted me late that November morning to say that she couldn't crash at Meadow's place *1 minute longer* and was coming over straight away. Then we could take my car and go back over and pick up the rest of her shit once Meadow had left the house. She had written all this in such a way that I couldn't really object or throw in any suggestions for alternative arrangements – taking me for granted, as I had always let her take me for granted.

And when she arrived, Dina began pulling all kinds of plastic bags and old canvas holdalls out of the taxi, breathlessly starting in on the whole story. It soon became glaringly obvious that Meadow (real name Sunette) had been waiting for the moment to contrive an argument so that she would have a reason for throwing Dina out of her home and letting her posh dreadlocked British boyfriend take her place.

"I can't believe I fell for that sisterhood crap, Jen, can you? My house is your house and all that kak."

As if I hadn't gently tried to warn her all along. As if she weren't clever enough to recognise from the outset that Meadow/Sunette was the kind of lazy liberal who accumulated SJW kudos for taking a homeless, beaten black lesbian into her huge, inherited house but whose performative variety of charity didn't extend to making sure that the arrangement had built-in protections for anyone but herself. As if Dina had had any choice, as she had pointedly explained to me when she had moved in with Meadow back around July, and reminded me over again now with respect to crashing at my place.

"I figure that Ed needs, what? – a yoga space or tattoo studio or some place to whip up batches of his evil gluten-free rusks or something? So she fixed to fight with me and then that gave her some excuse to chuck me out."

"A pretext then, that's what you're saying?"

"Yeah, a pretext. Thank you, Jen, that's totally right. Look, she was going on and on about how she was only going to the office later today because she had a bad night or something and needed to catch up on her sleep. Then she said it was because she was worried about the situation in Syria or something that she hadn't been able to sleep. I mean, jeez, serious? But when I asked her what it was about the situation there that she was so freakin' worried about and she couldn't say, I guess I must have rolled my eyes or sighed or something because it's the same old self-righteous crap as before: *I'm better than you 'cos in my endless spare time I keep up to date with how the world is rubbish on my brand-new iPad Pro, even though I don't actually do a damned thing about it ever except sign useless petitions.* And then she just started throwing her toys out the pram and told me I should probably leave."

I handed her a mug of tea, which she sipped, pulled a face over, then handed back, slopping a great deal of it onto the floor of my tiny patio as she did so. One of the old mutts, Toad, came over to take a sniff at the lemon-verbena-scented puddle, and Dina eased the bitch away with a decisive bare foot. I noted even more toe-rings than before. How did this girl even walk?

"'Kay so now I really, *really* don't have any place to stay except here now for the time being. Hope that's cool. We cool?"

As if I had any choice in the matter. Dina explained that she was no longer eating according to her star sign – having escaped Meadow's orbit and therefore her culinary diktats – and I mentioned lightly that this was some relief in the run-up to Christmas. *But not much*, I thought to myself.

❦

Dina had wanted to be the one to drive us back to Newlands when we set off a bit later that day to collect the rest of her gear. *See*, I guess Dina had wanted to suggest by pulling up behind the wheel of my ancient 2CV, *I landed on my feet. I have a real friend in Jen, and now she's invited me to go stay with her. And lets me drive her car even!* She seemed pretty confident that Meadow would still be at the house, possibly electing to help Ed move in rather than going to the women's empowerment project where she volunteered during the week, if Dina's hunch was correct.

On this occasion, I put my foot down however, since Dina was also apparently working on the assumption that I had forgotten the last time she had tried to drive my car, when she had stalled it in traffic on a bitter winter's morning months back and had got into a nasty argument with a businessman trying to manoeuvre around us as we waited, becalmed, for her to remember how to restart the car.

"I dunno why you keep that pile of kak. You can afford a decent ride, hey? It's as if you drive it to show that you are down with us poor folks," she had teased with her dirty contralto chuckle later, when we were lying under a pile of thick blankets on my bed watching TV and she was done imitating the red-faced apoplexy of Mr Alfa Romeo.

I had baulked a little at this but had let it go. With Dina, I had swiftly learned early on in our acquaintance, it was always wise to pick your battles. Although she was nominally Meadow's tenant already by then, she did spend a great deal of time hanging out with me at my cosy cottage and putting the world to rights, so the prospect of a skirmish was always on the horizon. Verbal sparring was one of her favourite pastimes, one at which her agile, voracious mind had made her particularly adept. But Dina was too mercurial to stick to objective, dispassionate argument for long, and any discussion therefore had the potential to deteriorate into a dust-up in the time it took to fetch her another drink.

Essentially, I had only the (rented) roof over my head and enough regular income to fill the tank with petrol once a month, do a frugal weekly shop, and cover my other few outgoings. My hair was turning grey in the absence of attention from a hairdresser, and a pedicure was something stamped on a voucher that one of my wealthy sisters might present to me on my birthday. I wasn't one of the poor folks really, though, and it would have been the height of disingenuousness to pretend I was. However, worrying about my lack of a decent pension kept me up some nights, and I wished that I could afford better food for my pack of dogs than the unappetising dusty kibble I ended up schlepping from the cash-and-carry every fortnight.

We now arrived that November afternoon at the magnificent old house that had been Dina's home until a few hours before. On the journey across town, Dina had casually dropped another little bombshell to add to the trail of destruction that seemed to follow in her wake wherever she went: the job at Lorenzo's Coffee Shop hadn't really been her thing, right, so for the time being she was without a job. But, you know, something would turn up, it always did …

Apart from the domestic worker we could see sweeping the highly polished hall floor through the massive open front doors, and the gardener pulling rotting leaves off the drain cover, no one else was about, it seemed. I waited on the street in the Citroën as Dina skipped through the opening electric gates with exaggerated nonchalance and the housekeeper greeted her under the portico: a tall, thin, world-weary older woman in a faded maid's uniform clutching to her waist this tiny, boyish imp who was bouncing up and down on her toes in the (less-than-enthusiastic) hug she had solicited. A figurative snapshot of Dina and her way of meeting the world – she threw herself headlong at people with such amiable force that they didn't realise they had caught her in a surprised, reluctant embrace until it was too late.

Then the two disappeared, only to emerge twenty minutes later with a pile of bedding I was pretty sure didn't belong to Dina; two fabric tote bags containing what looked like fresh vegetables; a thin white plastic bag with a tangle of cables poking out from the top; another, thicker sakkie that seemed to hold some folders and bits of paper … and a kitten. Dina was also wearing a long coat made of fake-fur material that completely swallowed up her tiny frame. The way she held the kitten aloft like a prize of great worth made me think that perhaps this squirming bundle of ginger fur was the real reason Meadow had tired of Dina's casual acquirements and divestments, her live-for-the-moment and plan-a-quick-getaway system for survival. About the coat and other liberated items, I didn't care one bit – Meadow could have that topic out with Dina herself if it ever came to pass that the addled, drippy old hippie even noticed that the things were missing from her cavernous, empty home.

Dina nodded in sly triumph as she scrambled back into the passenger's seat, leaving the housekeeper to stash all the gear in the rear of the little car.

"Oh yiss! Scored me my kitty!" she announced, as if there had been any possibility that Meadow – organisationally impaired at the best of times and barely able to take care of herself – would have wanted to keep the little thing, which was now bedding down contentedly in Dina's lap. It scratched ineffectually with an uncoordinated back foot at a large scab in front of its ear, in a way that set off an empathetic itching at my own temple. Anyone peering in through one of the car's windows as we headed back across town would have seen a careworn, almost middle-aged white woman patting at her streaming eyes with a wadded old tissue driving a black kid juggling a cat – both gender and age indeterminate in the case of the child.

"I'm allergic to cats, Dina? And also, what about the dogs?"

As if it made any difference. When Dina had reached up to embrace the housekeeper at the Newlands spread, I had spotted that her cut-off jeans – which must have been a large children's size rather than a small adult fit – were barely held up by the bones of her hips, and that the girl had no flesh to speak of rounding out her buttocks or belly. The shocking pity of it had produced a single sharp stabbing pain where I supposed my unhealthy heart to be – whether a coincidence or cliché I couldn't tell you to this day.

☙

Another snapshot, from later that same November day. Dina was standing on the little patio overlooking my lush courtyard garden with the kitten raised high in one hand as she tried to fend off the inquisitive attentions of my five panting dogs with the other. She was hopping from foot to foot and yelling, head thrown back and delighting in the attention, and carelessly kicking over the delicate little geraniums and pelargoniums in their plastic pots. My elderly neighbour, alerted by the noise in what was normally the quietest of streets, had emerged onto her own patio only a few metres away from mine and was also yelling in Afrikaans in a feeble, asthmatic voice, having assumed that Dina was being attacked. Having assumed, I assume, that Dina was a diminutive, jolly burglar.

Not really knowing what to do, I grabbed the stunned kitten and marched round to Mrs Green's place to explain the un-neighbourly noise, the new pet, and the appearance of Dina in my home. Mrs Green blinked mildly with damp, solicitous eyes, and nodded her approval at my charity. Did I know that she had herself once looked after the son of her maid for several weeks, back in the 1970s (she couldn't recall his name or the maid's) and ja, this is part of our obligation, our responsibility, to our countrymen and women, is it not? Mrs Green gingerly reached up and patted the terrified cat with an elegant, trembling clawed hand and there and then we struck a deal: she would keep the kitten until Dina moved on because it would be a terrible thing, would it not, for my guest to have her pet torn to pieces by my dogs? In return, I would give Mrs Green a few rand each week for cat food – an arrangement that seemed to me probably cheaper than paying for the animal to be patched up at the vets once one or other of the dogs got too boisterous with it.

On my return to the cottage, in a convulsion of sneezes, I realised I could turn this temporary adoption to my advantage: Mrs Green could hardly be expected to home Ganja permanently, and in any case, as soon as the kitten got bigger, he would start to wander back onto my property. Then we would have the same snot en trane over again with Toad and the other dogs. So straight away I was going to point out to Dina that she needed to be looking for other accommodation if she was going to reclaim her precious pet. That's how I would negotiate my way out of the quandary, deploying cynical tactics against a person I already knew had the ability to be a world-class manipulator herself.

Back on my patio, though, it was clear that Ganja was already a distant memory and that I would therefore be thwarted in trying to leverage his ownership when it came to questions of re-homing Dina herself. She was sitting in among the upturned pots and scattered compost with all the whining dogs piled up over her, several of them licking her grubby toes, with one hand still held above her head for some reason as she giggled in a slightly theatrical way.

"Look what that one brought me." She laughed, pointing at Tadpole, Toad's put-upon son. In her little brown fist, she was clutching something that was moving in jerky spasms and splashing drops of pinkish liquid onto the cracked terracotta tiles.

"Ima kill it but I dunno how," she sang out. Giggles, wriggles, killing, blood, barking. All this sudden activity, this unnecessary drama and noise, in my quiet, settled life. I reached down to help her disentangle herself from the tumble of canine bodies, but Dina misunderstood my outstretched hand and dumped into my palm a smallish mottled gecko that was missing most of its tail and was thrashing the ragged, bloody stump about in a fury. I was momentarily softened by her compassion for the little creature, which had been a regular evening visitor to the patio and kitchen. I was also confused that Tadpole had attacked it so violently – the dogs all knew not to pay attention to any of the smaller animals that lived around the cottage, and Tadpole was especially gentle and submissive. I immediately began to have my doubts regarding the tale of how the lizard lost its tail.

"Why kill it, Dina? It can survive. You can see them around the house sometimes missing their tails. And it's not in pain, I promise you that. So, no need to put it out of its misery after all, my girl."

"I didn't want to kill it for that reason. It's just disgusting. Me, I hate those siff things. How can you have those things live here?"

I placed the pulsing, marbled lizard in a shoebox in the dark, warm laundry room until – by the urgent scuffling sounds I heard coming from the box a few hours later – I ascertained that it had recovered. I then let it go in the bushes at the bottom of the tiny garden in the hush of the summer dusk. It scampered out at a clip, apparently none the worse for its ordeal, and then launched itself up the broken wall, blinking and gulping a little bit like Mrs Green. I whispered that it had had a narrow escape this time but should make an effort to avoid the house until Dina had gone. As the dogs had licked the reptile's pink blood off her hands earlier, she had announced with mock authority that as long as she was going to be living with me, she would not tolerate any dirty bugs or goggas or birds or wild animals in the house. Klaar?

છ

When I'd first met Dina, in May of that same year, it had been quite some time since I'd had to think about the day-to-day realities of a relationship of any sort. But I hadn't forgotten how mentally navigating the trajectory between affection and apathy could use up at least as much energy and time as the practical tasks required to cultivate and maintain a partnership.

Back when I had started dating the fellow student who would eventually become my husband, I sometimes caught myself wondering that Aubrey's rugged, rural appreciation of the world was so at odds to my own city-bred one. The first few awful weeks I spent with him on his family farm after our marriage had taught me that I had a surprising capacity to be tough – hard-bitten even – when I had little choice though. Much of the daily activity concerning the stock seemed to revolve around gore, slaughter, poison, traps, emergency operations and grisly death. I made a private promise then that for the sake of my husband – the easiest and most accommodating of men – I would face these horrors with the composure expected of my role but that I would never cause suffering to any living creature, no matter how small, if I could possibly avoid it.

Every year or two, Aubrey would amble across to the outbuilding where we stored our tools and open the rusting gun safe with a clang. I would then stand against the kitchen sink with my back to the window, clutching a tea towel until my knuckles turned to nuggets of bone. Soon enough would come the muffled noise of one thud, followed by a second, moments after. Jaspar, Jinx, Rotter, Butch, Belle, Tiff – how many old or sick dogs had he dispatched following just a few words to me as I got out of bed with the dawn?

"I'm going to do it today, Jen. It's time, and the poor thing is suffering. Keep out of the yard."

Afterwards, Aubrey would return to the back kitchen with the carcass wrapped carefully in a favourite dog blanket and offer me the chance to say goodbye. He always followed this ritual, and I always declined to say a sentimental farewell, because to me, the collection of ribs and legs and scars and smelly fur had no connection with the living soul who had shared our lives for so many years. I would simply pat the blankie and nod, the sign for Aubrey to take the body away and dispose of it. My husband's compassion on these occasions moved me almost as much as my grief.

I caught sight of this dear man sometimes, when he thought I was napping off a headache in the middle of the day, standing motionless in contemplation of the animal graves under the pepper tree at the far end of the weedy farm garden. He never asked me to accompany him down there, and he must have known that I never went alone. Many of our farmer friends had a child's grave in a similar site on their land, and maybe that's what he was thinking about, too, as he peered down at the dirt with his callused hands dug into his pockets, since we never were blessed with a child, either to raise or to bury.

Living together: alone, apart, separate, joined in tandem, bound, reflected. Until – a few weeks short of his thirty-fifth birthday, and as a result of a warthog on the unlit road one night, which leapt not right nor left but straight through his windscreen – we weren't. I wasn't.

There had been quite a few men since. Then there had been some women. Confidence can go a long way towards making up for an absence of the more conventionally appreciated aesthetics. Following the sale of the farm and my return to city life, I could walk into a party or book launch or reception and be assured that although almost every man in the room who was a stranger to me wouldn't give me a second glance, there would always be the one who suddenly realised that on the right woman some feature that he had previously considered unappealing – too many freckles, a gap between the front teeth, a stalwart self-possession – could generate an unexpected erotic frisson, even after the glamour of my being a new widow had worn off. And I would have been a wealthy one too, if I had had a rand for every time one of them had declared to me some variation on: "Well, no one would ever say that you are pretty. But there *is* something about you, though I can't for the life of me figure out what it is right now ..."

This was my cue to tell the man that the expression he was looking for was "jolie laide" and, without even asking for a translation usually, my new admirer would latch on to that second word, and so we would begin.

Without exception these chaps eventually demanded what wasn't on offer, my much-remarked-upon independence in the end always representing a reproach they couldn't live with. There would be the (initially polite) dance back and forth as we tried to figure out how I could remain desirable to them by virtue of my self-reliance, while at the same time tacitly agreeing to be cut down to size by them from time to time, for the sake of their egos. At some point, this accommodation would become more like a civilised sort of wrestling, until it degenerated into a power play, pure and simple.

By that stage, though, the mental effort required from me to second guess and pre-empt the elaborately prepared traps and the tiresome belittling made my exit inevitable. I would depart with a blast of repetitious, unimaginatively crude insults in my wake, and more than a few times, with the sting of a haymaker on my face.

And the women who came after, whom I met at the gym and the martial arts classes, tended to slip into similar roles, though largely minus the pugilism. It was pretty unedifying to learn that they were just as capable as men of masking their agendas and dishonouring their true intentions. The ones who always insisted that they valued honesty above all other qualities were, sadly but perhaps inevitably, the ladies most adept at an emotional sleight-of-hand.

Throughout my fourth and fifth decades, I found myself regularly flat on my back and wide awake in bed at 4 a m, trying to rehearse the correct formulation of words to get me out of the newest entanglement I had fallen into. The effort of making nice when I felt nothing but torpor; reckoning with email and text messages, and latterly Facebook as well, was too much of a drain on my psychic resources to be sustainable. A man ban was implemented, and a sister sanction eventually, too. I kept waiting to feel relief now that I no longer had to waste time trying so hard not to hurt other people's mixed-up feelings, but it was proving slow to arrive.

❧

Enter Dina, almost six months ago, like a hurricane-force rebuke against the carefully constructed third act of my love life. She danced between tables at the new café where I took my morning espresso on the way to work, a delighted, vivacious sprite. Who knew that the expression "force of nature" had been waiting through the centuries for her to emerge and become its embodiment?

And it wasn't just me: I noticed that many times when I went into Lorenzo's, at least one of the other tables was occupied by lone woman, avidly following the progress of this girl-child from customer to customer. I couldn't allow myself to lust after her – that would be tantamount to a mild form of perversion given her pre-pubescent appearance – but a spell had been cast, no denying. She bestowed her benedictions on each customer in turn, with a touch on the arm here, a conspiring wink there, until she appeared, one Friday morning, with a black eye on prominent display.

I knew her name by then – it was printed at the bottom of the café's receipts, although, as I discovered eventually, Dina is not the name she was given at birth. Her brinjal-coloured bruise and my gnawing sense of obligation compelled me to ask the question as casually, as brightly as I could. As if a perfectly innocent explanation might yet be forthcoming, idiot that I was.

"Hey Dina. Hi. I couldn't help but notice. Everything okay with you?"

Everything was not okay, she explained during a hastily convened break. She had been living with her older brother at his place in Khayelitsha, and when she (regularly and unambiguously) refused requests directed through him to sleep with his boss at the mini-mart, this brother had started demanding rent. When she couldn't make the payment in full this month, he had been obliged to smack her around a little bit. No, she didn't really have anywhere else to go because, despite a bewildering number of relatives spread all around the country (so it seemed to me), Dina appeared to have spent the past decade or so alienating and making enemies of them all.

"Because I'm gay. You see?"

Now she was sleeping on the floor of a basement room in a condemned building nearby, but she was regularly harassed by other people squatting in the property, as well as a white man who came by to collect "rent", in cash or in kind. She had only been there a few days, but she had to get out.

"Because I am small, and they can push me around so easy. You see?"

It was a performance of note. Even as she set out all her tribulations (her word, my surprise) for my consideration, I was fully aware of this fact. I hadn't failed to notice that on that fateful morning she had swung by my table in such a way that I was given multiple opportunities to survey the damage to her beautiful, tiny face, whereas the regular occupants of the other tables were not afforded such a privilege. What was it about me specifically that she had settled on as the answer to her prayers? This was a 4 a.m. question, if ever there was one. I had stopped making much of an effort with my clothes, hair and make-up since I had decided that I was no longer actively single and available, although several co-workers had said things like, "You know actually, that natural look suits you. Dignified, if you know what I mean." I felt this could be interpreted in one of two ways – at face value, or as acknowledgement that I had put myself out of the game and deserved respect for accepting, with dignity, the concomitant decline in interest in me.

All that has happened since then, and that led up to her taking up occupancy in my cottage long after she had taken up residence in my heart and my conscience, had taken off from the one innocuous statement I made to Dina then as my espresso grew cold at my elbow, and two other women looked on with envy at our intimate discussion.

"Okay, Dina. Let me see what I can do then. I should be able to shake up a few connections and help you make a plan."

She gave me her cellphone number but – I have a sense of observing myself weighing up and then making this decision – I did not reciprocate, neither did she then ask me to provide it. A masterful opening move on her part, because it helped to tamp down the unease I was feeling already, the fear that I was getting myself into something that it would be hard to extricate myself from later.

∽

Not long afterwards, through my professional contacts, I found Dina a place at a women's refuge by playing up her status as a victim of domestic violence and as a vulnerable member of the LGBT community. She had only been there a few weeks, though, when she caused some hectic drama and was asked to leave, which is how she ended up bedding down at Sunette-call-me-Meadow's place. Our local Stevie Nicks manqué had recently lost her last live-in social-responsibility project, a man calling himself Joopiter. Having turned her home into a large-scale drug den while she was away at the Glastonbury Festival, he had drawn the attention of her neighbours (one of whom had sampled the product first before calling the cops – you couldn't make it up) and been arrested. Dina moved in the next month, the perfect choice to take his place, ticking as she did a satisfying number of boxes for victimhood.

Meanwhile, I had managed to convince myself that I had established a clear demarcation between my semi-professional interest in Dina's plight and my emotions, which were by then in quiet turmoil. If I *had* started to have feelings for her, I told myself, maybe it was because she gave me an uncomplicated outlet for the affectionate nature I possessed but had been unable to exercise recently. In which case, I asked myself in my somewhat more bitter and inebriated moments, could it be that I didn't love Dina *specifically*? It was simply that I was primed – desperate – to love the next person who crossed my path, regardless of their suitability, and this just happened to be her.

Reciprocity was obviously not on the table, but I barely cared: being invested in someone else's happiness seemed to be its own reward – perhaps that was the definition of love as I grew older? And *perhaps* I had been too judgmental about Meadow, although I did still hate her tie-dyed harem pants and bloody wind chimes.

One day in July, Dina happened to be at my cottage using my computer to update her CV, when an ex-colleague of mine paid a visit. Dina put on one of her shows, conjuring up a perfect admixture of credible BS and childlike, heart-breaking wishful thinking. She announced that she had been a university student at one point (the first I had heard of this, though her erudition was something of a clue) and enchanted the poor man with her opinions about anarchy, subversion and subcultures. She had had to drop out because her family had no money; she had wanted to be a singer at some point as well, there had been talk of a record deal, some dubious character had taken the money she had raised to book a recording session. And so it went on.

After she had left (Karel having given her the taxi fare back to the mansion in Newlands), he gushed, "That girl's totally adorable. Just totally, Jen. Just such an interesting person all round. Is she, like, something to you, might I ask?"

"A young friend. That's all, really, I guess. She's had a few bad breaks, and I'm trying to help out. Without getting too involved, if you know what I mean."

Karel said he did indeed know what I meant. He also gave me a concerned look as if to say *Watch yourself before you become an old fool*, Karel himself, of course, having fallen into that trap – spectacularly and ruinously – with several young male friends over the years, to my certain knowledge.

After Karel left, too, I went to my home office to tidy up. Dina never left things in disarray when she visited to use the PC, but the office was so tiny – more of an alcove really – that any bit of paper put back in the wrong place could result in exponential disorder. The printer was still on, and when I reached over to flick off the power switch, I noticed that she had left a passport face down on the glass bed of the machine. Intrigued, I lifted the lid and took it out. How was it that she came to have such a costly thing when she regularly stressed how few opportunities had ever come her way, and how much she would welcome the chance to rectify that? I found myself flicking through to see what hairstyle Dina had been sporting when she had had her photograph taken.

For a long time afterwards, I really couldn't settle on which emotion had prevailed as I read her personal details set out on that page. Anger, because she had very deliberately obfuscated when it came to the specifics of her age, but at the same time happy – ridiculously, unreasonably happy – when I realised that she was, if one were to be fairly generous about it, almost my contemporary. The uses to which I might put this new information – the ways that it changed, or could change, the dynamics of our relationship – troubled me to the point of twitchy exhaustion for the next few days. Thoughts of what we might become to each other blew a hole straight through the middle of each night.

I had had a number of younger lovers through the years, and had also been involved with one man old enough to be my father, albeit briefly. As I examined these relationships over again, I remained certain that none had been cause for censure or scandal, certainly within my circle of friends and my few remaining (liberal-minded) relatives. Yet Dina, despite this new, incontrovertible evidence that she was almost 40, was a wholly different matter. She not only looked like a young girl, she acted and thought like one too – this I had to concede was a problem. She was not simply affecting a youthful mindset, pretending to like township rap and Marvel Comic T-shirts to hoodwink me, but was genuinely unable (not just unwilling) to act her age.

It was her own perception and presentation of herself – immature, trusting and vulnerable despite her street smarts – that placed her off limits to me, I had finally decided. Not the fact that she had deceived me, in effect, by closing down any conversations that might have compelled her to admit her true age. Nor that when we found ourselves conducting a particularly amiable conversation, she might make cheeky reference to me as an "old lady" or mention "people of your generation".

After the initial euphoria had worn off, my pragmatic nature had therefore delivered me back to the beginning. It didn't matter, in the end, what Dina's passport had revealed about her true age (or real name, as it happened), her childishness would always be an insurmountable barrier to passion. Ironically, I found that my own formless desires for her vanished completely over a period of a few days once I had registered that there was no longer any real constraint against acting on them, or attempting to.

Nonetheless, as an experiment, I tried to envisage what a seduction of Dina would be like (significantly, there was still no room in my imaginings for Dina to hit on me). Each variation on the theme, as it played out before me, featured the same denouement. Whatever technique I pictured myself using to draw her closer, however I made my advances, regardless of the tact with which I initiated my move, the playlet always ended with a blameless, confused girl painfully side-swiped by the change in our dynamic. And with me, sobered, mortified, and out in the cold.

I put the passport back in the scanner as if I had never seen it, and after Dina's next visit – Meadow had still not replaced the printer that one of Joopiter's associates had "borrowed" – it was gone.

໕

If you grow up on the farm, as Aubrey did, you are used to people coming and going, staying on and then departing on a whim. A big birthday bash means huddles of visitors snoring in sleeping bags the next morning on the stoep, their homes being too far away to drive back until the hangovers have worn off. Such an arrangement is barely a hardship when you have staff, and if folk don't expect variety in their meals. When we married, this continued – surveyors or other professionals passing through would be invited for a meal and then become regular drop-in visitors if we decided that they were good company.

It was only when I moved back to Cape Town after Aubrey died that I was reminded that not everyone kept an open house or enjoyed ad hoc accommodation arrangements. Little by little, as I got older, wiser, poorer, and more set in my ways, I also started to resent the upheaval that houseguests brought in their wake. My cousin broke my toaster by thoughtlessly shoving a fork inside it and never offered to replace it; precious books would get stowed in the luggage of departing visitors with a promise that they would be returned by post and a collective understanding that this would never happen.

As I downsized to smaller houses, and as fewer and fewer people came to stay, I guess I became less houseproud – not that domestic order was ever a priority for me, really. I would whiz about with a vacuum cleaner if I had invited people around for supper and try to get the matting of dog hair off the sofas, but I could only afford a domestic for one day a week.

It took Dina coming to live with me that November for me to realise the extent of the soft creep of slovenliness. Her own late mother had been a paragon of virtue when it came to a spick-and-span home, she announced. This statement caused me less grief from the implicit criticism of my slatternliness than by the comparison of her mother with me, as if we were contemporaries (which I knew by then would be a biological impossibility). I began to retrieve the old dog chews lurking under the sideboards; to separate out the towels we humans used from those I kept to collect up the woozy fledgling birds that had crashed into the windows on their inaugural flights.

Even my most prized possessions – my Linnware pottery filled with peacock feathers and porcupine quills, and my framed postcards from long-ago art exhibitions – suddenly seemed less like the contents of a tasteful Wunderkammer and more like cluttered, dusty junk. I ruthlessly picked out what I knew to be the best pieces and consigned the rest to crates I deposited in the garage of one of my sisters.

It became apparent that Dina expected meals when she came home from whatever she was doing during the day (I almost literally had to bite my tongue in an effort not to ask). I was content to oblige, substituting matzos and cheap cheese with homemade soup and wholewheat bread to try to add a few kilograms to her emaciated frame. Rather than being affronted by her presumption, as my sister rather thought I should be when I explained the set-up to her, I took quiet satisfaction from the fact that Dina did not try to ingratiate herself with me, or act like some charity case. For all anyone knew, she was simply my new – rather exotic – housemate, come to share the cottage and rent since I was struggling to make ends meet.

Every day as I tended to her small needs without acknowledgement, I asked myself repeatedly if I loved her, *how* I loved her. Like a surrogate mother? Like an older sister? Like someone with a lifetime's white guilt to assuage? Like von Aschenbach in *Death in Venice*, helplessly worshipping at the shrine of careless youth because he simply has no choice, because it is his destiny? And what would Dina do with this love if she discovered it – betray it, reward it, ignore it?

Did it make me pathetic, or abject, that I thought sometimes, in calm moments, of waiting for her through the coming years until she grew into my love for her and reached out with a grown-up but nonsexual love of her own? Living together as we grew older, friends rather than lovers. It wasn't as if I had any other offers on the table, or any prospects, so why not?

We went on in this way for several more weeks. To her credit and my slight surprise, Dina really did try to help out around the cottage. Not even once did she attempt to steer the conversation around to the return of Ganja, now a much bigger, more belligerent, tom cat who would no doubt have been able to take care of himself against the dogs. I started to enjoy having her around a great deal – but not so much that I didn't also look forward to the day when I would have the cottage back to myself. I did miss living alone, when I could wander about in just a flimsy kimono and no bra without worrying that Dina would feel I was hitting on her.

I relished the days when she messaged me that she wouldn't be coming back to the cottage for the cooked supper I was thinking of preparing, so that I could instead enjoy some crackers without having to make excuses for a pauper's plate. I noted, ruefully, that she had the manners of our generation and not the young, who my friends complained never texted to communicate revised plans.

Then Christmas came and went, and my resentful fears that she would sabotage the pleasure I always derived from planning and hosting meals for old friends proved unfounded. In fact, I ended up thoroughly ashamed of myself for having such uncharitable thoughts as I watched her jumping up unasked to serve people with more food, heard her captivating a visitor with some vignette from her colourful life, or noticed that she had snuck into the kitchen to quietly begin to tackle the mountains of washing up without asking me to help her.

"This is nice, hey?"

Dina would say it often and with sincerity, and I found myself nodding in contented agreement, sitting on the patio as the evening drew down, sharing a beer or two; or folding up the laundered sheets together with exaggerated care; or half watching some terrible show side by side on my bed late at night.

᭒

Then the parameters I had defined for my platonic affection, carefully plotted out with no regrets after I had uncovered Dina's true age, collapsed one February afternoon when I awoke with a start from a sweaty siesta. By then, caring for Dina had made me tired enough to initiate daytime naps over the weekends when I could. I felt both deeply aroused and thoroughly ashamed as I replayed over and over in a daze the dream I had just had of making fierce but tender love with her, there in my old bed.

At that moment she strolled into my bedroom without knocking, and a questioning look played over her sweet face. I felt more ashamed than if she had walked in on me watching some particularly nasty porn or snorting a line or two of coke (she was vehemently against drugs of any kind). For all that I suppose I had treated her like a potential thief or freeloader when she first moved in, never keeping much cash in the house and making sure that my pitiful bank statements were always locked away, I felt as if I were now the one guilty of a kind of betrayal.

From then on, I could not forget the dream that had ended with Dina jerking and bucking under my hands and mouth, nor could I stop replaying it in my mind, day and night. It was so real – I can't ever recall having had another so vivid – that it seemed impossible that Dina wasn't also aware of it in some way. It was too coherent, too graphic, to belong only to the world of sleep, and too all-pervading to be retained by just one mind. I came to regard it as a different kind of phenomenon altogether – a fervid conversation that our truest, deepest selves were having but that only I had been able to eavesdrop on, so far at least.

When she looked into my face now, how did Dina not know what my feral thoughts had done to her there in my bed? How could she fail to register my disgust at myself every time her physical presence forced me to relive them, before I found an excuse to leave the room? Since I did not have her permission to be intimate with her in real life, my keen sense of culpability informed me, I had no right to fantasise about her either, even unwittingly.

As a result of this dream, a dream Dina knew nothing about and that I could never mention to her, things had to change. There was no escaping the fact that this was entirely my fault, nor that this realisation brought on a further hefty dose of shame. I couldn't bear to occupy the same space as her, lost patience with her over insignificant things, and as a result she became snippy and sullen. Anyone now observing us would have thought that they were watching a demanding, unreasonable mother and her recalcitrant, brooding child. Not "daughter" or "son" however, because Dina had come home one afternoon soon after things began to deteriorate between us with a bleached flattop and her septum pierced with a heavy steel barbell – her gender was now even harder to place than before. A fragile, pretty boy or an edgy little tomboy – she seemed ready, charged, to revel in the ambiguity and in the confusion that her hybrid identity would cause in any number of situations from now on.

For the first time since she moved in, I knew I was being forced to size up a deliberate provocation.

"Yes, very nice Dina. Now no one knows who you are or how they must deal with you, and I suppose that was the intention all along. Perhaps you should think about growing up, rather?"

"How people deal with me, that's their problem, not mine. Do you have a problem with me now then Jen, is that it?"

"I don't, for Chrissakes, but you can see how this is going to make getting a job even more difficult for you now, can't you? It's just shutting down opportunities, and you don't exactly have a million offers of work as it is."

"I'd have hoped you wanted me to be an authentic version of myself. Not conform, just for some crap pay in a larney white deli somewhere."

I wasn't going to rise to this clumsy baiting just to give her the satisfaction of hearing me finally ask where she went all day, or why none of her job offers had panned out. Let alone enquire when she was going to make some gesture towards paying me rent or food money or – better still – save up for a place of her own.

Since that shocking dream, and my deep and lasting humiliation over it, this had become a most pressing, if unspoken, question for me of course. I recognised though, how completely selfish and unrealistic it was to expect that on the kind of pay she could earn – if she ever did manage to secure a job in her new, confusing iteration – she might be able to afford anywhere safe to live. I had even started wondering if I shouldn't just give Dina the money for a deposit myself so that I could reclaim my territory as well as my self-respect. Alas, we'd lived together long enough now that I had lost track of all the different places she'd told me that she had moved into, only to have to leave soon afterwards because of some threat to her wellbeing. It mattered not a jot that Dina herself seemed to be the originator of these dramas; I was sure that my beloved stray would find her way back into my home very quickly indeed if I paid for her to move out now.

Then one afternoon she was helping me unload the heavy bags of dog chow from the car and she asked in an artificially airy manner that I knew was leading us towards another confrontation: "This food then, Jen. How much does it cost to feed all those mangy dogs you have?"

I had no intention of telling her, and changed the subject promptly, but some hours later, when I was Skyping with an ex-boyfriend, Dina came dancing into the office waving the receipt from the cash and carry. Once more I was compelled to acknowledge the effort she made to respect my house and my space – when she saw that I was busy chatting, she put her finger to her lips in an exaggerated gesture of mock mischief and skulked out again. With bleak resignation, I brought the conversation to an end and steeled myself to walk into the ambush I knew Dina had prepared.

She was sitting on one of the sofas, painting her toenails with black nail varnish I hadn't seen before and pretending to scrutinise the receipt, though it had only six items on it, and she must have known them off by heart by then.

"Check this slippy. My Laaaawd. Do you know how many meals I could buy with the money you hand over to feed your dumb-ass dogs?"

"The dogs are important to me, Dina, and they were here before you came and will be here after you have gone. They're part of the family." I kept my voice even, but I could hear it wavering a little and hoped Dina wouldn't interpret this as weakness. If this was gearing up to be the fight that I hoped would precipitate her departure, I needed to stay rational and tough.

"You don't live in a house, you live in a freakin' petting zoo, and you expect me to share it with all those disgusting animals that you rescue or that must be allowed to live in the kitchen or what-what."

"They have as much right to life as we do, and they're not doing any harm. None of the animals have hurt you, Dina, have they? So I don't know what your problem is, really."

"You know what, you call out Sunette for being a crazy fake hippie, but you are just as bad, Jen. Yes, you are. Wasting money on animals when people everywhere are suffering."

"The animals are rescue dogs, and they didn't ask to be born. They don't have choices. Only humans have choices. The dogs all give me huge amounts of pleasure, and feeding them and giving them a good home is a small price to pay for that. It's my money, isn't it? That I work hard for? And I try to do the right thing in lots of other ways that you don't necessarily know anything about."

Though I knew I had argued her into a corner, I felt no satisfaction. Robbed of the ability to continue down this particular track by a statement she could not refute, Dina now tried another approach, one not worthy of her in her present circumstances, as well she knew.

Her discomfort showed in the way that she wrinkled her nose a little bit as she spat out, "Loving animals. That's a luxury only you rich people can afford. It makes you feel better when you go about ignoring actual people like me who need your help."

"You know that's not true, Dina. I have seen with my own eyes how people in the townships make huge sacrifices to look after their pets sometimes." I was on shakier ground here but thought there had to be a kernel of truth in this.

"No, no, no, no, no, no, NO! You know this man on the SPCA advert? Some black dude there in the squatter camp with his arm around his filthy cat? This is not me. I hate your fucking furry friends and all the other, ag, these stupid mice and beetles and whatsoever you let in this place. I kill them when I get a chance. You know that, right?"

I had had my suspicions for a while about the way Dina might be treating the smaller occupants of the menagerie behind my back, although she had established a respectful rapprochement with all the dogs almost as soon as she moved in. But really there was nothing now to be gained from interrogating her about this unlikely revelation.

You are a clever miss, but really not that good at the mind games people have to play in order to find an accommodation and live together. I'm not even that good at them, history has shown, nor do I want to make an effort again. That's why I have lived alone for so long and am about to do so again.

Dina didn't immediately register that she had said the one thing that was guaranteed to get her ejected from the cottage. Since animals were, honestly and instinctively, of no consequence to her, she was wholly unable to perceive how they might be of very great value to someone else.

Once she caught on to this, and as I set about calmly proposing a schedule for her departure, she backtracked furiously. Of *course* she hadn't actually meant that she hated the dogs – I had seen for myself how they loved her and made a fuss of her when she came home. And *seriously*, how was she going to catch the birds that let themselves in through the open windows or the bugs that ran around on the floors, and then kill them all? It was just a figure of speech. And she appreciated, she really did, I knew she did, all that I had done for her.

I told her that I couldn't risk it – a second pretext for eviction that she had had to hear in the space of just a few months. It was now patently clear, I told her, that she did truly hate some of the animals – yes, my friends – and how could I trust and share my home with someone who felt that way? At my use of the word *friends*, she narrowed her hazel eyes into a look of purest contempt, and I hoped that the dream of us together in the damp and tangled sheets would never bother me again. I now let her take her own parting shot. I owed her that at the very least.

"You are so up yourself that I don't even think you know how to love anyone anymore. You front all this caring for the pets and the other animals, and make this massive show of being the good person. But who do you love, Jen, you stupid bitch? And who loves you, come to that? Nobody does."

ℭℑ

The fight left us both shattered, and we went off early to our respective bedrooms at either end of the house with no attempt at even a "good night" from either of us. The next morning, I was resolved to follow through, regardless of any efforts at supplication or conciliation on Dina's part, but to my amazement, she meekly handed over my house keys and told me quietly that she had arranged to go back and live with her brother in Khayelitsha for the time being. She looked much, much sadder than I felt, and on the way out of the front door, she bent and buried her face in Toad's thick, wolfy mane for a several long seconds. I helped her load all her gear into the car that was waiting outside for her, and we agreed, without meeting each other's eyes, that we would no doubt bump into each other again soon.

In one brief, reckless moment after she and her brother had pulled away, I allowed myself to consider the possibility that Dina's apparent grief at parting was because she really did love me in her own fashion after all, and that this was something concrete to build a future on together, once life had forced her to grow up a little. Then I shook my head in irritation at my profound stupidity. Holding on to such ridiculous notions would leave me exposed and vulnerable if she ever reappeared in my life. Before I headed out to work, I blocked her number on my phone for my own protection.

I had a full day at work at the newspaper and some obligatory socialising to do afterwards, so it was already beginning to get dark when I let myself back into the cottage. During the day, I had continued to wonder if I might have lost something of value by asking Dina to leave. Compartmentalisation was a habit – or perhaps a defence mechanism – that I had perfected over the years for reckoning with emotional upheavals, and it had always served me very well. I was sure it would do so over again, once I could get Dina's stinging rebukes from the night before out of my mind, as well as the sound of my condescension as I fortified my defences against her.

Adjoining the kitchen was a breakfast nook with a narrow, cushioned window seat. I made myself comfortable there with a tub of cottage cheese and a couple of guilty-secret cheese grillers I had picked up on the drive home. As was their habit, the dogs all piled into the small space under the table to take their turns begging for a scrap of the gloriously greasy sausage, then slunk off to their blankets in a corner of the living room. I could hear their friendly squabbling and harrumphing sighs as they picked out the best spots for the night, and then took their leisurely time settling down.

I carefully scooped up a large tussock moth that was flittering along the inside window sill, his draped black-and-white wings looking like a miniature cape of regal ermine. I deposited him gently outside the kitchen door on a handy oleander bush, and swiftly closed up again before he was bewitched back inside by the tractor beam of the kitchen's glow. He left me a gift, a dusting of powdery scales on my hands.

Across the kitchen linoleum, and coming always at this time of evening from I don't know where, an enormous black-and-white beetle ardently pursued a slightly smaller version of himself, both of them making the very tiniest of pattering noises as they skittered here and there before disappearing into a cupboard under the sink. A cricket began an experimental warming up for the night's performance from its cranny behind the recycling bin in the same spot.

I then did the rounds of the other windows before shutting up the cottage for the night, collecting up one by one in both my hands and then freeing outside the various graceful, spiky mantids and dappled moths that always found some way to get inside at dusk. By morning, the smaller ones that I didn't manage to rescue were normally reduced to a pair of disembodied wings by the voracious, semi-tame geckos that patrolled close to the two lamps I left on for security.

I took my tiny glass of grappa into the living room and began to settle into my favourite deep armchair to read. Before I found my place in my book, though, I rose again to gather up a couple of massive shongololo millipedes that were patrolling across the rugs and dumped their coiled bodies out of the dog flap and into the soft rain that was just starting.

Above me now, in the space under the roof tiles, I could hear the erratic scampering of mice and on the roof itself the scrapings of the pigeons as they tried to gain purchase on a good roosting spot for the night. With the house drawing in on itself for the night, the swarms of ghostly bugs that collected outside on the windowpanes were arriving in their hundreds to worship at its illumination, rapping out the faintest tattoo as they busied themselves meeting, mating and consuming each other, a drama that repeated itself every night throughout the summer months.

❦

A solifuge is a fearsome-looking animal, an apparent cross between a spider and a scorpion that is actually not related to either, I'm informed. She stands off alone in her own biological realm, armed with terrifyingly large, hooked mouthparts that make her look like something from a science-fiction film. The cottage has a healthy population of them, and at night they can be heard shuffling around under the furniture and chasing off the smaller lizards that wait under the lamps for winged insects to crash into the hot bulbs and fall to the ground.

The solifuge that always joins me at my reading chair is huge, even by the standard of her large species, and she would not fit comfortably in my hand if I were foolish enough to attempt to place her there. One moment I am curling up and trying to find a position that does not place any strain on my creaking hips and the next, she will be there on the chair's armrest, having climbed up the fabric at the side with ease.

Even though she has been coming at night for a number of years now to keep me company when I occupy this spot, I always take a minute or two to admire her topaz body, seemingly glowing from within in the pool of light made by the reading lamp; the numerous fine hairs all over her fat abdomen and delicate thorax, and the sturdier bristles guarding her monstrous jaws. Her two beadlike intelligent and enquiring eyes are positioned high and central on her head, making her seem as if she were squinting slightly in concentration.

Whether I read for three minutes or three hours into the night, she will wait there with me until I unwind myself to leave. Then she will also hop down and rush for her refuge under the bookshelf before I switch off the lights and leave the room. Of all the animals in the house and garden – including the frogs in the tiny pond, the harmless mole snake one morning on the lawn, and the skinks behind the compost heap – it had naturally been this solifuge that had most disgusted and horrified Dina. She always refused to stay in the living room after its nightly appearance at the chair, and would regularly ask me, demand of me, that the creature be removed to somewhere far away, or that she be allowed to donner it to death with one of my heavy gardening clogs.

On this night I don't open my book immediately but gaze in renewed wonder at my solifuge, my old friend. I let my mind drift out to the handsome little bats I know are jinking above the garden now, to the spectral barn owl that I see occasionally on my gate post if I come home late at night, to the flights of termites that the steady rain will conjure up soon, to the little rainbow-tailed guppy fish breeding contentedly in the modest water feature below the patio.

I consider the varied procession of bird species that take their turns at the bird table and seed dispenser in the garden throughout the course of every day: the waxbills, weavers and sparrows, the pigeons and doves scavenging on the ground beneath, as well as the jewelled sunbirds that occasionally deign to use the sugar-water container I rigged up for them.

I make a note in my phone calendar to check the dogs for ticks over the weekend so that I can flick the apple-seed bodies of these disreputable characters down the toilet bowl in the hope that they will end up safe someplace where they can live out the rest of their lives without troubling my pack of hounds. My dogs, my five babies.

Each little life is mine to cherish and to care for. Every time I rescue, feed, protect or simply admire one of these animals that has made my home their home, I feel that I am calling up and repaying part of a debt that I could neither describe nor quantify. I had made a solemn compact with nature when I became a young farmer's wife, a contract to avoid harming her creatures if I could. It has always seemed to me an unfair apportionment of benefits – my notional pledge to aid and assist them all as they go about their business in return for the limitless reward that the sum of daily encounters with them delivers.

And *these* are my friends, if I tally up the joy that they ceaselessly bring, and the solace, and never find either lacking. Everything I give to them is in the form of the simplest of gestures – all they give me back in return weaves a new shining thread into the fabric of what is by any measure a happy existence.

Who is to judge if my affection is worth any less than that being found, traded, rejected, and forsaken all across the human world at the same time? It is my love, and it defines me, and it will never be lost. And that, this evening, is enough.

Virga

The bats had begun their swooping, figure-of-eight flights under the rafters of her house on the bluff when Toni finally heard the procession of distant cars labouring up the hillside below. She went out through the wide, timber-framed double doorway that opened the A-frame to the elements at this time of year and stood barefoot on the slatted wooden balcony as dusk descended. From here she could see the far-off headlights of the vehicle in front strafing the trunks of trees either side of the twisting route up to the top of the escarpment, then disappearing behind the huge, elemental mounds of boulders that lined the way.

The energy-sapping heat had now deserted the day just as the insistent, metallic zipping calls of the male weaver birds in the fronds of the palms planted in the lodge's grounds had ceased. She sighed, took a sip of her tepid drink, and braced herself for the tiresome evening ahead. The musky tang of wood smoke drifting across from the kitchen, her favourite smell in the entire world, failed to soothe her tonight. Toni wondered – a dull disappointment tinged with ennui – if her time here was coming to an end. It seemed that she could no longer summon succour from the calm of the twilight, the quiet chatter of her staff as they went about preparing for the guests' arrival, and the tentative zings of the nocturnal cicadas heralding the approach of evening.

The Italian film crew had been late leaving the airport at Dar es Salaam. She shut her eyes in frustration as she reflected on the inevitability of this and of the complaints she would no doubt soon have to field about African inefficiency. In fact, her head guide, Phillips, had managed to contact her from the airport terminal during the delay to explain that it was the group's many boxes of equipment – including supplies of coffee beans, tins of tomatoes, and other consumables – that were causing the hold-up, since they had brought along with them far more luggage than the six light aircraft they had chartered could safely transport. After conferring with the pilot who appeared to be in charge, as well as the local handling agent, Phillips had apparently explained to the group that an arrangement would be made for some of the less important or valuable supplies to come up to the camp in a day or two. It was during the Italians' resulting heated discussions concerning what constituted their critical supplies and what could be delayed, that Phillips had managed to slip away to explain to Toni on the phone why they would be late.

Phillips was a resourceful man, which was why he was the head guide, and a brave one – which was why he could confront these guests and their problems, when a younger, less-experienced person might well have panicked and agreed to demands that simply could not be met. She therefore doubted that there was any other solution to the problem, but already, before they had even arrived, this collection of characters had created a situation that held the potential to deteriorate into a crisis. Toni had already decided to get someone with authority from the group to sign the printed waiver she had cobbled together on the laptop an hour ago. This document would ensure that there were no misunderstandings about why there had been a delay in the transportation of the crates of supplies, or who would take responsibility for the safe delivery of the goods (not to mention who would be paying for the consignment to come up to the lodge). Only then would she contact the agent in town to release the food boxes from the office at the airstrip for their delivery to the filming location. *So it begins.*

Another sip of drink, to steel her against the objections and necessary explanations when she produced the waiver that would absolve her and her company of any responsibility for the provisions. The group had flown directly into the country, and had probably only glimpsed the few kilometres of tarred road surrounding the airport as they landed at Dar, since visibility tended to be low at this time of year. They could have no idea that to bring the food up by truck would take the best part of two days due to the parlous state of the roads and the certain un-roadworthiness of the vehicle that would be hired to deliver the crates. She had a map ready in case she had to explain this to them as if they were small, petulant children. Long experience had taught her that tourists who brought their own coffee beans, just like those who insisted on interrogating the cook about accommodating their various allergies, would not be easily mollified. And it was often the wealthiest clients who turned out to be the most parsimonious, too. Consequently, she felt sure that she would have a fight on her hands to convince whoever held the purse strings to finance additional flights for their precious provisions, rather than paying only a little less for delivery by truck. And she couldn't help but hope that, in the event that a decision was made to transport the goods up by road against her advice, the rented truck would have a spill on the potholed route, and that all the exotic contents of the boxes would disappear into the local villages and settlements, as if by magic.

While she had been taking her shower, soon after having received the call from Phillips, another thought occurred to her that exacerbated her foul mood. The arrangement was supposed to be that the film crew would spend each day out in the bush filming, but would return every evening to the lodge. This made sense from an organisational point of view and meant that they were, for all intents and purposes, simply guests, like any other. The fact that they had brought along their own supplies of food now strongly suggested that they would ask instead to stay out in fly camps for at least part of their visit, which meant organising a cook, camp dogsbody, drivers, and armed escort to accompany them the whole time they were away from the lodge. Furthermore, they had insisted on the provision of a small fridge for their exclusive use for the duration of their stay but had never explained its purpose.

The group had finally taken off very late for the 30-minute hop to their destination; the vehicles bringing them to the lodge from the airstrip in the wide valley to the west would have raced the pink sun flattening itself against the horizon but still, the very last section of the drive would now be undertaken after nightfall. Strictly speaking, this was against lodge policy, since the risk of a car hitting a large animal on the road was high, but now there was no choice. The sound of all the vehicles would scare off every elephant, hippo, and giraffe for hectares around, anyway, she was sure. The convoy would therefore arrive after an exhilarating sprint from the airstrip through the swiftly cooling open grasslands, then a slow climb between rocky outcrops from where they would still to be able to make out the long, low shadows of the crocodiles that clustered on the sandbanks of the river, and finally a series of loops through the trees along the top of the escarpment in the dark. A grand beginning, at least, to their laughable adventure.

Toni's resentment towards them was irrational at this point – petty and premature. She knew this, and her acknowledgement of her unprofessional attitude was simply further feeding her annoyance. Although this was the first film crew she had hosted in her five years as a lodge manager, she knew Italians a little, since her father – an embarrassing, perpetually drunk playboy – was one. Through friends in the same line of work, she had also heard horror stories of the inconveniences and dramas that filmmakers had caused at other places. She was supposed to be on her scheduled leave by now, but the boss of her company had begged her to stay on to facilitate a successful trip for these important guests – the first of what he hoped would be an influx of big-spending TV documentary-makers to his chain of upmarket destinations across the region.

The "film company" seemed to comprise a spoilt young film-studies graduate, some of his unemployed dilettante friends, and a collection of technicians he had hired for three weeks. A few days previously, one of them had sent her a long email detailing the historical context to their "journey of discovery into the past", as they predictably called it. Presumably, this was the same nonsense they had used to entice gullible backers for their enterprise and that they would later use to drum up interest in the finished product. *At least it wasn't yet more packs of wild dog chasing and ripping apart yet more antelope.*

She had scanned the message in case it contained anything relevant to her work of keeping them entertained and happy, but it didn't really. It simply explained, in florid but quite acceptable English, how Mauro – the soon-to-be boy-wonder director of the film – had heard or read the tale of the two "native" manservants of a pair of soldier brothers in the war. She couldn't recall now which war this was, nor the nationality of the brothers. The African servants had conducted themselves with bravery during a skirmish or something? As a result of the courage of these two characters, the officer brothers had managed to effect a lucky escape from the field of battle, though the servants themselves, naturally enough, had both been mortally wounded.

Toni wasn't sure if they had been bayoneted or shot or blown up; there was something lost in translation in the email that led her to believe they may even have been hurt in some pathetically mundane way. Before they succumbed to their injuries, the hapless pair had managed to extract from their young masters a promise that their bodies would be taken to their home district for a proper burial – which the brothers did once the war was over. Only this aspect of the story had managed to make an impression on her; the solicitude of the soldiers seemed to belong to a very different era altogether.

Mauro had done some detective work or – more likely – had paid a researcher to do it for him, and had lit upon a trail of evidence that strongly suggested that the two brave natives were buried somewhere along the long ridge to the east of the lodge. He had raised enough money to hire a crew for three weeks to record him looking for the burial site, after which they would all be compelled to return to Rome. In their time in the area, they hoped to locate the grave (or graves), get some footage of the surroundings and the wildlife, and capture Mauro doing some pieces to camera about the nameless, faceless locals who made such a sacrifice in the wars of their colonial masters. If there was time, the whole outfit would then fly back to Dar to capture some contemporary local-colour footage.

Toni had to admit that her disagreeable frame of mind had perhaps led her to imagine the bit about the post-colonial revisionism that would weave its thread through the narrative, but she did suspect that the finished film would be sure to show up the young filmmaker in a sympathetic, woke light. She also already had a bet on with her senior staff that the crew would ask Phillips and the other guides to engineer an elephant or hippo charge in the event that nothing of that nature took place spontaneously while they were filming, just to add excitement to their footage.

❦

In fact – and this was the dilemma that was making her feel mean-spirited about the whole enterprise, she supposed – Toni was pretty sure that completely by accident, she had already discovered where the graves were situated when she had been on the trail of an elusive animal that she'd always wanted to see just recently.

She had been working at various lodges and tented campsites in the Tanzanian bush for five years now, so there were few animals that could excite or surprise her anymore. But one evening, a few months ago, Islam – one of the younger and keener guides – casually mentioned at supper that he thought he had briefly spotted a pangolin under a lightning-struck tree on the east ridge during that evening's game drive. Toni had taken a car out by herself in the crystalline dawn of the following day to try to locate this most secretive and mysterious of animals. She had found some scratch marks in the dust at the place Islam had pin-pointed and spotted a strange spoor, which she assumed was caused by the drag of the pangolin's heavy, armour-plated tail, but that was all. She then used the ladder fixed to the side of the jeep to clamber onto its roof in order to try to see if there were any other signs of the creature in the surrounding area. This was when she had noticed some large, flat half-buried stones placed in a surprisingly orderly manner among the leaf litter under a spreading fig tree nearby, so she climbed back down in order to investigate.

Although some of the massive, slate-like slabs had shifted and tipped at an angle either side, what she eventually concluded that she was looking at were two low, rectangular platforms of rocks that could only have been arranged by human hands. At the time, she had decided that they had to be the graves of large dogs, probably placed there by a hunter during the time when the area was too full of tsetse flies to attract anyone but the keenest of sportsmen.

Only once she'd read the recent email explaining the purpose of the film-crew's visit in detail did she ask herself if a pair of human corpses, preserved for a time while a ragged war had played itself out, could have been interred there instead. Certainly, there was something still and strange – though far from sinister – about the secluded spot, quite unlike the busy, noisy activity of the bush around the lodge. With no clients in the camp that morning who might need her, she had stopped under the deep, cave-like shadows of the enormous tree for several moments to take in the view across great distances of tawny plain towards the swiftly rising new sun, and to attune her ears to the soft, secret sounds of the waking bush. By six in the morning, she was usually too occupied with her many routine and not-so-routine tasks to appreciate the soft, plangent calls of the little doves patrolling the ground under the lodge's tree canopy with their tiny, bobbing steps. Or to make out the confiding twitters and muffled crashes of a troop of far-off monkeys as they started searching for fruits in the riverside vegetation below the dining area for the day.

The lodge guests rarely missed an opportunity to tell her what an idyllic life she led, surrounded by this unspoilt paradise, and away from the stresses of modern life. The reality was rather different. Toni couldn't recall the last time she had been able to take time off to accompany the guides out on a game drive or routine patrol, or to break away from the camp as she had done that morning to seek the refreshment of solitude.

This spot was very different from the bush around the camp that she knew so well – it was impossible not to be struck by its singular lack of birdsong, the absence of the usual furtive rustlings of small creatures in the undergrowth, and the constant tumble of falling leaves. She might have expected the loud flaps of a large hornbill to explode from a branch above her head, or to hear the alarm calls of a family of baboons disturbed in their foraging.

Instead, Toni was struck by the almost complete absence of any sounds or signs of the animals that she knew ought to be there. There was just the lulling drone of a million insects, near and further away, a single, complex humming accord composed from the intermittent, lazy buzz of the waking flies, the scraping chirrs of grasshoppers in the brittle grass, and above it all the high-pitched, monotonous one-note zithering of the day cicadas. The noise seemed to reverberate and compound itself to hold her in a soporific trance – she found she had to fight an urge to simply slide behind the wheel of the car and drift off to sleep.

Toni shook herself out of her inertia and into a consideration of the tasks that would fill the rest of her day. A shred of something long lost was urging itself into her consciousness, though. What *was* this? "No whit less still nor lonely fair" … She didn't know where this lovely phrase had come from – so unlike the usual practical thoughts that occupied all of her time – but she couldn't rid herself of it as she drove back to camp. She would Google it as soon as she had a moment's quiet and the internet was working.

Yet by the time that precious combination of circumstances was available to Toni some days later she had forgotten the words entirely.

༄

Toni really hadn't decided yet what she would do with this crucial piece of evidence concerning the graves that she had stumbled upon purely by chance and that she was certain no one else in camp knew about. Would it be unkinder to mention it tonight, before Mauro and his team had even started filming their quest, or to contrive to withhold any hint of the information until she decided that they were either worthy of it or their time was almost up? A chance existed that they might find it for themselves perhaps, but the ridge was several kilometres long and only by viewing the burial site – if indeed that was what it was – from an elevated vantage point and at a particular angle, might it be possible to discern the giveaway shapes put there by human agency.

It bothered Toni to have such control over these people, whom she was yet to meet but already actively disliked. It troubled her even more to think that she could be tempted to do something spiteful to thwart them, if she chose.

She roused herself, eased on some presentable flip flops, and left her house to greet the guests she could now see wearily climbing the shallow steps to the lodge's reception area. The larger group of three men and two women was just how she imagined a film crew would look. Judging by their affectedly jaded demeanours and defiant assortment of slightly worn T-shirts, cargo pants and board shorts, it was immediately clear that they had worked in Africa before and were anxious not to be mistaken for first-timers – hence the choice of clothing in every colour shade except khaki. Four other men, however, were carefully dressed in new, expensive safari-wear: beige waistcoats with lots of tiny pockets; ungainly, uncomfortable-looking heavy boots; freshly laundered tan trousers; and a discreet trimming, here and there, of zebra skin print.

Two among this quartet immediately caught her eye and piqued her interest: a tall young man with tightly curled black hair she was already sure was Mauro stood slightly apart from everyone else, while a much older, somewhat shorter man had his hairy, tanned arm draped awkwardly around Mauro's slim shoulders. His mouth was deep within the boy's unruly locks as he whispered something conspiratorially in the younger man's ear, and he was rearranging his own dramatic mane of very long, thick grey hair with his free hand. The guarded, slightly embarrassed way that Mauro peered about him while keeping his head perfectly still to listen to the older man's urgings made her loosen her grip on the comforting assumptions she'd made about this group of guests. By the moment, Mauro was starting to look less and less like the entitled, spoilt scion of some wealthy family – which was the personal history she had concocted for him. He was clearly neither in charge of this strange assortment of people who had been drawn together to help him realise his dream, nor was he even remotely happy to be there.

☙

The evening had not turned out to be the ordeal Toni had predicted. The members of the professional film crew kept themselves apart, smoking and talking among themselves mostly, so she was able to focus her attention on the four other members of the party. Using that sixth sense that made her so good at her work, and watching closely the interactions between the boy, his father, and the two young friends, Toni came to understand that the driving force behind the entire project, and its likely sole financial backer, was the father, Alessio. Mauro just appeared to be reluctantly along for the ride.

Toni had already observed Alessio organising those around him with a quiet word and a small pat on the back. Or he would stand slightly apart, raising his leonine head to cast about him with a slow, appraising gaze, as if to reassure himself – like a vain priest at the pulpit – that his entire flock was in view and at his command, and that all was therefore well in the world.

Curiously, though, Alessio would self-consciously and deliberately defer to his son every time it was necessary to make a decision or to discuss some organisational matter. She could see that it was requiring an agonising, almost physical effort on the part of the father to cede authority to the disinclined son. An elaborate, and so far indecipherable game of family politics was playing out here at the lodge, as it must have done on the journey out and, even before that, during the planning of the whole elaborate project. Despite herself and her disinclination to get involved in the lives of clients, Toni couldn't help but wonder what, exactly, was going on between the sternly affable and instinctively commanding parent and his ill-at-ease, bashfully sincere son – who seemed to resemble him so little in manners or attitude.

Several times during the course of that first evening, she had found herself alone with either Alessio or Mauro when they had separately left the group and followed her on a turn by the bar or to the office. Alessio flirted with her in a dutiful, mechanical manner during their exchanges, in a way that would have been a bit insulting if she had given it any thought. Mauro chased after her like a desperate puppy when the time came to check over the legal waiver on her desk; she felt a little squeamish about the power his father obviously held over him and that he was so eager to escape. *I know that feeling well enough.*

҂

The next morning produced a new, confusing development. Young Junior, the night-watchman, had come to her house before dawn and had knocked softly at her door as she was getting dressed. Something about his distressed agitation, and that he had never before disturbed her in this way, made her usher him in. As she brushed her hair and teeth, he told her through the crack she left open in the bathroom door that soon after everyone had gone to bed and he was making his rounds, he was sure that he heard a movement between two of the huge rondavels that were arranged a little way back along the lip of the escarpment, rooms which comprised the guest accommodation.

He went to investigate, he said, expecting to disturb a bushbuck that had recently taken up residence in the garden of the lodge.

However he was sure – here Young Junior looked at the ground and picked at a scab on his elbow – that one or more of the guests had been moving quietly between the rooms, which were placed some thirty metres from each other for the sake of privacy. This was strictly forbidden, and indeed after supper the previous evening, Toni had given her little spiel about the regulations that were enforced at the camp for the safety of the guests and staff. Staying inside your accommodation after dark and summoning help, if necessary, by ringing a large bell provided in each room for that purpose was principal among these. She had explained, as she always did to a new influx of clients, that some years previously, a woman had walked across to her daughter's room in the night to bring her the malaria tablet the teenager had forgotten to take at supper. Even though the guides had only finished accompanying the guests to their rooms some twenty minutes previously, the mother had chanced upon a leopard on the path and had been very lucky not to have been attacked. This story, which happened to be true, always impressed the guests in the manner intended, and there had been no repeat of the episode until now.

She managed to extract from Young Junior the numbers of the rondavels concerned and asked him if he had approached the guests to let them know that they were placing themselves in grave danger by wandering the pathways at night. Again, he looked about him but didn't meet her eyes: no, he had thought it best not to get into any kind of discussion with them in the middle of the night and felt it better if Toni dealt with it now. Fair enough, she concurred.

Toni wanted to raise the matter immediately after breakfast, in order to impress upon the culprits the seriousness of their behaviour. Aware of the potential for embarrassment, however, she was anxious only to confront the guests involved, rather than create a scene in front of the whole group. So she made her way to the reception area to confirm with Constance, the staff member who had checked in the guests the previous night, which people had been placed in rooms 11 and 12. She was taken aback to find it was Alessio and his son – she had assumed that Young Junior had witnessed a tryst taking place between a female member of the film crew and one of Mauro's friends, perhaps. She noted from the signing-in book that the two men had different surnames, which was far from unusual, of course, and also that Alessio had "Doctor" appended to his name. She had heard him called *professori* a few times in the course of the previous evening, but had assumed this to be simply an admission of his senior status and authority within the group. Her own father used to joke that anyone in Italy who had done a fortnight's evening course in basic plumbing could call themselves "Doctor".

Toni also noted that while Mauro lived in Rome, Alessio had given Berlin as his home town. Again, she was perfectly well able to see how they might live in different countries – after all, she and her own father had done so virtually her entire life – but then she cast her mind back to the previous evening and tried to recall at what point it had emerged that the two were related. She was still puzzling over this when she met Phillips, Islam, and Juma for the daily guide conference and asked them the same question, then asked it one more time when Jephter and Mary, the other senior staff members, joined them. It turned out that while no one on the film crew had corrected her or the staff when they had alluded to the paternal relationship between the Alessio and Mauro, at no time had any of the Italians actually said anything to confirm it. Juma, the most cosmopolitan of the senior staff, finally said what everyone else was now thinking about the nature of the relationship between the two men. Mary, the least worldly by some measure, ostentatiously spat in the dust as she left the office once the discussion was over.

Toni joined the guests as they were finishing up their buffet breakfast, curious to watch the interactions between them all so that she could try to verify the newfound suspicion that was at that very instant fanning out through the staff quarters. They had not had any openly gay clients stay at the lodge before – the fact of Tanzania having a large Muslim population definitely militated against this. When she had worked on her stepfather's fazenda in Brazil at the start of her career, she had become aware of the power of the pink tourist dollar and the growing importance of catering to gay clients – but she was pretty sure that it would be a long time before most African nations would provide a welcoming destination for this subset of visitors.

Once again at breakfast, Alessio was dividing his fulsome, slightly unsavoury (as it seemed now to her) attention between Mauro, whom he sat next to with his seat turned around so that he faced him directly as he spoke, and the wider group. When he held off his private conversation with his young companion, he would raise his head in that regal, self-satisfied manner and regard the collection of people he had gathered at his command, narrowing his eyes slightly as his focus shifted along the table. For all his well-groomed, expensive sheen there was something disreputable about the man – a person you would not want as an adversary if a business deal went bad, and definitely not a man you would want homing in on your just-adult child in a sexual manner. Without making it obvious that she was doing so, she continued to scrutinise the two men as she briefed everyone for the day ahead.

"Guys, guys. Can I have your attention one moment please? *Grazie mille.*" Slowly, the five members of the crew; the two young, indistinguishable friends; Mauro; and Alessio paused in their animated conversations, and with varying degrees of attention, listened to her announcements while picking at the remains of their fruit platters, sweaty salami and cheese.

"So, yes. Today we start your exciting hunt, and my team and I want you to know just how thrilled we are to be part of this amazing adventure." At this there was a smattering of applause from the staff, all lined up along the walls of the dining room for this first briefing.

"It's a whole new ball game for us, and even though I know some of you have been in Africa before" – here she nodded at the film crew collected in a casual knot at the far end of the table – "it's really important that we are all on the same page regarding how to make a success of your trip and send you all back safe and well and with a great film in the can!" Although she had a professional obligation to deliver a pep talk liberally dosed with such expressions of faked enthusiasm, Toni was surprised and encouraged to discover that she was actually beginning to be caught up in the novelty of the enterprise, and that as she spoke her jaded appetite for the project was reviving a little.

Toni looked at Alessio as she went on, and observed how his gaze dropped and he started fiddling with his discreetly expensive watch as she continued. "Last night I told you how critical it is that you stay in your rooms after dark, *si*? In fact, last night we had a visitor to the camp, a large puff adder, and one of our deadliest snakes, and if one of you had wandered about and met this guy then your quest here would have been over even before it began. So. *Allora*. I want you to pay special attention to all the safety instructions that you are given now so that we can continue to avoid any problems." She felt sure that this information, untrue though it was this time, had had the desired effect. Alessio looked sideways at Mauro from underneath his flamboyantly bushy white eyebrows, and she could have sworn that the boy smirked very slightly. Her staff nodded gently in appreciation of her imagination and tact.

"My job is to oversee all your practical arrangements and to try and make sure that there are no hitches. I will therefore remain in camp most of the time to take care of organising, *logistica*, and Phillips and his team will be with you in the bush for the whole time of your stay. Within reason, you can ask them to take you any place and to assist you in any way – with lifting stuff, moving stuff and so forth. But. And I want to be most clear on this. When you are out on the cars, Phillips here is in charge, no question, and you must, *must*, do as he says instantly if he asks you to, no matter how odd the request might seem to you at the time. He is taking care of you and making sure you come to no harm. That is his job. I don't care if you have just set up the best shot in the whole world. If he says to jump in the vehicle you do that, pronto. Agreed?"

She was aware that she had probably overstepped the mark somewhat in her efforts to make sure there was no repetition of the previous night's clandestine rule-breaking, and essayed a little joke against herself to compensate for the strange mood that she sensed was settling over the company. "I know that you are thinking probably, we pay all this money to come here and now we are treated a little bit like children by this tiny bossy woman. Well, let me tell you, it is a major headache for all concerned if one of you sits on a scorpion or something, and really, I am just trying to avoid a great deal of paperwork and administrative stress for myself. Plus, if one of you gets carried out of here in a body bag, I would have to dismiss Phillips, and we are all pretty fond of him."

The mood lightened, as she had hoped it would, and she handed over to Phillips and Juma, who would plan the day with the group by going over maps, then get them and their equipment, plus the coolboxes of filled rolls, muffins and drinks, out of the camp before it got uncomfortably hot. She beckoned Mauro to accompany her to her office and noted that as he got up to join her, Alessio also stood and made as if to move out from behind the table, then reconsidered and sat down. Again, that little pat on the back. Reassuring or patronising, she couldn't tell.

Mauro stepped inside the small, neat office as she pulled out a typed, laminated list of phone numbers from a drawer so that they could try to liaise with the handling agent in Dar.

"Was it really a serpent that was in the camp last night? For definite? How do you know?"

"We have two night-watchmen. These guys are super observant and very knowledgeable about the animals that can come into camp when it gets dark. Also, in the past, poachers would move around the area at night sometimes, but not now. One guard saw that a big snake had been between two of the huts, 11 and 12 I think, only a very short while after you all went off to bed. We sweep all the dirt around the huts and paths while you are at supper so that we can check for spoor, for prints, the morning after, but in this case, the night-watchman actually saw the snake."

"So even in the camp we need to be careful?"

"Even in the camp. And especially after dark. All kinds of things on the prowl …"

Toni gave him what she hoped was a slightly ambiguous look, so that he might read as little, or as much, into this remark as he cared to. Then they got down to the business of trying to figure out what to do with the crates of food that had been left in Dar. Toni ventured that she hoped, really, *really*, hoped that all the food left at the coast was dried or in cans, because dealing with the illegal importation of rotten hunks of Asiago cheese or pancetta was not something she relished.

Mauro allowed Toni to lead him towards the conclusion that there was no hurry to move supplies just yet, and that the goods – non-perishable, it seemed – could remain in Dar for at least another week. If it became obvious that the crew needed to ramp up their search efforts and start fly camping, they could revisit the idea of moving the supplies from the coast later. Mauro was so manifestly pleased that he had successfully tackled some logistical aspect of the project himself that she felt inclined to ask him to tell her a little more about how he had come to be part of this odd trip and, if possible, make some innocent enquiries as to what Dr Orsi's role in it all might be. But at that moment, Phillips knocked at the open door to say that they were ready to start loading up for the first reccy trip, and could she come to help them with checking the drinks and lunch packs to go on the cars.

✧

That had been a number of days ago. Since then, there had been some small-scale alarms as the team set about locating their objective: one of the moping friends had scraped his head on a branch leaning out of a window as the cars raced along a little-used track and, bored by the whole enterprise already, had wanted to be flown home. Toni talked him out of that by flirting with him shamelessly as she dressed his small wound. Then one of the camera crew turned out to be a vegetarian and objected to being offered an omelette with rice for supper twice in one week.

And one somewhat stranger incident happened when a member of the housekeeping staff went to see if it was necessary to restock the small drinks' fridge that had been placed in Alessio's room and found it to be full of medical equipment. Toni went to investigate and discovered unused syringes in sealed plastic bags, packets of scalpel blades, and tiny bottles of reagents. This, coupled with the conviction now shared by everyone that the older man was Mauro's lover, led to some general concern about his possible HIV status and its repercussions for the staff. She was swiftly able to dispel these, even though she herself remained extremely curious about the purpose of the fridge's contents.

Then one night just over a week later, the convoy arrived late in camp, just as the kerosene lanterns were being distributed along the pathways to guide the guests to their rooms after dark. Mauro bounded up the steps and took her hands in his. With palpable relief mixed with excitement, and abandoning temporarily the English that they had all been using for communication, he told her that they had just found two strange shapes made out of rocks on the escarpment. He described their position in such a way that Toni knew instantly that the team had finally of their own accord, stumbled on what might turn out to be the graves they sought. Phillips came up behind the boy, grinning with pleasure, and confirmed all that had been said. They would set off early tomorrow to record a re-enactment of the discovery when the light was better and spend the rest of the day filming around the site and doing the scripted pieces to camera.

It was impossible not to get caught up in the sense of excitement and noisy vindication – especially since she and Mauro had set aside the morning of the following day to begin making expensive arrange-ments to fly up the crates still stored in Dar so that the fly camping could start in a few days, if necessary. Now they wouldn't have to do this, and as the drinks flowed and the tension that had been building swiftly dissipated, only Alessio seemed less than overjoyed that they had maybe found their objective. That evening for the first time he looked old, tired, and alienated somehow, and excused himself to go to bed early after he had made only a perfunctory effort to join in the celebrations. In place of the previous bluster and bonhomie, Toni now detected a sad, weary resignation.

"Your father seems exhausted tonight, Mauro. Is he okay?" Even after more than a week, she and her staff were still pretending they believed in what they were all now quite sure was a fictional relationship. None of the visitors seemed inclined to correct them – the opportunity for that had apparently passed some time ago. She was concerned because Alessio's odd response to the find was so very different from what she had been anticipating. Toni wondered if he was coming down with malaria, perhaps, or some other similarly serious illness. Mauro was by this point very drunk, and the departure of the older man seemed to release something in him – an ebullience, but also a defiance.

"Actually, he is not my father I have to tell you, Toni. He is more like, I think we could say, my mentor? He is a friend of my father, actually. He wanted to sponsor me at the start of my career – help me to make a film that would get me some attention in the industry?"

"He doesn't seem really all that pleased. Well, not as pleased as all the rest of you anyway. Not as pleased as I would have expected?"

"I think he is just tired. Maybe he sees this as the end of something, can we say? The end of his little adventure, when to me it is actually the beginning of mine. This film is my passport. No, I don't know the word. *Comme se dice?*" In Italian he called out a slurred question that she couldn't catch to one of the celebrating crew members and got his answer. "No, it's my calling card apparently." He enunciated the words carefully, for effect but also because he was struggling now to hold on to his English. "I make this film, and after that I will no more have to beg for finance for what I want to make. No more favours, no more making nice with people not nice." There was something unappealing about his new-found cockiness and his eagerness to move on and move out of whatever situation he had got himself into.

Then Mauro went off in a huddle with the two beaming, equally drunk friends, and Toni was left to ponder how quickly he had changed from a sulky, resentful acolyte to the centre of the team's energy and focus. She even found herself feeling a little sorry for the older man, side-lined now that he had fulfilled his purpose and, doubtless, soon to be told he would no longer be welcome in the boy's bed and would also no longer have any role to play in his future success. She had decided early on that Mauro's friends were feckless and vacant in a way that she hadn't previously acknowledged it possible for men, and especially young men with money and energy, to be.

Her mother, a calculating but compassionate trophy wife, had always tried to impress upon her daughter the strategic value of vapidity, or the illusion of vapidity. Being slight and girlish, Toni was not always above using a little flattery and an appeal to old-fashioned male chivalry to get what she wanted in a small way. But these two friends – even now she couldn't for the life of her recall their names – were a whole new species. Interchangeable in looks, identical in height, the same gap-year beads at their wrists, they seemed to have no role other than to provide Mauro with people of his own age to interact with so that he would stay docile and happy.

She assumed this was why they had been brought along, although perhaps they also functioned to create some kind of physical shield at times between Mauro and his lover, and Mauro valued them for this, too. As far as she could tell, all their conversation revolved around student friends at home, clubs they frequented, skiing holidays they had enjoyed, drugs they had taken or hoped to take, and plans to travel to exotic, vaguely perilous places after this trip. It seemed that they didn't think of Tanzania as exotic or dangerous at all, and were about to join a trip to support a first ascent in Peru to score some adrenaline.

෴

The next morning, two hours after the team's early departure for the possible grave site, she went over to Alessio's room and let herself in using the master key. Earlier, as she had seen off the excited group, she was relieved to see that Alessio was back to his usual, domineering self. It was also clear that he and Mauro had had a fight and were not speaking – were, in fact, studiously avoiding each other. The effort Dr Orsi put into maintaining the impression of energetic good cheer was heartening to her, but no one could fail to note that he and his toy boy had departed in separate cars for the day.

Despite Alessio's restored vigour, Toni wanted to know what she might be up against if, as seemed possible, he was taken ill again. When she opened the little fridge in his room, she was surprised to find it completely empty, even though previously it had contained scalpel blades, five or six syringes in Ziploc bags, and bottles of clear liquid in vials a bit bigger than the ones that vaccinations come in. Where had all this gone? And why had it gone? Was its disappearance linked to Alessio's sudden partial collapse in spirits the night before and his remarkable recovery now? A look through the contents of the waste bin in the bathroom shed no light.

She locked up the rondavel and observed that a few high, drifting clouds had started to sweep overhead in the short space of time that she had been indoors. She also noted with satisfaction under a galleon-like cloud on the horizon, many kilometres distant, the smoky, dark veils of virga – rain that was already falling but then swiftly evaporating as it met the updrafts of hot air rising from the parched land underneath.

Some preliminary showers would make an appearance any day now – a prelude to the colossal storms that would arrive in earnest in a few weeks. She was glad for the filmmakers that they had probably found the graves and would be holed up in some editing suite in Rome long before the weather enveloped the escarpment in thick curtains of grey, cold rain, and the camp officially closed up for the season as the roads became rivers of swirling, sucking brown mud.

Toni snuck into her office in the hope that she could grab a few moments to herself. Something was bothering her, and she wanted an opportunity to nose around her suspicions before a member of her staff came to her with an intractable problem only she could solve. She went back to the recent email she had received from Mauro outlining the motivation for his film. Reading it now, she could tell that Dr Orsi had written some, if not all, of it – she could hear his low, seductive and yet disdainful voice as she scanned it over again.

The story was all there, and she was struck again by how poignant it was, an echo from a time when a man's word was his unbreakable promise, even when it was given to a native servant by an officer just out of his teens. She wondered how it was that Mauro – or more correctly Alessio, she supposed – had first stumbled on this tragic little tale, and she typed a few words into the search engine to see if she could track back to the genesis of the project. As she did so, she realised she had also started to piece together the other narrative: that of a directionless, unformed teenager from a modest background perhaps, who had allowed himself to be swept up in the middle-aged fantasies of an older, wealthy family friend. He'd found in Dr Orsi a mentor attractive enough to be tolerated, at least for a while, until the younger man figured out how to make a seemly escape.

It must have been Alessio who had bought them both matching, expensive watches. And surely it was the older man who had come up with the idea of this "calling card" film, so that he could keep Mauro in his orbit a little longer and, of course, make him always beholden to him for the funding he graciously supplied when he sensed his boy slipping away from him as the last term of university approached.

She found a website and started to read more about the tragic servants: some few bare facts, some conjecture, some tantalising blank spaces waiting to be filled in. And then the gracefully simple answer to the question of long-ago logistics that she realised had been bothering her from the outset revealed itself.

In the reception area, some distance down the dim passageway, the two-way radio crackled to life, and she heard Constance answer the call in her low murmur. Then the sound of slapping running feet.

"Toni you need to go out to Phillips. He says you must come straight away."

"Has there been an accident, Constance? What did he say?"

"He said you must come straight away. No accident, but you must come."

She found Islam cleaning the smaller open jeep that they used for taking pairs of guests, honeymooners usually, out on game drives alone and told him curtly to get into the passenger seat. She thought she knew a shortcut through to the site of the graves, and as Islam handed her the keys and started to ask her what was going on, she tried to remember where the little-used road began.

She had nothing to tell Islam except that if Phillips had asked her to come quickly, there had to be a bigtime problem, though Phillips had reassured her, through Constance, that there was no medical emergency, which is why she was not anticipating scrambling the medevac plane. She corrected herself: he had told Constance there had been no *accident*, and now she thought back to the empty fridge in Alessio's room and his exhausted, sullen demeanour the night before, as well as his miraculous recovery to his bellicose self this morning. As speculation was pointless, she kept her suspicions to herself, but as she steered the little car up the barely discernible track, she had a sickening premonition that whatever the problem was, Alessio would be at the epicentre of it.

❧

Thirty minutes or so had passed since she and Islam had left the lodge, and the oddest of tableaux started to reveal itself through the low trackside bushes as she pulled the car to a dusty halt. Some fifty metres away, the film crew and their vehicles were assembled a little higher up the hillside, close to the flat stones. Now that the surrounding grass had been trampled down and someone had hacked back the higher scrub that might have blocked a camera shot, it was easier to see the flat rocks under the fig tree without having to climb on top of a vehicle. Toni thought that perhaps some of the smaller ones had been disturbed recently and moved aside. She switched off the engine, and as she and Islam walked closer to the other cars, the full scene gradually came into view.

Phillips was pacing up and down in extreme agitation in front of the stones, throwing his hands out in front of his face as if in self-defence and yelling at the top of his voice in Kiswahili. Most of his words were being lost in the gusts of desiccating wind that always came a day or so before a short, inconsequential shower, but something in his anguished tone made her heart start to reverberate in panic. Before she trotted further up the incline, she instinctively reached in to grab a rifle out of its rack behind the cab of one of the cars.

Four of the film crew had remained in, or returned to, their vehicles. They were slouched low in the seats of their respective cars as if hoping they could thus be rendered invisible enough to be relieved of any responsibility for whatever was happening. Juma and the other two junior guides squatted motionless in their habitual resting postures next to the drivers' doors, with nervous or guilty expressions on their young faces. The remaining crew member, a mournful, jowly man, had shouldered his equipment and was filming something that was, for the moment, blocked by his large, heavily perspiring body.

Mauro appeared out of nowhere at a tripping trot, followed by the two ridiculous friends, who ambled along behind him, clearly fed up. The boy was behaving for all the world like a wronged child racing to his mother for help and assurance, even though there could only have been four or five years between him and Toni at most. He stood in front of her, wholly lost for words; panic and confusion were rendering him incapable of saying anything meaningful to her, in either English or Italian. The friends looked just as they always had done throughout the trip – malleable hangers-on, disinterested bystanders with no emotional investment in Mauro's film, and mute enablers of Alessio's skilful predation if it meant a free trip to Africa and their names on a film's credits. Their transparent boredom at least gave Toni some reassurance that no one was dead.

She saw now that the cameraman was filming Dr Orsi, crouched over the stones at the edge of the shade of the fig tree near the apex of the hillside. He seemed to be speaking for the benefit of the camera, though at this distance his words, too, were being lifted away by the capricious wind. Of the large group of people gathered around the tree, only Alessio and the cameraman weren't watching her intently now.

Dr Orsi was concentrating on some task and didn't even seem to notice that Toni was approaching. He had rolled up his sleeves and removed his gorgeous watch, which he had placed on a flat rock nearby. His bare left arm was buried up to the elbow in a hole that had been excavated at the edge of an area of disturbed stones. A small polystyrene box that she hadn't seen before was at his side, as was a fluttering collection of grubby strips of once-white cloth, held in place under a large plastic water bottle. As he gently wormed his fingers further and further into the loose dirt and leaf litter, he suddenly raised the volume of his voice without looking up. He must have registered her presence after all, though it had not stopped him in his task. The slight quaver in his voice – from his exertions or from nervousness, she couldn't say – gave her at least a little confidence that he was not quite the master of the situation that he wished to appear. Every so often, he would lift his hand out of the hole and add another small strip of fabric to the collection growing under the drinking bottle. He looked at each scrap he pulled out with some obvious distaste.

"So I think now I can say we have reached the climax of the expedition. Once I have cleared away just a little more of this winding sheet, I believe I will be able to access the body itself and take the necessary samples for identification to confirm my findings."

He continued to scrabble away in the growing hole, focusing on his work with such determination she couldn't tell if the loud explanation for his actions was intended to accompany the footage being shot or was really now for her benefit. The fat, baleful cameraman continued to circle around carefully, glancing up from his viewfinder every few seconds to make sure of his footing on the incline. Phillips, now sitting collapsed in despair on one of the dislodged rocks, looked up at her with tears streaking through the dust on his handsome face.

"He is going to dig them up, Toni. He is going to mess all the bones together and take some away. Then how will they stay to rest here?"

Toni spoke with as much command as she could muster, though she felt right then as if she were about ten years old. Orsi had disregarded the requests, then the commands, that Phillips must have directed at him once it was clear he was going to desecrate the grave. She had no real reason to believe that he would pay any attention to her either.

"He's going to do nothing of the sort, Phillips. Would you mind getting your arm out of there please Alessio? I'm sure Phillips has already told you to, and you decided to ignore him, but now I am telling you to do it as well."

The cameraman sighed loudly and switched off his equipment. Alessio carefully retracted his arm and, stumbling just a little, rose to his feet. Even though he was not a tall man, his calm, patient anger and elevated position above her on the slope gave Toni pause for thought. He took in the rifle at her side in a bemused sideways glance and smiled, then having wiped his dirt-caked hand on a pressed handkerchief he removed from his trouser pocket, brushed aside a hank of his long, damp hair.

"You thought we could come all of this way, my dear, and just film a few rocks and say 'Yes, here they are. We found the graves'?"

"So you're taking away some bits of these poor people, so that you have proof, and no one can call you or your little boyfriend a fraud, are you?"

She was struggling to speak with equanimity to match his. Although she could detect no change in his coiled composure, she realised that she had just made a very poor choice of words. Too late, she acknowledged that she ought to have been able to find a way to defuse the situation that would have allowed Alessio to discontinue his plundering with his dignity intact. Toni was used to people-dramas she could fix with a phone call, a complimentary drink, and a soothing reassurance. She wasn't at all sure what would happen if her words failed to stop him, and Orsi returned to his excavations. If she went up there to try to intervene, would he hit her perhaps? Would the others try to defend her, or him? She thought of the useless, clueless pair of friends, of Mauro's capriciousness, and the professional interest that the film crew had in getting the story told. She appeared to be on her own, although she knew she could count on Phillips, distraught though he was, if the need arose.

The doctor's fake affability, the becalmed attitudes of the group members – like amateur actors waiting for their cue on stage – the strange stillness of the place, made her next words seem all the more sharp and savage.

"This isn't a fucking crime scene, you bastard. This is a sacred grave site, and you've no business disturbing it and taking away your samples in your little test tubes. These bones must stay where they are, all of them. That's what Phillips told you already."

"*Si* … yes. But how can we know for sure that this is what we all hope it is? We cannot go back with the film and with that question not answered. I am sure you can see the position this would put Mauro in?"

Dr Orsi seemed to believe that by addressing her thus, as if he were the only reasonable adult on the hillside, he had conclusively regained the upper hand. With some difficulty, he began to crouch back down to resume his macabre work, then stood again, as if he thought better of it for the moment. In doing so, he upended the heavy water bottle and the little scraps of material started to lift and disperse in the eddies of hot air. Mauro, standing behind her, remained silent and detached – as she knew he would now that she had taken on the task of deputising for him. She hated Mauro and his little coterie with an all-consuming fervour.

"Anyway Miss de Souza, you will be pleased to know that I don't even need to take any bones away with me, though a shot of me lifting a skull from out of the dirt would make a most dramatic moment, I think."

Still chuckling, he started to approach her with a smirk of conciliation and then stopped when he saw her shift the position of the gun a little in her wet grip. At that moment, one of the smaller rocks that had been moved aside the better for Dr Orsi to access the grave, slid from its position on a larger slab with an eerily loud, hollow grinding. This was followed by the soft trickle of disturbed dirt sifting into the hole Alessio had made with his arm.

"I do know that, actually. You need to just get some soil samples or a scrap of cloth from next to the body to see if either of them contains honey."

He snorted in the patronising way that her father used to do when, having not seen her for the best part of a year, he'd been taken aback at something Toni had said that revealed either her precocity or the results of her expensive education.

"You have done some little homework I see. So yes, *e vero*, it is honey that I am trying to find. Not so exciting as bones but still, everything I need. It would be too much coincidence if someone else was buried here with honey on the body."

This is what she had found out in the course of her morning's research. That the two soldier brothers who had made that solemn pledge early in the last century had been compelled to preserve the bodies of their menservants until they could be returned to their home villages for burial. And, since they had no idea how long the war would continue, they had had the naked corpses stuffed into two old wine barrels and had filled the little remaining space with honey – a natural preservative that was readily available.

"So if you would just let me finish here and be filmed getting my samples, then we can all go home and have a happy result."

Without turning his body, or taking his eyes from hers, Alessio started to retrace his steps backwards up the hillside, retreating with care as he placed one foot behind the other on the uneven rising ground. A few bits of the winding cloth that he had stripped from the corpse he had been uncovering had caught in the branches of the fig tree and were fluttering in the rising wind. Everything about Orsi's deportment implied that he felt his victory against her to be now settled for good.

It took him some moments to regain his position at the head of one of the graves, and in that time, it dawned on Toni that he was lying. If a soil or cloth sample impregnated with honey was truly all he was after, he would have explained this to the embarrassed crew, the three foolish boys, and the sheepish junior guides. He would have placated them all and made his peace with Phillips, especially after the head guide had started to react with such disgust and obvious distress. It had been human flesh and bones that he had been digging for all along.

It was going to be up to Toni to call his bluff now and take whatever action was necessary to bring this shabby episode to an end. Once more, she shifted her grip on the rifle and wondered if discharging it into the air would convince Orsi that she was serious. As soon as the thought occurred to her, she was already chasing it from her mind. They had enough problems already without having to deal with the legal fallout from such a spectacularly ill-advised move.

Dr Orsi was bending down now and had taken his eyes off her in order to resume his gruesome work. Clearly, as a man always accustomed to getting his own way, he believed the discussion was over and the matter closed. As she was walking back to Phillips to seek his advice on their next move, she became vaguely aware that Islam had started the engine of the open jeep the pair had driven up in. The Europeans – scattered behind and below her on the incline – were also beginning to rouse themselves, and a few of them were exclaiming surprise in words she couldn't catch. So the spell was broken, and they, too, appeared to believe that Alessio had trounced her objections with his fictitious counterpunch. He could be left with the cameraman to film the gristly climax of the quest, a scene straight out of the charnel-house that no one else wanted to stick around to witness.

∞

Above the low, guttural pitch of the diesel engine, she could make out the thrumming of a distant motorbike approaching. She turned to Phillips for an explanation for this latest unexpected development and saw that he was rising from his perch on the rock in haste, his horrified look plain for all to see. Toni listened with more care.

"Into the cars right now, everyone!" she yelled, and then repeated this in Italian. Phillips had reached one of the cars, and the younger guides – who had realised that a new, more serious situation was swiftly unfolding – had begun to launch themselves into the vehicles. They were looking around as they did so in fright, perhaps still unsure of what it was they were suddenly fleeing so desperately but convinced by Phillips's obvious terror that it represented some dangerous escalation in the drama.

Now everyone was in a car except Toni, Alessio, and his cameraman, who was gingerly negotiating his way down the hill in tiny pattering steps. He had abandoned his equipment and appeared to be transfixed by something in the sky above the dense scrub some way off to his right. She knew without looking what it was now, but nevertheless glanced over at the huge swirling, smoky cloud. She heard him finally tumble his bulk into one of the other vehicles and turned to Alessio with a beseeching look. All the man's concentration remained focused on excavating his samples, however, and he was oblivious to the threat now almost upon him. The noise that they had all initially thought was a motorbike was now so loud there was no point in even trying to call out to him.

Her dread rising, Toni tried to calculate how much time she had left before the mass of bees descended on the pair of them in a relentless, lethal swarm. She threw herself into the passenger seat of the jeep next to Islam and turned to finally take a proper look at the billowing, deafening cloud of insects now blackening the sky only a hundred metres or so down the hill. The full cars had already started to drive off as fast as the broken route would allow, the terrified faces of the passengers pressed up against the hastily closed windows. At least one of them, she noticed, was recording the unfolding scene on a phone.

"Up. Up!" was all she could say, but already she knew it was too late. Alessio still had his arm inside the cavity he had made, but now he was trying to bat away the first bees with his other hand. Islam stared at her in anguish; he was still young and unmarried and didn't want to lose his life in this senseless way.

Toni leant across and yelled in his ear, "Islam drive up, go up. It's fine." He looked at her imploringly as she plucked at the tiny amber body that had settled on his chin but had not stung him yet.

&

Islam pointed the jeep up the hill and revved the engine, but there was no obvious direct route he could use to get to Alessio without risking overturning the little car. By the time they reached him by driving in short zigzag bursts across the face of the hill, Dr Orsi was desperately trying to flatten himself against the ground under a growing heap of purposeful movement. The infuriated shrieking buzz that the flying swarm had made previously had been replaced by a deeper, more contented susurration now that they had found their quarry. Alessio was moaning loudly and was trying to sweep away the dense clouds engulfing him, but every wide arc of his arms simply lifted the massed bodies briefly until they settled back down with renewed determination. Scraps from the shroud had become stuck to the hairs on his arms, and it was here that the bees were gathered in the thickest, seething mounds.

"Alessio, Alessio. Can you get in?" She and Islam were both shouting instructions at his thrashing body from within the car, but one of them would have to get out and physically lift him and help him into the back of the jeep. She already knew she couldn't ask this of Islam, who had a fear of wild bees far more atavistic than her own.

Islam's padded canvas jacket was on the backseat of the car. She could use it as a kind of tent to cover herself while she tried to reach the human buried underneath the bees, so she grabbed it, buttoned up the neck opening, then swung the whole heavy garment over her head. Islam helped her to do up the lower buttons, leaving just that small opening for her face. Thank goodness she was the size of a teenage girl, and Islam was a large man – the whole assembly came right down to below her bare knees, and the long sleeves fully covered her hands. She swung down and made a rush for Alessio, crouching low so that the hem of the jacket swept along the ground now peppered with the twitching bodies of dying insects.

Dr Orsi was now prone and motionless under his own black-and-gold shroud, and at first, Toni thought he must be dead. But then she heard a single gasping groan underneath the murmurs of the settling blanket of satisfied insects. She shoved her sleeve into the mass of carpeting animals where she thought his lower arm might be, already conscious of the sharp prickles of stings in her palm and on her wrist. Finding, then clutching, his left hand, she dragged and yanked until she saw the shape beneath the pile of bees bunch and raise itself onto all fours. Alessio was now beginning to laboriously inch himself along, his back mantled with a living, shimmering cloak, the exposed parts of his face and neck already hideously swollen and crimson from the merciless attack.

On his knees, he pulled himself forward in slow jerks as Toni continued to tug on his hand with every ounce of her strength. The insects – still matted in his hair, on the curve of his back, and clinging to his tidy trouser legs – were not going to relinquish their victim easily. Here and there, though, they began to fall away, and Toni saw that Alessio had somehow managed to replace his precious watch before he had disappeared under the living cloud by the graveside. Her nose also detected that he had soiled himself.

After several minutes of terrifyingly slow, creeping progress, they reached the open back of the jeep, and somehow Alessio found the strength to haul himself upwards and into the rear of the vehicle, with Toni and Islam hoisting him by his ankles from behind. Most of the bees came too.

Islam started to reverse the car back down the incline in the same direction in which they had come, switchbacking and jamming on the brakes at each turn in an effort to dislodge the cloak of bees flowing over the prostrate body and over the jeep's open bed. Toni had found herself back in the passenger seat, a decision she hadn't been conscious of making at the time and one she could do nothing to rectify now, despite her shame at abandoning her stricken client.

A moment later, she was startled by a vibrating bang, as if something large and heavy had fallen behind them onto the car. Toni swivelled round in alarm to see what could possibly have landed on top of Alessio and was confronted by the sight of Mauro crouching next to the older man, shovelling armfuls of bees away with his bare hands, his mouth grim in a closed rictus, and his pretty, tanned face wet all over with tears. As the car lurched and bumped down the slope, the bees seemed to lose interest in continuing their assault, and at first in narrow ribbons, then in thicker strands and loops, they began to peel away and disperse into the still, silent air in aimless, lazy flights.

სა

By the time their car met the others at the bottom of the slope, Toni could see through the window behind her that Mauro and Alessio were miraculously free of their attackers and only a few dead or dazed little creatures remained on the rutted metal on which the pair was sprawled. Mauro jumped down, shaking and ruffling his black curls in an effort to rid himself of the bees that had inevitably become trapped there. She joined him at the tail of the vehicle and observed that he had largely escaped being harmed, though he was holding up his lightly stung hands in front of his face and scrutinising them with wonderment.

In the meantime, Islam had moved swiftly to jump into the car's rear with a thick blanket they always kept on hand for emergencies. He had swaddled Alessio as best he could, but the appalling damage was clear – the stings were so numerous that there wasn't even the tiniest patch of skin that was not livid and grossly swollen, his eyes had disappeared into puckered, bright red pillows of flesh, and his lips were ballooning into a grotesque circle of magenta tissue.

Alessio seemed determined to pull away the covering now that the danger of further attack appeared to be over, however, and he was attempting to haul himself slowly and painfully up into a seated position. He reached both arms out in a gesture of supplication that made the heavy blanket fall from his shoulders, and at first Toni thought he was attempting to enfold her in a thankful embrace. But at her side Mauro was already mounting the open tailgate. He slid down next to Alessio, then tenderly removed the watch that was embedded deep in the flesh of the older man's terribly engorged wrist, and carefully wove his slim hands through the matted grey mane. Then he gently eased the older man sideways until he was cradled in the boy's shaking arms, his knees drawn up to hide the shameful stained crotch and his clutching fingers trying to find purchase on the material of Mauro's shirtsleeves.

Alessio's face was only a mask now, a taut travesty of scarlet flesh and rivulets of sweat, but nevertheless Toni saw that he was smiling – really for the first time since she had laid eyes on him many days ago. His mouth was contorting into the smallest upward curving of the distended lips, as a last, bedraggled straggler bee swung out from the spittle collected in one corner and launched itself away into the cool dusk.

Census Night 2010

Being an enumerator for the government population and housing census is an interesting way to spend a few days if you want to see how other people live. I'm pretty sure that's why a lot of young people do it – though certainly the allowance you receive is an incentive as well, I guess. My friend Wongani, who has already been active surveying across the city this week, told me he had to be prepared for some not-so-nice experiences, especially with respect to people's dogs and security guards, or sometimes an angry person not understanding initially that they were under a certain obligation to answer the questions. *That is the law*, I was to explain politely, *and there are penalties for not complying.*

During their training, enumerators are always told that it is critical to focus on the printed form, with its codes and checkboxes, and not get into a beef. And just keep on emphasising the citizen's responsibility to answer the questionnaire as "fully and honestly as he or she can in the interests of national development". Nearly all of them come around in the end, Wongani had told me.

It was 6 p.m. on an evening three days into the surveying process, and I was in a deserted cul-de-sac that led down to a group of three old, dilapidated apartment blocks, arranged in a kind of C shape around a small central parking area. I had never been to this part of town before, and something about these low towers and the similar roads with similar rundown blocks in this neighbourhood was pretty depressing. If I had to say why, I would probably be thinking about how difficult it would be to create any sense of community in these places – where people tend to come and go a lot, I'd imagine. Parking spaces take priority over any area where children might play or people gather to chat. A dank stairwell is no place to converse, really, although my guess would be that most residents are very much temporary occupants and not the type of people to be especially neighbourly.

The shabby entrance courtyards in front of the individual blocks were not nice places to dwell either: many of the paving slabs had been removed, with clumps of long yellow grass sprouting from the bare patches of dirt left behind. Also, I don't believe that the rubbish bins had been emptied for a long time. Certainly, as I cycled in, small groups of rats were nosing around discarded food wrappers, and one was even running around with a used sanitary towel in its mouth. A big green, shiny stain was smeared right down the wall of one of the external staircases where a pipe on an upper floor must have been leaking for ages. Mosquitoes had collected above the stagnant, stinking puddle that was formed on the ground underneath, where the overflow ought to have been carried away into a drain but wasn't, because the grating was blocked with broken house bricks and old newspapers. The few balconies were caged with security panels and were all being used as storage spaces, rather than for relaxation.

Several large floodlights, like those directed onto a prison yard, were trained on the open gateway to the compound so that cars entering and leaving wouldn't hit the crumbling gateposts. A smaller one was pointing at the main doorway to the westernmost block. Other than that, most of the space was in darkness, apart from the glow coming from behind tatty blinds in the windows of some rooms, and a few bare bulbs in the stairwells that flashed on and off intermittently.

As I padlocked Wongani's bike to a railing guarding the steps down to a squalid basement area, I made sure to keep my mouth closed: the floodlights had attracted huge swarms of flying insects – I had never in my life seen so many. Beyond the razor-wire fence at the rear of the empty lot behind the blocks and across a void of unlit wasteland, the lights of the city pulsed under the seething lavender-and-gold clouds of early evening.

As Wongani, Edgar and I had planned, I started on the top floor of the left-hand building and rang each doorbell in turn. Maybe twenty separate occupants – sleepy young men mostly, barefoot and muscled in vests and shorts – opened and answered my questions politely as they scratched their chests and looked up towards the filthy light-fittings, trying to get their stories straight. With only a handful of exceptions, they all claimed to be business students – yes, they were doing a "bee com". Various older men and women who just opened their doors a crack said that they had done the questionnaire already the week before but were amenable when I pointed out that this couldn't be the case because interviews at the Orchid Gardens apartment blocks had not yet been carried out.

Certain people lie easily but don't seem to mind being caught out, and I made sure to stay polite with these characters at all times. Some even seemed to think that being caught out in a lie was funny; they remained unembarrassed and eager to draw me into their harmless joke by offering me a beer or soft drink from the fridge. *Thank you for your kind offer but enumerators may not interact socially with citizens taking part in the census.* They would then mumble vaguely about their line of business being something to do with "import-export" and I had to be content with inputting that onto the form.

Even from the parking area, most of the apartments had seemed to be vacant, though, and this I didn't mind because I was most anxious to be out of that place as soon as possible. After I had finished here I could go home.

It took me much less than two hours to work my way down the block, since at least half of the apartments were indeed empty. The doorbells didn't work when I applied my finger to them, and no sound could be heard coming from within in response to the few moments of knocking that followed. The official census protocols printed on a piece of A4 paper made clear what I should do next: when a dwelling appeared to be uninhabited, mark it as "vacant" using the correct checkbox on the top sheet and just move on. Don't ask any neighbours to try to supply information on behalf of anyone who might have lived there until recently, or who might return at a later time.

Each questionnaire took only a few minutes to complete, actually – although more, obviously, if people had to think about how to spell the names they wanted to provide; or wondered aloud how to categorise what they did for a living; or started describing to me the distant, far-off relatives occupying the outermost branches of their family trees. I didn't mind – it gave me a chance to improve my interviewing technique so that I would appear to be an old hand.

It seemed to me that some parts of the form I was using belonged to another time and place completely, asking questions about the name of the senior person who was "head of the household" and the marital status of each adult member present: married, divorced, single, widowed, cohabiting … Quite a few of the women just gave a careless shrug when I asked them these two questions, and I ticked the boxes I felt best approximated their individual circumstances after I had asked a few friendly leading questions. "It is not for an enumerator to judge, only to record" Wongani had reminded me. This was my appointed role at that point of the evening.

At two of the apartments, a large dark-wood TV cabinet could be seen through the open door, totally dominating the living area and surrounded by a cluster of noisy young men sprawled on L-shaped sofas watching the soccer, a coffee table covered with beer cans at their knees. At both places, I was invited in to join the little crowd for as long as it took to record everyone's details on the form, since it was an activity that would take quite some time and would draw their attention away from the match if they each had to come to the doorway to answer my questions. Since Man U was playing Liverpool, the man inviting me within each time must have thought there was a pretty good chance that my team was involved in the night's fixture. I would like to have joined them for a while, but I had to explain that my schedule was tight and *protocol prevents enumerators from entering any home* in any case, to protect the female census-takers from any unfortunate misunderstandings.

Many of the women I spoke with seemed anxious for company or conversation. Only a few had children on their hips or at the breast, or mentioned that they were busy preparing food. The rest seemed trapped in a kind of limbo in their tiny individual flats, looking out into the hallway over my shoulder as if waiting for someone, or anyone, to materialise in the flickering of the strip lighting. One of these women smelt, deliciously, of coconut oil, and clacked her long nails against the doorpost as we spoke. The invitation in the eyes of this girl, Mona, was so frank as to be disturbing. By now I had had enough evasive answers to my questions about employment to form a pretty clear picture of what many of the women – young and not-so-young – did to get by. In case I failed to get the message, Mona followed up her slow winks during the course of my questioning with a bold suggestion that no male could have misinterpreted, and few might have been able to resist. But I had forms to complete, a timetable to stick to, and Wongani had insisted that I had to be out of the building by 8 p.m. at the very latest.

By the time I got to the final apartment, my stomach was hollowed out with hunger. The soccer fans had all been eating burgers or fried fish, waving handfuls of food around as they urged their players on with tender racial epithets. Mona had been nibbling on a piece of pawpaw, and the juice had been dribbling down her dimpled chin in a slow fragrant trickle before splashing on the floor as she laid out her proposition for me and I promised to think about returning later, a lie neither of us really believed.

Several of the other apartments, those with occupants from other parts of the country or DRC, had emitted savoury but less-immediately recognisable odours when the doors were opened. And a few were just plain rank with the sweat stink of onions fried days ago in windowless kitchens with no ventilation. The combined effect of the smells of cornbread, peanuts, chillies, stewed chicken and fresh, peppery greens was making it hard for me to focus on the vital task in hand when I knocked on the last door at the end of the unlit passage on the first floor. I would treat myself to some leftover nshima and relish when I got home. I hoped that Wongani would remember he was supposed to buy some dried kapenta on his way to our place, as well, to reward me for my role in his clever scheme.

The way that the door swung inwards in a wide emphatic arc after I had been knocking for a whole three minutes let me know not to expect from the angry man who opened it any of the courtesy or mild ribbing I had encountered up to that point in the evening. I was surely glad this was destined to be my last survey of the night before Wongani took over again, but the disputatious look on this character's damp, pockmarked face told me that it was going to be the longest by far.

❧

Of course even if I hadn't known in advance who was going to be visiting Apartment A14 at this time of night, I would perhaps have recognised him from his sporadic appearances in the *Lusaka Times*. He was a mid-level official who seemed unable to keep his fat fingers out of hot pies, and who had been implicated – though never charged – in various kickback scandals over the years. His wife, who kept herself out of the public eye in Ndola, was known to be rich through her connections to various mining companies, but the young lady hovering at his shoulder now could never have been mistaken for his spouse by anyone, of course. In fact, the "lady" standing behind him wearing a short silky kimono and dirty, once-white mules was evidently no such thing, given that she was working at an itch under the stocking cap that covered her head with the badly manicured index finger of one huge hand as she twirled a cheap-looking long blonde wig in the other.

Her wrap was printed with big, cartoonish pineapples and, although I had known full well what to expect when I arrived at this final flat, for some reason the woman's attire struck me as profoundly sad in this place of many sad things.

Neither the girl with the mocking look on her face nor her middle-aged companion seemed anxious to say anything, though the man kept swinging the door back and forth a little on its hinges in an irritated manner, causing a gust of musky hot air to buffet me each time.

Eventually, he opened his ugly toad's mouth and spoke, "Get back there, you. Get back into the house."

He was obviously talking to the woman, since he was flapping a hand at her behind his wide back, though he continued to stare right into my face with a challenge. *Click, clickety click*, the woman tripped off on her heels into a back room through an archway that cast an aqueous blue glow out into the shadowy corridor. She poked her head back through the opening a little though, so she could continue to make eye contact with me as I interrogated her paramour.

"What are you wanting, my friend?" asked the man, in a tone anything but amicable. He was wearing a grey work shirt that strained against his belly and tartan boxer shorts that bunched up between his wobbling thighs in a way that made me feel slightly sorry for him, despite myself. No man likes chafing, especially not in such a delicate spot. He reached between his legs and pulled the ruched material from out of his crotch area and down towards his knees, but the fabric looked unlikely to stay put for long.

I started in on my explanatory script as he fake-yawned with every muscle in his face, delivering a hot, garlic-infused blast at me with a contempt he didn't even try to disguise.

"Yes, but why are you here at *this* moment, my friend?" he interrupted, looking behind him now to check on the whereabouts of his girlfriend, who had luckily anticipated this and ducked out of view. I repeated the part of the script about the legal responsibility of all adult occupants of any dwelling to answer the questions of an appointed enumerator within the period allocated for the census activity. As I completed my spiel, I pulled on the lanyard of the laminated accreditation card tucked inside my T-shirt so that he could see the corner and know that I was for real.

"Yes but, you see, I don't live here, so you are wasting my time. I have business to attend to. You can see this, perhaps. You need to be on your way now."

I tried very hard not to move my eyes from him or let my own face betray my amusement because behind him, his cheeky mistress was silently mimicking his self-important, puffed-up way of explaining himself. If I allowed myself to become distracted, it could be game over.

"I can go just as soon as I have completed the form. One section for each person who is presently at this address tonight …" I tailed off as he drew the door closed behind him with an impatient sigh and took a step towards me so that he and I were belly to barrel belly. He looked like a walrus, or some other small-eyed, flabby creature, and he stank – the unmistakable funk of unwashed, unprotected, protracted sex.

"I am not living here. How can I make this clear? Are you a stupid person or is there some other reason why you are failing to understand me?"

Naturally, Wongani had coached me on how to handle a situation that mirrored this one – reassuring any householder who, for his or her own reasons, would rather not be placed on record at their present location. Just like, of course, this last one now.

"Sir, it is not really private information that we gather, believe me. Only statistics on sex, age, job, type of property and that kind of thing. Education, too. All that can be used confidentially in the interests of nation-building and progress." I gave a weak smile that was intended to come across as ingratiating, if not pathetic. *I'm just doing my job, sir, and would like to be on my way as soon as you have assisted me.*

He started a sentence that sounded as if it were going to be another contribution towards his litany of excuses, and that would no doubt end with him trying to slam the thin particleboard door shut in my face. Then he stopped, as if considering an alternative that might work more in his favour. He was now trying to adjust his uncomfortable underwear by tugging at the shorts from the back, yanking the seam away from the place where his pendulous buttocks met as he looked towards the ceiling and pondered his predicament in silence. His next questions were most revealing of the man and his methods and they came as no surprise whatsoever.

"What happens if I refuse to answer you, let's say? Your people are going to waste time trying to come looking for me? What purpose is that serving when you don't even know where I live, normally? Or don't even know who I am?" The last sentence was tacked on as a speculative afterthought.

"Well, we mark the sheet with your address and indicate that one of the residents at the time was not forthcoming. Then it will be up to the administering body to take measures as they see fit. People in the past have been prosecuted. I am advised to tell you that, sir."

It wasn't a fatal blow, but it had him wavering – just as we intended. I was certain, too, that I was being reappraised: against census protocol, I had employed long words that the older man was unsure of, in a language I knew that he was uncomfortable using. Had he also recalled from the recruitment notices in the papers that enumerators had to have at least a high-school education, perhaps? Did he at least know that, for all his bloviating ignorance?

"Just, just …" But he seemed to have nowhere to go with this. His hands moved away from prying his boxer shorts from the crack of his butt, and he wiped his palms against the front of his shirt. I had to speed things up to get out of the block in time to liaise with Wongani, and I had just one final, but crucial, tactic available to me.

"How about you think about how you want to proceed with this while I question the other resident, Mr Cheyeka? I must do that as well before I leave."

He placed the flat of one hand against my upper ribcage, over where that ID badge was trapped inside my T-shirt, and steadied himself against the door jamb with the other. Despite his corpulence and evident lack of physical fitness, he was still an imposing man – as Edgar had warned me he would be. If I'd any fear that he might harm me, this move on Cheyeka's part would have been a truly disconcerting one, but I trusted that the trump card I'd just played would protect me. He was visibly deflating at the mention of his name, his licentiousness leaking out and leaving behind only a wary truculence once the implications started dawning on him. I didn't think that violence at his hands was on the cards for me this evening, though I was already worried about the extent to which he would be taking his resentment out on his companion after I'd gone.

"I can answer for that other person. You don't need to be bothering them, my young friend." He was using a conciliatory tone now, peering at the sheet on my clipboard to try to see if his name was to be found there, perhaps. But the printed forms were not personalised in any way, so he had to know that I had recognised him from someplace – TV or the newspaper – despite my lowly status at the bottom rung of the data-crunching ladder.

"You are saying that you are the head of the household, Mr Cheyeka? And that the young lady is in some way related to you or is a dependent? For example, that she is your spouse?"

I sensed I was still on dangerous ground, but this was the body blow that we had all planned and that everything else depended on.

Cheyeka seemed to have accumulated a maw full of spittle that he couldn't dispose of. His fat pink tongue was working the bolus of saliva back and forth from cheek to shiny cheek as his convulsive swallowing failed to clear it away. Just for a half-second, I did wonder if he was going to spit at me, then dismissed the idea. I knew shameful calculation when I saw it; the unedifying sight of a man weighing up the consequences of his forthcoming self-serving, tawdry actions and trying to decide if his conscience would let him live with them. Asking himself if he has the balls to survive a public fall from grace in the unlikely event that his scruples win out. Did any married man ever opt for the second course of action? Had Cheyeka a conscience to live with in the first place? Wongani, his brother and I were counting on the answer being "No" to both questions tonight.

For just a moment, though, that reckoning with decency was postponed. The front door slowly opened, and the coquettish face of the girlfriend, not even nineteen years old, peered around and looked enquiringly from Cheyeka's face to mine, lips pursed in a practised half-pout. She was taller, by almost half a metre, than either of us, even though – as I was already well aware – her bare wrists and ankles were no thicker than a stick of firewood.

"Are you done here, Cletus?" she simpered, effectively barring for good the only escape route he possessed out of public exposure and this whole undignified mess.

"Do it. Ask her. Do it," Cheyeka growled in surrender as he barged past her and into the dim passageway behind, where he stood listening and mashing one meaty fist against the other.

The initial questions that respondents usually had few problems with – name, sex, age – our girl seemed hesitant to answer. Instead, she just waggled her index finger at me in silent, amused chastisement, promising that we would get back to all that eventually. She did, however, watch with pride as I completed the entry line for "employment". She offered that she was a part-time student but also an entertainer: she sang and gave performances and that sort of thing. I was only allowed to enter one code to try to capture the rich, varied forms of work that she was alluding to, so I gave her a lopsided grin of complicity instead. This made her bark out a series of deep raucous laughs while behind her, Cheyeka cursed almost as loudly in his mother tongue.

His lady friend now mentioned that her *professional* stage name was Mizz Mangoes. She said it twice more as I debated how I would enter this information and where on the form it should go. She said it one last time so slowly and emphatically that it came out as Miss Man Goes, and she nodded gleeful encouragement as I printed out the words on the line where freelance and consultancy activities could be captured. Her huge feet must have been uncomfortable in her towering heels because she was shifting her weight from foot to foot as she spoke, and eventually she removed the mules altogether and threw them behind her into a pink raffia basket under a coat hook on the corridor's wall.

"Um, I have to indicate if there's a family or other connection between occupants and if ..." but I didn't get to finish my sentence. Cheyeka covered the distance to the door in two long and surprisingly swift strides and threw it wide open, hitting the young woman on the inside of her arm with the curved metal handle as he did so. Other than rubbing thoughtfully at the spot where the skin immediately began developing an angry red graze, Mizz Mangoes didn't even acknowledge the blow, either by look or remonstration.

"No. Seriously, no! How is this information important for your purposes? You can just leave that bit blank. Or write out that there she gave no answer."

"Mr Cheyeka, it's not only the case that you are breaking the law if you refuse to be included in the census. I can also get into lots of trouble myself if I don't perform the duties I've been paid to carry out. The electoral authorities have even trained certain undercover officers to behave just as you are doing now, to try to identify enumerators who do not take their responsibilities seriously. Who just take their payment for doing the interviews without doing all the work."

Cheyeka had already swallowed a great many half-truths that I had served up to him, and in his bovine stupidity had altogether failed to spot them. Another few would make no difference, either way, to him now.

Here we were then. The moment of truth – or it would have been if anyone had still been interested in the truth by that point of the evening. Cheyeka grunted as if, a man of the world, he had seen the next development coming all along, and then he just came out with his offer. "What can we do to make this little issue between us go away then?"

Being an enumerator for the government census activity is a challenging way to spend your time if you want to try to maintain your integrity. My varied encounters at the Orchid Gardens apartment block had shown me this. I'm pretty sure that's why a lot of honest people don't want to do it – though certainly the different kinds of informal offers that you might receive from place to place may constitute an incentive of sorts, I guess. Wongani, who had already spent a few days conducting real questionnaires, told me to be ready for some shocking behaviour from respectable-looking people during the course of my few hours' as his replacement, and here was just the most blatant example of such, presenting itself now at Apartment A14, right where we had been expecting to find it.

Cletus Cheyeka was truly as dumb as he looked, which was pretty dumb in my estimation. It took some time to explain to him, through increasingly desperate hints, how I might be persuaded to assist him with his dilemma. I led him through the sections of the census form that could be completed in such a way – not exactly lying but certainly manipulating the truth here and there – that no one collating the data would ever be able to tally up the details and use them to identify him or associate him with his teenage shemale friend and the flat he provided for her. He couldn't prevent himself from boasting that he was the head of the household, I noticed however, despite also admitting that he visited only rarely.

Once I told him that we were done, he took the clipboard from me with shaking hands, and where I indicated that I was supposed to print his name in the space provided, he wrote out some half-approximation in a childish scrawl. He then signed with a perversely legible signature on the first page at the place I showed him next to the unique barcode.

That done, I stood in the doorway patiently and waited for his deviousness to displace his profound idiocy. As I was really running out of time now, I tried to speed the process along a little.

"If it's found that I helped you to falsify some of these details, Mr Cheyeka, then I can be in a great deal of trouble. I could receive a very big fine myself, in fact."

"Let me get this thing clear then. That if someone finds out that this form is not completed correctly, then you are going to say that I am responsible, my son? You would implicate me?"

This fool. Honestly. He could barely string a sentence together coherently, let alone read and sign a simple form, but he knew how to use that word "implicate" just fine, no doubt through longstanding familiarity with the concept and prior experience in its nefarious uses.

"It's been a long evening, Mr Cheyeka, and I am tired and I am hungry. At times like this, my memory isn't what it should be. I imagine that perhaps it will be difficult for me to recall your name and exact address by tomorrow. I do have to survey lots and lots of people, after all."

"Perhaps" cost him ZMK900,000. Towards me feigning amnesia in the matter of the name of Mr Cletus Cheyeka, but also for striking through the response already given by his companion when I'd asked over again which box on the census form I needed to tick for her sex – which turned out not to be the one immediately obvious to many eyes, maybe. Cheyeka complained that he hadn't all that money on him, though he did have a great deal of it for someone hanging out in a rackety neighbourhood after dark. He would go to get the rest right away, and I could come back to collect it from Mizz Mangoes at some point the following day. Cheyeka suddenly recalled that he was heading overseas on urgent business the very next morning.

He stalked off, presumably to put on some trousers before he went in search of more cash. A handshake didn't seem appropriate, so I just blew a kiss at the girl, her expertly painted eyebrows raised high in delight at the speed at which we had concluded business, and I left.

෴

I cycled fast to get home. The mid-week streets were quiet, and so I wasn't in trouble with Wongani when I arrived back at the crib we shared, only ten minutes later than expected. As good as his word, my old friend had a grease-blotched paper bag of dried fish waiting for me on the kitchenette table, and I got to work straight away preparing it. Being party to a complex deception had left me famished.

Wongani was an experienced enumerator by now and could make up the lost time easily when he went back to Orchid Gardens to survey the other two blocks on his schedule for the night. The cooked fish would be ready for us to share on his return.

I handed over the lanyard with his accreditation card plus the key for his bike padlock, and then gave him the borrowed clipboard with my thanks. He removed my pile of competently completed questionnaires and replaced them with blank ones from an orange nylon courier bag he had slung over one shoulder. Not wishing to keep him in suspense any longer, I then produced the thick wad of kwachas from my inside jacket pocket, flicked them so that he could hear the gratifying sound they made, then placed them with care in the bread bin for safekeeping until we could divide them up between the three of us.

As Wongani checked to make sure he had everything he required to complete his night's work, I took the bogus census form I needed from the pile he'd placed on the kitchen table and checked it over. Where Cheyeka had made a mess of printing his moniker, I now put a line through his words and copied out his real name very clearly with large capital letters. I might not be a real enumerator, but I do like to see things done properly. Then I took close-up photos of all the sections using a camera we had borrowed, taking care to make sure that Cheyeka's signature, which he had forgotten to disguise, was captured clearly on one image. I also filled in the box giving his lover's true sex over again and took a series of photos, for added insurance.

I heard Wongani letting his brother in by the front door as he manoeuvred his bike out through the narrow space and into the night. Then I heard Edgar locking the bathroom door behind him to attend to business in there before he came out to greet me. It was a good ten minutes before I heard my friend's fraternal twin come out again, but finally he stuck his wet head around the kitchen door, smirked as he sidled in, and gave me a high five.

If I hadn't met him a few times already over at Wongani's mother's place as he was getting ready to go out to work for the evening, I would never have linked this rangy but otherwise unremarkable boy in a Miami Heat tracksuit with the exotic glory that was Mizz Mangoes less than an hour ago. Gone was the thick foundation and false eyelashes, and of course, the slinky mini-kaftan and the shoes the colour of spoilt milk. The only giveaway was the long, straw-coloured wig poking out of the plastic bag that he flung on the table next to my pile of completed forms and the paper bag that had held the pungent fish. Wongani's height and the clear family resemblance would have pegged him for Edgar's sibling to anyone who saw them side by side, however, which is why the pair had inveigled me into standing in for Edgar's twin for a few hours tonight, just in case Cheyeka wasn't quite as clueless as he seemed.

Edgar pushed up his too-short sleeve, delved into the plastic tub of water, and peeled off the tiniest sliver of dried kapenta from the pile soaking there. That boy really did have a taste for strange foodstuff these days. The action of popping the piece of fish into his mouth exposed the disproportionately large, dark bruise that had already covered all the skin on the inside of his elbow where the door handle had hit him not so long ago.

I had seen Edgar just the once in his full Mizz Mangoes guise, belting out Céline Dion hits at a private-members club in the middle of town where he had flirted effortlessly with the shy male clientele between numbers. Ordinarily, Edgar and his brother were men of few words. That night a month ago, when we had hatched our plan of wealth redistribution and revenge, had been notable for the number of sentences the twins had each contributed, as well as the times they pretty much said the exact same thing simultaneously.

He chewed the little morsel contemplatively then wiped his fingers delicately on a paper towel I offered him. He turned and unzipped his worn jacket so that I could see the fresh, four-fingered bruise that was just starting to emerge on the right side of his collarbone.

"That from tonight, Edgar? He gave that to you just a moment ago?"

He nodded at me wistfully. "As we were in the car out collecting the rest of your gift for forgetfulness. And just because, you know? There doesn't have to be a reason …"

"In that case you had better take more than a third, it's only fair. Wongani and I just facilitated – it was basically your idea."

Edgar wasn't aware that I possessed a secret of my own. I had found out from Wongani that a regular beating wasn't the only damage to his brother's young body that Cheyeka had inflicted and Edgar's share of tonight's takings would not end up going far when he started to need treatment and care.

"Nooo now. You two can keep that for yourselves. I made a little deal with Cletus of my own. Along the lines of what was I going to do if his wife *somehow* found out about the two of us now and made a claim in court against little old me for damages to her pathetic lie of a marriage?"

"Edgar, you continue to surprise me, my man. I did *not* know that was still possible these days."

"I wasn't a shitty-correspondence-course law student for nothing, my friend. And … truthfully, I'm not even sure people actually can still do that these days. But as you may have noticed, old Cletus isn't exactly spilling over with intelligence." He chuckled, but sadly.

From out of the bag containing his wig, Edgar drew a bundle of new banknotes bound up in an elastic band and counted the balance that was due to Wongani and me for our role in the fake census scam. Since he was still left with a substantial fistful, I didn't concern myself too much over the finer details of the disbursement; neither did my own conscience trouble me one little bit concerning my side-role in the shakedown. The combined value of the contents of Cheyeka's drinks' cabinet in his villa in a smart part of the city probably added up to more than all the proceeds of this evening. It was a matter of public record that he was a career crook and bully of old who had escaped his lawful fate many times over, more by luck than judgment.

This was fair. This was justice. That was my view. The new bruises on Edgar and the virus even now laying waste to his body just reinforced my sense of righteousness.

I looked him over – his thin, thin wrists, the little line of foundation that Mizz Mangoes had failed to remove, caking at the side of one cheek. I remembered how, as he sang his power ballads at the club, he would throw back his head as he hit the key change and drink in the wild applause.

I hoped that by the time the next census took place, Edgar's alter ego would have moved onto less dangerous ways of making ends meet, assuming that he was still around, of course. Ten years can seem like a very long time in the future though, depending on where you stand.

Glossary of terms

asseblief (Afrikaans): please

bakkie: a pickup truck, with or without a canopy over the back

botsotsos: criminals, street thugs

cheese grillers: smoked sausages made from spiced pork mixed with cheese

donner: beat up

dropper: upright fence post of solid wood

fly camping: a way of exploring the bush on foot. Staff set up a basic camp ahead of clients on foot and prepare food and tents so that they can spend time away from fixed accommodation and out of vehicles

frikkadels: meatballs

goggas (originally from the Khoikhoi): insects or creepy-crawlies

Intercape: southern-African inter-city scheduled bus service

kambashu: a small basic dwelling, often put together from materials such as corrugated iron and wooden boards, and usually located in an informal settlement

kamboroto: a regular sexual partner, but not the type of girlfriend you are likely to introduce to your family

kapenta: a small freshwater fish resembling a sardine

klaar: finished, over

Kombi: Volkswagen campervan

larney: posh, upper-crust, smart – or aspiring to be

magwinya: deep-fried bread doughnut, also known as fat cake

mbira: a musical instrument consisting of a wooden soundboard with attached metal pegs, played by holding the instrument in the hands and plucking the keys with the thumbs

munt: derogatory colonial-era slang for a black African

nshima: white cornmeal porridge cooked to a thick, paste-like consistency *panga*: a large, broad-bladed machete

PE: colloquialism for Port Elizabeth, a coastal town in South Africa, which is now named Gqeberha

relish: an accompaniment to nshima, made with either a protein base (meat, fish, peanuts or beans) or vegetable base (leaves or cabbage) in a sauce

rondavel: a westernised version of an African-style hut, frequently used as accommodation at tourist lodges

siff: gross or disgusting

sjambok: a heavy leather whip, traditionally made from an adult hippopotamus or rhinoceros hide and commonly used in former times for meting out punishment to black Africans

skelm (Afrikaans): a crook, thief, or untrustworthy character

slippy: a receipt

slops: rubber flip-flops

snot en trane (Afrikaans): snot and tears, i.e. misery and/or drama

TIA: acronym for This is Africa, a dismissive catchall phrase meant to denote how unlikely it would be for things to function properly

tokoloshe: a tiny and malevolent spirit

vetkoek: savoury deep-fried bread dough

Acknowledgements

My thanks go to Team Modjaji Books (Colleen Higgs, Nerine Dorman, Leanne Johansson, Andy Thesen and Monique Cleghorn).

My thanks also go to Anna Cloete, who shared with me some of the ideas upon which the story "Mother's Milk" is based.

I extend my special gratitude to Derek Workman of the *Kalahari Review* online magazine, where these wandering stories first found a home.

Marisa (Mel) Kelly is originally from Manchester, England. She worked at London Zoo as a senior keeper and then in veterinary nursing before going on to study film theory. An English-language editor and writer since arriving in Windhoek in 1998, she also manages a small-scale women's upcycling project, Sew Good Namibia. Her fiction has appeared on the *Kalahari Review* website and she has also contributed regular opinion pieces to *The Namibian* newspaper on social, cultural and economic issues.

Printed in the United States
by Baker & Taylor Publisher Services